P
Murder o

Carpe Ski 'em

a Murder on Skis Mystery

Other **Murder on Skis Mysteries**
by Phil Bayly:

Murder on Skis

Loving Lucy

Back Dirt

Witch Window

The Man Who Had 9 Lives

A Small Mountain Murder

CARPE Ski 'em

a Murder on Skis Mystery

Phil Bayly

CARPE Ski 'em
a Murder on Skis Mystery

©2025 by Phil Bayly

WWW.MURDERONSKIS.COM
ISBN: 978-1-60571-657-2

Cover Design: Carolyn Bayly, Debbi Wraga &
Ruslana Chub / istockphoto.com
CSA-Printstock / istockphoto.com
Ievgen Radchenko / alamy.com
National Museum in Krakow / alamy.com
Author Photo: Carolyn Bayly

Printed in the United States of America

Carpe Ski 'em is a work of fiction. All the people, groups and events in this novel are the work of the author's imagination. They are used in a fictitious manner.

The Craters Ski Resort does not exist, nor do the ski resorts of Minnie's Gap or Snow Hat. Those last two are apparitions from previous MOS Mysteries.

There is also no real Cameron County or town of Placer in Colorado.

Beyond those boundaries, I aspire to be as accurate and faithful as possible to the histories of Colorado, the Cache La Poudre, Cameron Pass, Larimer County and the people who first inhabited this beautiful setting.

To Carolyn. I was found, barely breathing,
on a mountainside and she nursed me back to health.

"Life in itself is neither good nor evil. It is the scene of good or evil, as you make it. And if you have lived a day, you have seen it all."

— Michel de Montaigne

"This is a wonderful world, but it's got a weird cast."

— JC Snow

1

❝❝The skis clattered when they hit the rocks. They landed on jagged granite one hundred feet below the chairlift.

A ski helmet came next. It bounced a few times before coming to rest.

The body followed. There was no chance of survival and none attempted. A note was found in the woman's pocket. It read:

"Please forgive me for what I am about to do. I can't go on thinking and brooding. There is nothing left but memories.

The dear Lord was good to me."

Aaron Aguayo stood atop a scree slope and fingered the note nervously as Sheriff Brush labored to reach him.

Deputy Aguayo was a young man, and he was fit. His face showed the scars left from childhood acne. But it was a handsome face. His dark hair and features displayed Colorado's proud past when First Natives were in charge.

"When did I get old and fat?" the sheriff panted as he finally climbed up to Deputy Aguayo. Sweat droplets coated the sheriff's forehead when he removed his cowboy hat, despite the air temperature of only fifteen degrees.

"I don't know, sir," Aguayo responded dutifully. "I only joined the sheriff's office two years ago."

"So, I was already old and fat by then?" the sheriff asked, still breathing heavily.

"No, sir," the nervous deputy blurted, realizing he had insulted his superior. "I didn't mean that."

"I know what you meant," the genial sheriff laughed and patted the young deputy on the shoulder of his standard-issue down parka with multiple pockets.

The air was thin at this altitude. The top of The Craters Ski Resort, on Bald Mountain, was 10,847 feet. And they were close to the top.

Sheriff Jerry Brush was also dressed for the coldest weather. He wore his own durable down parka. It had a star on the breast pocket.

He was acclimated to the high altitude, but it was still a steep climb in thin air.

The sheriff squinted his eyes and craned his neck to look high overhead. He studied the chairlift, swinging slightly in the wind.

"Boy," the sheriff said, his hands on his hips. "That's a long way to fall. She just slipped off?" He turned to Deputy

Aguayo for an answer, as Aguayo had been the first one to respond to the scene.

"She might not have slipped," the deputy cautiously suggested to the sheriff. He did not want to contradict the more experienced law officer. He was raised to respect the beliefs of his elders.

"How do you figure?" the sheriff asked.

Aguayo handed him the note. The sheriff studied it.

"So, she may not have slipped," the sheriff said. "She may have jumped."

The sheriff told his deputy to place the note into a plastic evidence bag. The handwriting was graceful and neat. It was written on stationery from the most expensive hotel at the base of the ski mountain.

Aguayo had discovered the note tucked into a zippered pocket on the woman's stylish Obermeyer one-piece ski outfit.

Sheriff Brush again stared at the chairlift overhead. He winced a bit when he pictured the long fall to the spot on the rocks, the splashed blood and the dead woman next to him.

"Pretty woman," the sheriff mumbled.

He and the deputy stood on the steep slope. It was too steep to hold snow when hit by the Colorado sun.

The sheriff had passed a ski helmet on the rocks as he climbed up to meet the deputy.

"You'd better get that on your way down," Brush told his deputy. "It could be hers."

"Look down there," the deputy said, pointing downhill, beneath the cable for the chairlift. "There are two skis. Could they be hers too?"

The sheriff looked in the direction of the skis.

"Could be," the sheriff said to Aguayo. "If that might be the case, leave everything where it is. I'm going to ask the crime-scene technicians to come up and take a look before we disturb anything."

The chairlift was designed to carry four people to the top of an expert run called "Heart Attack." But after investigators from the sheriff's office interviewed the lift operators, they were confident the woman had climbed aboard the lift alone.

A brochure promoting The Craters Ski Resort boasted that the high-speed quad would suspend skiers and snowboarders higher above the ground than any lift in the entire country. That was possible. But then, the nation's ski industry was never short on hype.

Upon hearing of the incident, the resort's management ordered the chairlift to be stopped after being emptied of riders. Then, the very chairlift in question was moved back into position above its last rider.

Two frantic snowboarders had reported what they witnessed as soon as they reached the top. They were apparently the only ones to see what happened.

"You saw her fall off?" a sheriff's investigator asked them.

"I'm not so sure she fell," one boarder stated. "She looked like she jumped."

The other snowboarder agreed. They described the woman kicking off one ski and then the other.

"Those skis took a long time to hit the ground," one of the witnesses said. "But she didn't seem bothered by it. Then she pulled off her helmet and just tossed it."

CARPE Ski 'em: a Murder on Skis Mystery

The witnesses told the investigator that they had noticed her in the lift line. They described an attractive woman. They said brown hair flowed from beneath her ski helmet.

"It was crazy, man," one of the snowboarders said. "She just chucked her skis and helmet, lifted the safety bar and sort of slid herself off the seat."

"Without skis and with no hope of surviving the fall," the investigator said.

"Crazy, man," the snowboarder said. "Reminds you to live for today. You never know what's going to come tomorrow. Carpe Ski 'em."

2

T hat's not a chairlift, that's a *scare* lift! You're one hundred feet above the ground?"

Bip Peters made the remark as he read the newspaper story about a woman's death at The Craters Ski Resort. Her name still had not been released.

The television news photographer was sitting at a table having lunch with his girlfriend, Sunny Shavano. The two news reporters whom he most often worked with also sat at the table, JC Snow and Snow's fiancée, Robin Smith.

They had agreed to lunch at Casa Bonita, a suburban Denver landmark. The restaurant was best known for its engaging ambiance. Built inside a former department store, the interior was turned into a detailed replica of a Mexican village. In the middle of the sprawling dining room was a waterfall where cliff divers plunged into a small pool below.

"Alright, we're going to go shopping," Bip said, putting the newspaper down and standing. "I would say that we're going to buy your wedding present, but you haven't picked a date yet."

"Yeah. We're worried we won't fit into your busy social schedule," JC responded.

"I'll be there," said Sunny. "Even if he can't fit you into *his* calendar."

"That's why you're my favorite," JC told her.

Sunny was a raven-haired Ute with beautiful brown eyes. She didn't talk a lot. JC thought she was still coming out of her shell. But when she did speak, there was a melody in her voice. She almost sounded like she was singing.

She met Bip when he was covering a story on the Western Slope of Colorado. She moved to Denver to be closer to him. She was still adjusting to big-city life, after growing up in a small community in Utah populated mostly by other Utes. In Denver, she was still going through a bit of culture shock.

The dining room at Casa Bonita was dimly lit. JC and Robin sat at a replica of a patio at a Mexican hacienda. Little stars beamed from the ceiling. The walls and floors had colorful tiles with birds and flowers on them. The conversation was periodically interrupted by the splash of a cliff diver hitting the water.

"Do you want to help me or not?" Robin asked when she and JC found themselves alone at the table.

"Of course, I do," JC told her. "But I want you to plan the wedding the way you want it to be. Make choices that make you happy. If you're happy, I'm happy."

"If you say, 'Happy wife, happy life,' I'm going to call it off," Robin told him, smiling. "You will live alone until you die alone, always wishing you had been nicer to me."

"You sound dangerously close to coming to your senses and dumping me," JC responded. "How may I help?"

"Let's look at the menu again," she said.

"Yes, ma'am," he replied.

"Don't call me 'ma'am,'" she told him. "I'm not your grandmother."

"Yes, ma'am."

"Stop it!"

"It's a sign of respect," he told her.

She shook her head. It was a sign of disbelief and defeat. "What kind of hors d'oeuvres do you want?" she asked.

"There's more than one kind of hors d'oeuvre?"

The response came as no surprise to Robin. Scientists have determined that the fruit fly has the shortest attention span of all living things. That supplanted the goldfish, whose three-second span of attention had previously been heralded as the leader of the pack.

"You remind me of a fruit fly," she said.

"They're kind of gross," he responded.

"In the kitchen," she said more specifically. "You have the attention span in the kitchen of a fruit fly."

She actually thought that JC was brilliant and intuitive. But she understood that for all of her fiancée's knowledge about a wide range of things unknown to most humans, he had a broken neurological switch when it came to cooking.

"Name an hors d'oeuvre that you want at our wedding, JC," she commanded in an "or-else" kind of way.

"Oh, I know," he said, buying time. Then he announced triumphantly, "Chicken wings?"

"You want servers to mingle with the crowd carrying trays of chicken wings?" she asked. He thought she sounded a bit judgmental. "Should we give them napkins or just let our guests wipe their hands on each other's nice dresses and sport coats? Or should the dress code be blue jeans and wool shirts?"

"So, I guess that's a no," he deduced. "How about Rocky Mountain oysters?"

Her eyes studied him, perhaps looking for evidence of a head injury.

"No," she finally said.

"Why not?" he asked, sort of instantly regretting it.

"Because," she said. "Some of our guests from the East Coast will throw up when they learn what Rocky Mountain oysters really are."

"That has happened on occasion," he agreed. "Jackalope drumsticks?"

"I should have made you take a test before I agreed to marry you," she said, sounding aggravated.

"A cooking test?" he asked. "I would have failed."

"I know, sweetie."

JC looked at Robin and was astonished by her beauty. That's how it always was with him. He looked at her red hair that curled at the ends and the smile that always seemed to be there. She had smarts and energy. And he thought she possessed an almost supernatural empathy for others.

"Will you give some more thought to the hors d'oeuvres on your flight to Wisconsin?" she asked.

"Yes, ma'am," he replied.

She winced.

"Are you certain you don't want to come with me?" JC asked again. "You can experience the real-life drama of being inside a maximum-security prison full of women. I hope they all wear short shorts and tight work shirts like that movie we watched."

"That was fiction, honey," she reminded him. "And not very good fiction."

"Potato potahto," he said with a smile.

A woman approached their table. She stood over them for a moment. JC smiled at her. He didn't recognize the woman, but it wasn't unusual for television viewers to approach him and say hello.

The woman tossed a folded piece of paper onto the table.

"They've got it wrong," she said in a voice bordering on gruff.

JC picked up the piece of paper and looked at the woman.

"You don't recognize me, do you?" she asked.

That put JC on the spot. He made an effort to give a moment of his time to every fan who approached him. But there were precious few whom he could name.

"We were at Colorado State University together," the woman continued, still just a notch below sounding combative. "We took some journalism classes together. Agnes Mason."

"Of course, Agnes. How could I forget?" And it was an honest answer. "Agnes" was not a common name in this day and age. "You said they have it wrong. What did they get wrong?"

"Read it," Agnes ordered, pointing to the note.

He did and then slid the paper across the table so that Robin could read it. It was a copy of the suicide note recovered from the body of the woman found at The

Craters ski area, the one who jumped or slipped off the chairlift.

"Did you know her?" JC asked the woman, who continued to stand over them.

"My sister," Agnes replied in the same brusque voice. "Her name was Loretta Sopris. Different last name than mine. She was married and divorced. I never married."

"Do you know what happened?" Robin asked.

"No," Agnes responded. "But this doesn't make sense. It's not who she was."

"You don't believe she committed suicide?" JC asked. He was trying to be as gentle as he could be with someone who had suffered a terrible loss.

"I'm not even saying that," Agnes said. "Maybe she did. But then she had a good reason. That's all I'm saying."

"Do you think she was murdered?" Robin asked.

"Maybe," the woman replied.

"The newspaper says that she was alone on the chairlift," Robin said gently.

"Doesn't mean she wasn't murdered," Agnes replied.

"Not in the customary fashion, I suppose," JC told her. "Have you told this to the sheriff?"

"Yes," she said bluntly. "They don't agree."

"Did John Washburn show up for work this morning?" Sheriff Brush asked his next-in-command, Rock Bush.

Captain Bush was chief of investigations in the small sheriff's office. He had a wide mustache with ends that rose slightly, like a handlebar. He looked the part of a frontier lawman from the old days.

"No," the captain answered. "And his wife hasn't seen him for four days."

"Didn't she think that was odd?" the sheriff asked, running his hand over the top of his red hair.

"She said that she spent a long weekend in Fort Collins," Bush told him. "She said that she telephoned home, but he didn't answer. She figured that he was in the shower or out on a walk or something."

"Did she call him more than once?" Brush asked.

"She was sort of vague about that," Captain Bush said. "I get the feeling that the coals in that couple's campfire have cooled."

"How much older is he?" Brush inquired.

"Thirty years," the captain responded. "John is seventy and Charlie is forty. She was only twenty years old when she married a fifty-year old man."

"Well, who are we to judge," the sheriff mumbled. "Take another look around for him this morning. Go down to his office and see what they know. By this afternoon, if we haven't found him, we'll have to put out a BOLO and call him a Misper."

It was Monday morning. This was the routine that Sheriff Jerry Brush and Captain Rock Bush carried out every Monday morning.

They were not unaware of the odd similarity of their names. They liked to say, "We are Brush and Bush. We both grow wild and sometimes catch fire."

Each Monday morning, they sat in the sheriff's office, shared a cup of coffee and asked about each other's lives. Then they rehashed the weekend and set the table for the week ahead.

"Anything new on the suicide?" the sheriff asked.

"Not really," Rock told him. "The family called and said there must be more to it. But they didn't know what that would be."

"It must be a terrible thing to deal with, the suicide of a loved one," Brush commented. "Anything else?"

"We had a rescue late yesterday," the captain reported. "A couple of teenagers from Wyoming took a wrong turn off Pap Smear and skied out of bounds. They had a nice run down a gully until it got flat and box-ended. Then they were lost and scared. One of them climbed up a rock face to get a phone signal and dial 9-1-1. Pretty daring climb. They're okay now."

"Good," the sheriff summed things up. "Well, it looks like we have our work cut out for us. Let's find John. We'll be getting calls soon."

3

"Mr. Emerson, you are on trial for attempted assault with a deadly weapon."

The district attorney stated the obvious for the benefit of the defendant and the jury. "You were already on probation for prior offenses."

"Nothing that was that big a deal," Horace Emerson, the defendant, responded, summarizing his prior convictions.

Despite the disapproving expression on the district attorney's face, a few of the jurors smiled a little at the defendant's attempt to bring context to his criminal background. Cameron was a small county. Everyone on the jury was familiar with the defendant's record of petty thefts and misdemeanors.

"This time, you were having a disagreement with a man," the D.A. asserted. "What made you go get your gun?"

"I was loading my skis into the back of my pickup truck," Emerson explained. "I was in a hurry to get first tracks on Montgomery Pass. There was a ton of new pow pow."

The D.A. scratched his forehead. A few more members of the jury chuckled at the defendant's informal manner of presentation.

"Pow pow is fresh powder snow?" the district attorney asked.

"Yes," Emerson replied.

The district attorney was a man named Frank Steen. He was from one of the few Black families in Cameron County. But he could trace his roots in Colorado further back than most people.

Steen's great-great-grandparents had moved to Colorado when they were freed as slaves in the Deep South. They were among a number of ex-slaves who settled in the Pawnee Grasslands in Weld County and took up farming.

The families scattered during the Dust Bowl when their crops were wiped out. Steen's family came to Cameron County.

"So, back to the point," Frank Steen said. "What made you go get your gun?"

"Okay. So, I'm loading my skis into my pickup truck and I hear a boom!" Emerson explained. "Suddenly, the top third of my skis disintegrate! I'm like, 'What the fuck?'"

"Mr. Emerson," the judge cautioned. "Please be mindful of your language."

"Sorry, Your Honor," Emerson responded.

"Pick up where you left off, Mr. Emerson," the D.A. ordered.

"So, I say, 'What the fuck?' And I turn and see that guy holding a gun," Emerson said. He was pointing at a man sitting behind the prosecution desk.

"And what did you do?" Steen asked.

"I went up to my apartment and got my hunting rifle," Emerson told him.

"Wait," the D.A. said. "Did this man continue to shoot at you?"

"No," Emerson said.

"Were you injured?" Steen asked.

"No," Emerson told him.

"Do you think you had an opportunity to run away?" the prosecutor asked.

"From what?" Horace Emerson inquired.

"From the man with the gun," the D.A. told him.

"Dude, why would I run?" the defendant asked. "He just shot my best pair of skis."

Despite their best efforts to remain composed, a few of the jurors laughed.

"So you didn't consider running to avoid escalating the confrontation," the D.A. summarized. "You just went to get your own gun?"

"For sure," Emerson confirmed. "I told you he just shot my best pair of skis. They were ten years old. You can't even get a pair like that anymore. And they rip!"

A couple of jurors giggled.

"So, you shot at him?" the D.A. asked.

"Yes, what would you do?" Emerson asked the prosecutor.

"Well, I think I'd run for my life," the D.A. said, looking at the jury.

Horace Emerson, the defendant, considered this.

"Well," he finally said. "You must not have very good skis."

Most members of the jury erupted in laughter at the defendant's response. The judge hung his head, but he was laughing too, before banging his gavel to return quiet to the courtroom.

In Cameron County, where everyone knew everyone else, this answer made a lot of sense. No one was actually injured. And the next day, Horace Emerson was acquitted by the jury of his peers.

The story of his testimony quickly circulated around the county seat of Placer and for a short while, Horace became known as the "Celebrity Dude."

The district attorney had not misstated Horace Emerson's background. He was much more talented on skis than he was at evading capture when he broke the law. But he was a small-time offender. And members of the jury knew that.

The existing misdemeanor resulting in the probationary status that the D.A. referred to in court was the result of a Friday night when Emerson "borrowed" a fire truck to drive across town to get to his job in the kitchen of a restaurant.

"It occurred to me that I pay taxes," Emerson had told Deputy Aguayo when he was apprehended. "Therefore, I sort of own that fire truck. I paid for it with my taxes. My pickup truck was broken down, and I only needed to borrow the fire truck. I wasn't going to keep it or anything."

It was actually one of two times that Horace Emerson stole a piece of firefighting apparatus. The other offense involved a ladder truck. He told a deputy that he needed to patch a hole in the roof of the apartment house he rented. He said rain was getting in.

On yet another occasion, Emerson showed up at the small hospital in Placer with a gunshot wound to the hand.

"Numbnuts here says he shot himself with a ghost gun," Captain Bush had explained to the sheriff. "His story makes no sense. But, frankly, he lost me after calling me 'Dude' for about the fifth time."

The sheriff took a crack at questioning the suspect and determined that the young man was actually trying to cover for a friend who accidentally shot Emerson with a ghost gun. The friend was tried and convicted. Emerson wasn't charged.

Horace Emerson was twenty-nine years old. His blond hair was long, and a silly expression seemed to be cemented on his face. He was a backcountry skier. He was rarely seen within the boundaries of The Craters Ski Resort. He seemed to resent that The Craters was there at all. But he knew the chutes and couloirs and plunges of the backcountry around Cameron Pass as well as anyone.

He came to Cameron County when he was adopted by a local couple. He had been living in a foster home in Longmont. Both of his adopted parents died when he was seventeen years old, one succumbed to Covid and the other to cancer.

Horace immediately dropped out of high school. He had only a few months to go before he would have received his diploma.

"Make your education laws strict so your criminal laws can be gentle," county Treasurer John Washburn had lamented. "But if you leave youth its liberty, you will have to dig dungeons for ages."

It was a quote from 16th century philosopher Michel De Montaigne. The county treasurer often liked to quote Montaigne. That one proved to be prophetic.

Since dropping out of school, Horace Emerson had worked as a dishwasher in a restaurant or as a day laborer. He'd been arrested a half dozen times. But he stayed in Cameron County. He loved to ski up on North and South Diamond Peaks, Montgomery Pass and The Nokhu Crags.

The people in Cameron County knew Horace, marveled at his skiing ability and accepted that the bad choices he made rarely inconvenienced anyone other than himself.

"He has a brick for a head, but he has a good heart," the chief of investigations had said. "He's harmless."

Sheriff Brush was overseeing efforts to find John Washburn, the Montaigne-quoting county treasurer. Evening was arriving and there was still no sign of him.

Washburn had lived elsewhere for forty years. He'd come from somewhere in Kansas. No one knew exactly why he settled in Cameron County. It was an odd match.

In a community where lumber shirts, Carhartts and work boots could be worn to the best restaurant in the county seat of Placer, Washburn showed up each day at work in the county building wearing a three-piece suit made in France. He always had a pocket square that matched his tie. His shirts were custom made and he wore cufflinks.

He was well-read and often liked to quote great philosophers, Montaigne being his favorite. He was a dashing middle-aged man when he swept the pretty town bookworm off her feet, a girl named Charlene but better known as "Charlie." She was thirty years his junior.

But John Washburn hadn't been seen since last week. He hadn't shown up for work or called in sick. His car was gone. It wasn't like him to just disappear. And it wasn't easy to hide in a county where everyone knew your business and noticed when your car drove by, especially *his* car.

Sheriff Brush declared Washburn a Missing Person. A BOLO was sent out. Law officers across Colorado, Wyoming, New Mexico and Utah were alerted to be on the lookout for John Washburn.

4

"Don't stare at anyone," she said. "Be careful who you go to the movies with, because movie night is shack-up night. Nothing wrong with that, just know what you're getting into."

Shara Adams Kelly recited the lessons she had learned so far at Taycheedah Correctional Institution in Fond Du Lac, Wisconsin.

She sat on a plastic chair at a table across from JC Snow in the visiting room of the women's prison.

"And you need cigarettes if you're going to get along with these women," Shara continued. "They love to play poker, and cigarettes are money."

JC reviewed his conversation with Shara as he emerged from the modern glass-and-concrete visitors entrance of the women's prison in Fond Du Lac. He was back in a world where he was free to go where and when he wanted to.

"There is no privacy in here," Shara had told him. "Zero. I think that's the worst of it. It takes some getting used to."

The sliding glass door closed automatically behind JC and locked him out. To him, the locking mechanism sounded like a hammer. Even though he had been a guest there, he was glad to emerge from the concrete walls and tall fences that were topped by razor wire.

He looked at his cell phone. He had to store it in a locker before he entered the actual prison. He stuffed it in his jeans pocket.

The skies were cloudy and spitting a little rain. He heard the sound of seagulls fishing at Lake Winnebago, only a few blocks away.

The visitors entrance at the correctional facility belied the age and disagreeable nature of the complex behind it.

Taycheedah crammed over nine hundred women inside its maximum- and medium-security sections off County Road K. Shara was in the maximum-security prison. After all, she'd killed a man.

She was still getting adjusted to her life in prison. She told JC that she was assigned to wash the floor outside the library.

"They knew I had a college education so they thought I should be near the library."

Shara said that she was also assigned to anger-management training.

"I'm not angry at anyone," she told JC. "I was, but I took care of that."

Shara Kelly was charged with second-degree murder. She shot a Wisconsin state senator to death. But a strong defense and sympathetic jury reduced the ultimate conviction to negligent homicide. She was sentenced to ten years in prison.

The news media devoured the criminal trial; murder charges against a beautiful white redhead whose husband, a crusading journalist, was murdered. And Exhibit F through Exhibit J were photographs of Shara's murder victim, a married state senator. The pictures were taken while he was romping with naked senate interns.

"There's not much trouble here, really," Shara informed JC. "There was a suicide the other night, poor thing. And there's a teacher here who hired her students to murder her husband."

JC and Shara had history. They enjoyed a love affair in college and shared talk of marriage. Then she did a disappearing act. Then there was their second love affair. Eventually, all the drama exhausted them both.

JC had no desire to travel down another path with Shara. He had found Robin. She was perhaps a version of Shara, only emotionally stable.

"There are religious services offered here," Shara told him from her plastic seat and the table across from him. Touching wasn't allowed. "Do you know that four-percent of the women here think they are witches?"

JC had brought her some books. He made the trip to Wisconsin to check up on her. But he wasn't really worried about her safety. Shara's parents named her after a warrior princess. Shara shot and killed a man who deserved it. She would survive this.

"I know a guy who used to be a corrections officer in New York," JC told her. "He said that, with patience, inmates can saw through the metal bars with dental floss."

"JC, hush!" Shara barked and whispered at the same time. "These conversations are monitored. They'll think you're trying to help me break out. I've got enough trouble. I'll just quietly do my time."

"I was just making conversation," JC smiled with false innocence.

"You are a devil," she smiled back.

Their allowed time was coming to an end. JC rose from his seat but leaned forward.

"Can I mail you some dental floss?" JC whispered to Shara.

"Mail me cigarettes," she replied.

5

Big Phil the Cannibal was a Colorado mountain man whose legend befit his name. He was a large man for the middle of the 19th century, perhaps six and a half feet tall. And he told anyone who would listen that in dire times and facing starvation, he had consumed more than one companion.

Cameron Pass, most of which was now incorporated into Cameron County, was roamed by the likes of Big Phil the Cannibal as well as Kit Carson and John Fremont in the first half of the 1800s.

In 1849, a Cherokee found placer gold in the Poudre River. It triggered a brief gold rush that didn't pan out. Then, there was a silver rush that lasted about three years, and then another short gold rush.

The gold rush of 1886 proved to have the most potential. The promise of riches inspired prospectors to endure the harsh winters at the headwaters of the Poudre.

Towns like Manhattan and Poudre City sprang up overnight. They had hotels, supply stores, saloons and brothels to feed off the prospectors and miners.

But the gold veins quickly played out. The gold in Poudre Canyon never amounted to the rich rewards reaped in the mountains west of Denver. Before long, the bustling communities in the Poudre became ghost towns.

Later, a lucrative timbering trade blossomed. Railroad ties were cut to use on the transcontinental railroad. But that brief boom ended too. Cameron County became a relic of the past.

The hardy settlers who remained, like John Zimmerman, left their cabins on Cameron Pass and sought a more survivable climate just down Poudre Canyon. Zimmerman built a hotel. Today, at the foot of Cameron Pass, there is Zimmerman Lake. And nearby, Agnes Lake is named after Zimmerman's daughter.

Today, Cameron County clung to the windy frigid top of Cameron Pass and the Medicine Bow Mountain Range. It was the second smallest county in Colorado. There were nine hundred forty-three permanent residents.

But in the 1970s, Cameron Pass was paved and for the first time, snowplows kept it open all year. A remarkable amount of snow was measured there each year. A ski resort was built called The Craters. And now, during ski season, the number of people bedding down in Cameron County swelled into the thousands. Those were numbers not seen since the gold rush.

The county seat, in fact the only incorporated community in the county, was called Placer.

Placer gold was what made poor men rich, simply by sinking a pan into the river and finding gold nuggets that had already been separated from the hard rock where it had spent millions of years.

At an elevation of 9,921 feet, the town of Placer was constructed as close to Cameron Pass as its settlers could still hope of surviving the harsh winter. The *average* low temperature in January was three degrees. The high was twenty-nine. The town once received twenty-nine inches of snow on Mother's Day.

Placer was a long narrow town that sat on the northern shore of Joe Wright Reservoir and was split in half by State Highway 14. That was Main Street.

There used to be more of Placer. But when the reservoir was built and flooded in 1908, it submerged the schoolhouse and a half-dozen homes. Plenty of other homes burned down over time.

The three-story county courthouse on Main Street, the tallest building in town, was built of granite. There were a few brick buildings in town, but most of the commercial buildings and housing stock was made of wood. It was old wood scarred by fire, water and the weather's fury. The four oldest buildings in Placer were log cabins.

There were stores in Placer with names like Tie Hack and signs with fish and bear. Tie Hack sold work clothing for men and women. In the winter, it also sold skis. The name Tie Hack used to identify the men who fashioned the railroad ties out of fresh-cut timber and floated them down the Poudre River to a spot near Fort Collins.

There was a café called the Lady Moon, named for a washerwoman in a mining camp who became nobility when she married an English lord.

There was also a fishing store and a gas station. And there were a couple of hotels, rustic and affordable. They offered alternatives to the more expensive lodging at the base of the ski mountain. But the expensive ones were within walking distance of the base lifts.

The closest town to Placer didn't even exist. It was called Manhattan. It was a gold-mining town. Its population peaked in 1886, with 300 people and a post office. But Manhattan had long become a ghost town.

Placer remained. It was the last man standing.

The town was just west of the line from Larimer County. At the other end of the Cache La Poudre River and Poudre Canyon was Fort Collins and the north end of Colorado's Front Range.

JC Snow was spending the day on assignment just outside Fort Collins. He was doing a story about an old log cabin on Overland Trail Road, *The* Overland Trail. A new plaque said that a French trapper built the cabin in 1858.

"So, I was speaking with the old guy who lives behind the cabin. He owns the property," JC told his assignment editor over the phone in Denver. "The old gentleman says he has befriended a ghost who lives in the cabin and sometimes they have long talks about the old days. I mean, the old days when there were cowboys riding horses down the road."

"Did he tell you this on camera?" the assignment editor, Rocky Bauman, asked.

"Yeah," JC responded with wonder and delight. "This is a great tale."

"Are we going to embarrass him or get sued when we air it?" the ever-concerned assignment editor asked.

"Sued by who, the ghost?" JC asked.

"Probably not," Rocky stated. "I was thinking about the old man or his family."

"I don't think so," JC told him. "He's a nice old guy. He gave me permission to interview him on camera. Bip was right there with the camera on his tripod. You'd have to be blind to miss it, and I don't think the guy is blind. He said that he doesn't have many years left on earth and he doesn't care what anyone else thinks."

Rocky, the assignment editor, was silent. JC knew that he was thinking over whether their boss, the news director, would be okay with running the story.

"It's a great story, Rocky," JC said into the phone. "I'm not saying you have to believe in ghosts or believe the story is true. But it's a cute slice of the Old West and he makes it sound real as hell. Every story we run on our news can't be about crooked politicians, murder and who is threatening to blow us up with a super weapon. People love these stories."

"I'll make you a deal," said Rocky. "I'll try to sell this story to our boss if you'll agree to pack a bag and go spend a few days up in ski country, starting tomorrow." Their boss was Pat Perilla. He was the news director they both worked for at their Denver television station.

"Seriously?" JC asked. "That's your asking price? An all-expenses-paid ski vacation?"

"There's a county treasurer missing up in Cameron County," the assignment editor informed his reporter. "You're almost halfway there, already. But come home and pack a bag. You and Bip can drive up tomorrow. You'll probably only need one night there. But I don't think this is going to end well. I think we want to get on top of the story."

"I may need a producer," JC said, though he knew he wasn't going to fool Rocky.

"No, you don't," Rocky said. "And your fiancée is not a producer anymore. She's the best reporter I have when you are out of town."

"But she inspires me," JC persisted, knowing he couldn't win this one. He was just in the mood to torment his assignment editor.

"Paintings inspire people," Rocky told him. "Keep an eye out for an inspiring painting when you get up to Placer."

"You're being kind of a homewrecker," JC teased.

"If she hasn't learned that she's too good for you by now, which she is, there probably isn't any hope for her," Rocky laughed.

"Okay," JC acquiesced. "I agree to your difficult terms. I'll do your assignment at the ski area, and I am willing to allow you to pay for my hotel room there. You drive a hard bargain."

"Yes," Rocky agreed. "I am a difficult taskmaster. My plan is to slowly crush your hopes and dreams. I suppose you'll be taking your skis with you."

"If that is the only thing that is going to make you happy," JC replied, "then I'll take my skis, and Bip will bring his snowboard. There is no end to the sacrifices I make for my art."

"Come home, get your ghost story on the air tonight and pack your things. I'll have some information printed out for you on the Cameron story and arrange a satellite truck to meet you there tomorrow for the evening news," Rocky said, winding up the conversation. "Get an early start. It's a long drive."

"I may go ask the ghost where this county treasurer has disappeared to," JC said. "He sounds very insightful."

6

"**C**an you think of anything harder to stop than a torrent of water?"

Bip Peters glanced at JC, awaiting an answer. JC Snow, the television reporter riding in the passenger seat, was giving his answer some thought.

"A crazy conspiracy theory on social media is harder to stop," JC finally answered.

"Okay," Bip said after thinking about JC's answer. "It's a tie."

Bip was behind the wheel of the unmarked news car. A news photographer nearly always drove when news crews were on assignment. The vehicle, a sturdy SUV in this case, was considered a piece of the photographer's equipment.

Bip had raised the issue while pondering the rushing waters of the Cache La Poudre River, running alongside Colorado State Highway 14.

It was January. Temperatures were in the twenties and falling. Some bodies of water froze at that temperature. The rumbling water of the Poudre rarely did.

The car drove west and up to higher elevation. At the top, snow that lined the road was probably three feet deep. The snow pile's height was aided by snowplows.

There was ice on twigs and dormant flora along the riverbank, but the Poudre River itself continued to crash down the path it had carved out over thousands of years. The water was cold, but it was still rushing water.

The drive west through the narrow forty-mile canyon took them past the Ten Bears Winery and roads with celebratory names like "Wonderful Place."

Small collections of log cabins would appear and then disappear in their windows. They had names like Poudre Park and Rusty Buffalo and Indian Meadow Lodge.

There was a legend that the famous scout, Kit Carson, had a string of trading posts along the Poudre River. But legends and outright lies could be hard to separate when recounting tales of mountain men.

There used to be a stagecoach that ran up and down Poudre Canyon to Cameron Pass. It carried mail to homesick silver and gold prospectors.

The Cache La Poudre got its name from French trappers. The story goes that they became stuck in a particularly severe snowstorm at the mouth of the canyon. They had to lighten their load if they were to move forward and survive.

So, they buried much of their supplies, including gunpowder. They would return later to retrieve it. The translation of Cache La Poudre is something along the lines of "Where one hides the powder."

Bip Peters was a talented news photographer. And if that wasn't enough to make him JC's "weapon of choice," Bip was also a skilled snowboarder.

He had just turned thirty-one. He had subtly spiked hair and a face so handsome that women caught themselves staring in his direction.

JC Snow was Bip's elder by eight years. He too would be considered handsome, as long as he wasn't competing against Bip. JC's face would be considered "rugged." He had dark hair and a dark mustache, though he noticed gray hair sneaking into the ranks of both.

JC was fit. He had an athlete's build. He had been a ski racer at CSU in Fort Collins during college. He still entered the occasional ski race among fellow adults. They called their category "Masters Racing." JC didn't feel that he had "mastered" it all.

But he still skied a lot. It was probably why he had never married.

At first, his girlfriends would find ski racing and his ski racing friends exciting. But when racing filled every weekend during the winter and took them only to colder climates, those girlfriends became ex-girlfriends. It was a common casualty of the sport.

Now, Bip and JC were driving up the skinny paved path in Poudre Canyon. There was only enough space between the canyon wall and its wild river for two lanes of Highway 14.

Bip kept one eye on the road and one eye on the scenery. He was sad to see the bare pines, spruce and cedar trees blackened by a recent wildfire. But groves of small aspens were growing in their place.

As JC studied notes he had compiled for the news story they were covering, Bip would interrupt when he spotted the occasional bighorn sheep on the canyon wall.

"I would like it on record that history is gender-biased," JC proclaimed after a long period of silence and a drought of bighorn sightings.

"How so?" Bip asked.

"I'm reading a magnificent history about Cameron Pass, the Poudre and the Medicine Bow Range. But it only talks about the men."

JC held the hefty volume up to Bip so he could look at an old photograph.

"These pictures of old cabins built by pioneers often include images of women standing next to the cabin," JC said. "But the written history only names the men, Mr. Provost or Mr. Davis or Mr. McGinnis. I'm guessing that the woman in that picture didn't just stand around all day and watch the man work. I suspect those women were pretty tough too. I just think they should get their share of the credit."

"And I am sure those women are, at this moment, applauding you in their graves," Bip told him.

As the canyon opened up, much taller mountains were revealed. The road over Cameron Pass had an elevation of 10,276 feet. Mountains around the pass exceeded 11,000 feet. Mt. Richthofen was 14,000 feet.

The snow lining the road outside their SUV grew deeper. Ahead was the Medicine Bow Range. To the south was the Mummy Range.

They passed a turnoff for The Craters Ski Resort but continued west up Highway 14.

JC spied a pair of backcountry skiers and pointed them out to Bip.

"Didn't a backcountry skier just die up here in an avalanche?" Bip asked.

"Yep, a woman," he said. "And another backcountry skier died up here last winter. Backcountry skiers love it up here, but avalanches are a recurring problem."

They passed a sign informing them that the speed limit had dropped to thirty miles an hour. A few old wooden buildings and a rusted pickup truck appeared, half buried by the snow, and they entered the town of Placer.

Bip parked their car in front of the county building. It was an impressive structure built a long time ago with blocks of gray granite. There were pillars in front that reached from the front porch to the roof.

The day was sunny, but it was cold. It didn't look to JC like snow melted there very often. Aside from the sidewalks and plowed streets, everything was covered in snow.

Walking up the shoveled stairs and inside the county building, they entered a dark lobby that was two stories tall. Gray pillars filled the space and office doors lined the walls. Stenciling on the frosted window of a door to the left told them it was the treasurer's office.

"When is John coming in?" complained a voice as JC and Bip entered the office. Bip was carrying his camera and, unnoticed, began to gather footage.

"I can't make sense out of his bookkeeping," the clerk's voice continued. The two journalists could see that the complaining was coming from one of three men on the other side of a glass partition. The partition stood on a service desk that extended the width of the room. Employees were allowed on one side of the glass, and the public would be tolerated on the other.

"Nobody knows where John is," an employee standing on the other side of the glass answered impatiently. "Even the sheriff can't find him."

"Well, he is the only one who can balance these books. So, he has to come back," the first employee said tersely.

"Don't worry," a third male employee said. He was sitting at his desk. "John will know where the money is. He always finds it."

"I don't know how," the first employee said, sounding exhausted. He sat at his own desk and had logbooks open in each hand. "I can find entries stating who paid their taxes or who paid for a permit. But I can't see where the money was deposited. I'm looking at the line I should be looking at. It's just blank."

"John will know," the other sitting employee said. They were used to John taking the lead. They were finding that they really couldn't function without him.

"I see there is no record at all of our allowances," the fraught employee continued. He looked across the room at the employee who was standing. "Jed, you took a fifty-dollar allowance out of your cash drawer when you went out to lunch last Thursday. Have you paid it back?"

"John said I don't have to pay it back until my next paycheck," Jed responded after rolling his eyes. "He didn't have a problem with it. Why do you? And have you paid back the allowance you took to buy a birthday gift for your niece?"

"I always pay mine back," the first employee snapped.

"But have you?" Jed persisted.

"Not yet," his colleague mumbled as he buried his head back in the books.

"Excuse me," JC finally interrupted, so he could get some dialogue going. "Do you know where we can find the treasurer?"

"No, do you?" the first employee asked, noticing Bip's camera. "And you can't do that in here. Stop that please."

Bip continued to record the conversation. It was a gray area when it came to videotaping public employees in a public building.

"Does he go missing very often?" JC asked.

"And who might I be speaking to?" asked the first employee.

JC told them that he and Bip were TV journalists from Denver.

"I had hoped he would be found by now," JC said.

"We do not have any comment," the first employee said. "You'll have to speak with the sheriff."

"Has the sheriff asked you where Mr. Washburn goes?" JC asked. "Who is in charge while he's gone?"

"I am," the man sitting with the office books said. "I'm the deputy treasurer."

"Did the sheriff share any theories with you?" JC asked. "As far as Mr. Washburn's whereabouts?"

"You'll have to speak to the sheriff about that," the deputy treasurer responded. "And I should be getting back to work, if that's all you need."

"And Mr. Washburn hasn't been seen since when?" JC inquired.

"He called in sick Thursday morning. We haven't seen or heard from him since," the deputy treasurer stated in a haughty tone. "And now, is that all?"

"One more thing," JC said. "What's an allowance? The thing you and your co-workers were just talking about."

"I am not at liberty to say," the man responded. His eyes shifted to his colleagues.

"Should I ask the sheriff about that also?" JC inquired with a smirk.

They left the office and looked for a stairway. The sheriff's office and the small jail were in the basement of the county building.

They found polished granite stairs in the back of the lobby. After climbing down to the basement level, they walked through a single glass door with a push bar. The metal bar felt sticky. From behind a long desk, a receptionist sat next to equipment that suggested she was also the sheriff's dispatcher. She advised them that the sheriff wasn't in his office. JC left a business card and said he would be calling.

"What's this allowance thing about?" Bip asked, after climbing back up the stairs and walking out the double doors at the front of the county building.

"I don't really know," JC admitted. "They were talking about their allowances when we first walked into the office. To me, it sounded like they were taking short-term loans from their cash drawers. I can't imagine that's legal."

7

"**D**id you hear that?"

Bip called JC's attention to a BOLO issued by the Cameron County Sheriff's Office. It told law officers within earshot to "be on the lookout" for a new Citroën C5 Aircross.

They had been driving away from the county courthouse. While JC was writing notes, Bip fiddled with his phone and opened an app to pick up local police scanner frequencies.

"A Citroën?" JC said, to make sure he had heard the BOLO correctly. "The French Citroën?"

"It's a Citroën version of an SUV. Nice car. Thirty-three to forty-three thousand dollars. You can get the fossil-fuel version or electric."

"I'm guessing this one is fossil-fuel," JC said. "Where would you plug in an electric car around here if you couldn't reach your own garage?"

"Maybe you get a long plug that extends from France," Bip quipped. "There can't be many Citroëns around here. I don't even know where there's an official dealership."

"You know something about cars," JC said. "How come you never want to talk about auto racing with me?"

"Because when it comes to history, ski racing and auto racing, you're a motormouth. The discussion of last Sunday's F1 race would last longer than the race itself," Bip said with a smile. "I dabble in motorcars, and I like unusual things. Citroëns are unusual here."

"You think that's the county treasurer's car?" JC asked. "Could he possibly drive a French SUV? It *is* missing. That's something the car and the treasurer have in common."

JC's phone rang. It was the sheriff's secretary and dispatcher. She said that the sheriff could talk to them if they could be at his office in ten minutes.

"Turn the car around," JC told Bip. And they headed back to the courthouse.

The rear entrance to the sheriff's office was in the parking lot in back of the county courthouse. To enter the sheriff's office from outside, their visit began with six granite steps going down to the basement. It was a common layout for county buildings built in that era.

"Gentlemen," Sheriff Jerry Brush greeted them. He extended a hand to shake. "What brings you to Cameron County during the warm season?"

41

"If this is the warm season, how do you survive the cold season?" JC asked.

The sheriff laughed. They were standing in the small lobby of the sheriff's domain.

"It's always the cold season here," the sheriff smiled. "Even in the summer."

"Is that the county treasurer's car you have a BOLO out on?" JC asked. "The Citroën?"

"That is a fact," the sheriff answered. "I can't tell you much, though. John Washburn hasn't been seen since last week. We have no reason to expect anything has happened to him, but we can't find him."

The sheriff agreed to an interview on camera. He thought it would be useful to get the word out on the missing man and his car.

He showed them into his personal office, behind a wall of frosted privacy glass. The walls were concrete building blocks painted white, now a dirty white. The whole of the sheriff's office-space, the workplace for the sheriff and a dozen deputies, looked as though it could use a scrubbing. It reflected a county that didn't have a lot of money to spend.

"What can you tell us about the car?" JC asked. "He really drives a Citroën?"

"John is a bit eclectic," the sheriff told them. "I would ask your television viewers to keep an eye out for the car. It's platinum gray. Gray interior. He's got a mechanic in Denver who services it for him. He could turn up there."

"So, the car is missing. Could he have slipped off the road?" JC asked.

"That certainly is a possibility," the sheriff told them. "There aren't a lot of places, locally, that it would easily slip off the road. As you have seen for yourself, the snow here is about three feet high along the side of the road. Nature's guardrails."

"Do you have any suspicion of foul play?" JC inquired.

"I have no evidence of that," the sheriff replied. "We can suspect things all we want. We have no reason, however, to suspect foul play."

At the end of the interview, Bip wrapped up his equipment. Off camera, there was another question JC was curious about.

"What is an allowance?" JC inquired. "I was in the treasurer's office, and I heard employees there speaking about an allowance two of them had taken out of their cash drawers. What were they talking about?"

"I can honestly tell you that I don't know what you're talking about," the sheriff replied.

"You've never heard something termed 'an allowance' here in the courthouse? In the treasurer's office?" JC asked.

"I'm not familiar with that term," the sheriff said. "When John turns up, you can ask him."

"John Washburn, the county treasurer?" JC asked. "You honestly think he is just going to turn up?"

"I have no evidence to the contrary," the sheriff said.

The interview over, JC handed the sheriff his card and headed outside. The drive from Denver had eaten up much of their day. As the sun set, JC and Bip met the satellite truck that was parked outside the courthouse. Climbing inside the box, they edited their story and then reported "live" back to viewers in Denver on the disappearance of John Washburn.

They were in darkness by the time JC, Bip and a satellite truck operator named Jem Norvell were done with their work.

JC and Bip climbed into their car and turned east, headed for The Craters Ski Resort and the place they'd call home for one night, the Clark Hotel.

Jem said he'd check in later, after tidying up his truck. JC and Bip smiled at each other. They knew that, when on overnight trips, Jem used the impressive satellite truck as a babe magnet.

He would find a bar to park in front of, strike up a conversation with a woman and invite her to take a tour of his high-tech news-gathering ship. Sometimes it worked, sometimes it didn't.

Bip and JC turned up Long Draw Road, less than two miles south of Placer. It was the access road to the ski mountain, the resort village and the Clark Hotel.

A plaque inside the lobby of the hotel told them that it shared a name with a hotel built on Cameron Pass in 1881. A man named J.A. Clark erected the original. A store was built next to it and a post office opened in a small cabin next to that.

The check-in desk at the *new* Clark Hotel was long and made of dark, polished wood. The hotel lobby was sprawling. Skiers and snowboarders traveled with a lot of gear. The lobby was big enough to accommodate all their baggage.

Staff at the Clark Hotel all wore green jackets. There was a man in the lobby wearing a green jacket and standing next to a door with a sign overhead that said "Valet." Skis and snowboards were allowed no further in the building than the lobby. Sharp metal edges on those skis and snowboards would not be allowed to scar the hotel's woodwork and furniture.

The new hotel had old-world charm. Aside from a wide-open lobby, there were nooks where guests could squirrel away to read a book or talk on the phone or enjoy an après-ski drink.

The builders of the hotel took care to give it the feel of an inn that would have been there for skiers a long time ago. The interior was full of white walls and polished wood. The lighting was mounted on wall sconces, carved to include the shapes of wildflowers, moose and bear heads.

There were carved mantles over the doors of the rooms. They blended shapes of mountains and pine trees. And on the walls hung paintings, visions of how life looked when gold miners and tie hacks and their women endured the elements up there.

Checking into their rooms, there was little to see out their windows other than the dark ski mountain and dots of light high up. That's where groomers were already starting to prepare the slopes for skiers the next day.

JC and Bip walked out of the hotel in search of dinner. A restaurant and bar called Chambers' Revenge had been recommended. It was only a few doors down.

Sliding into a booth, JC ordered a dark beer brewed by New Belgium in Fort Collins called 1554. Bip followed his lead.

"You want to hear a story about that beer?" The voice came from the table next to them. A man and woman were looking at them, smiling. The man had short hair and wore glasses. And he had a larger-than-usual Adam's apple. He looked a little out of his element on Cameron Pass, not a skier or snowboarder and certainly not a lumberjack. He looked a little vulnerable.

45

"Henry Marvin. Everyone calls me Marv," the man said as he shook hands with the two journalists. "This is my girlfriend, Mercy."

"Hi," Mercy said with a big smile. She had shoulder-length brown hair and wore a necklace made from leather and ceramics that was visible only because her shirt was unbuttoned to reveal the top of her breasts. She was average-looking, but her energy, and maybe some sex appeal, moved everything up a notch.

"Yep," JC said. "Tell us about the beer."

"It's an old recipe for Belgium black beer," Marv said. "But the real story is how the brewer in Fort Collins found it. The recipe was buried in some old volume in the basement of Colorado State University's library. A beer aficionado stumbled across it and wanted to bring other brewers to the library to view his find.

But the next day, the Poudre River flooded and filled the library basement with water! The recipe was lost. Long story short, I think they went to Europe and found the recipe. And here it is!"

"Glad your tuition paid for something useful," Bip said, nudging JC.

A waiter came to their table. JC and Bip ordered dinner, one order of chicken wings and one order of nachos. They'd split the two plates.

"Want to hear a great story about this bar?"

"Yep," JC answered Marv, who was again leaning from his table toward their booth.

"The story is about why they call this bar Chambers' Revenge," Marv said. "It's a true story."

"Stop him if you get bored," Mercy said with a smile. "He could go on and on. His brain never sleeps."

"No, I actually like this stuff," JC told her.

"Thanks," Marv said. "So, Robert Chambers and his son moved to Cameron Pass in 1858. They built a camp. The lake, by the way, is now named Chambers Lake. It's the headwaters of the Poudre River.

Anyway, the Chamberses trapped for beaver and hunted bear and all that stuff while they were living there. But when the son was away getting supplies, some Indians attacked the camp and Robert Sr. was killed. He put up a heck of a fight, but he was killed. The son returned and made some vow to get even, get revenge for his father's murder. And apparently, he did. The son went berserk, killing a lot of Indians who he felt were responsible for his father's death."

"I told you," the smiling girlfriend said. "His brain never sleeps."

"Do you two live here, in Cameron County?" JC asked.

"We do," Mercy told them. "I've lived here all my life. Marv showed up a couple of years ago. He's a genius in hiding."

"A genius?" Bip asked, turning to Marvin. "What have you done with your beautiful mind?"

"You know that GPS that gives directions but also taunts you and makes wisecracks? It's funny as hell," Mercy said as she began to pet her boyfriend. "My baby invented that."

"The one that says, 'If you're done driving like my grandmother, we might get there before dark. Turn here?'" Bip asked, laughing.

"That's the one," Mercy said smiling. Marv just lowered his head. He didn't seem to be looking to impress anyone.

"That makes you 'Mad Marv,' doesn't it?" JC asked. "You're 'Mad Marv, Boy Genius'?"

"Holy crap," Bip said.

"I told you he was a genius," Mercy affirmed. Marv just flinched, not really comfortable with the adulation.

"Seriously, I have seen turtles drive faster," Bip said laughing, imitating the voice that ridicules drivers who buy Mad Marv's GPS.

"It's probably time to get you home," Marv said to Mercy as he took a long look at his wristwatch. It was an impressive timepiece, lots of dials within the dial and a vintage leather strap.

"Enjoy your dinner. It was a pleasure to meet you," he said to JC and Bip as he rose from the table.

Mad Marv exited the restaurant with Mercy, smiling in tow.

"Did you see that wristwatch?" Bip asked. "That's like an eighteen-thousand-dollar watch. It's a Breitling Aviator 8."

"He paid that for a *watch?*" JC asked. "How do you know about his watch? Are you going to buy one?"

"Pffft," Bip spat. "I paid that for my car! Eighteen-thousand-dollar Breitlings are unusual watches. They only made like two hundred and fifty of them. I told you; I'm interested in unusual things."

"Like Citroëns in Cameron County," JC suggested. Bip nodded.

"What else is Mad Marv known for?" Bip pondered out loud. "I remember reading something."

"Yep. I do too," JC said. "I can't remember what it is, but I don't remember it being a flattering portrayal. His girlfriend said he was hiding up here. She may have meant it literally."

8

"That is so Johnny," she told JC.

JC and Bip had awakened early at the Clark Hotel. They grabbed breakfast at the Lady Moon Café in Placer. They wanted to take advantage of the day, before they reported one more time, live, for the evening news and then drove back to Denver.

JC told Bip to head up the hill on Medicine Bow Avenue and turn left onto Never Summer Street. They were going to pay a visit to Charlene "Charlie" Washburn, the wife of the missing man.

On the hill overlooking the rest of Placer, there was a row of old Victorian houses on Never Summer Street. They were painted in bright colors. Someplace else, they'd be called ostentatious. But in Colorado's old mining towns, they were lovingly called "Painted Ladies."

John and Charlie Washburn lived in one of the painted ladies. Compared to some, the paint scheme of their home was subdued. It was a sky-blue house with red trim and white posts and railings on the porch.

"Do I understand that he drove a Citroën?" JC asked. "Why go through the inconvenience of driving a French car with practically no dealerships or maintenance available to him?"

"That is so Johnny," Charlie Washburn answered. "He loves everything French. His car is from France, his suits are from France, and he loves to quote a French philosopher named Montaigne."

"Is he French?" JC asked.

"No," Charlie laughed. "He's from Kansas."

Charlie Washburn was forty years old, three decades younger than her husband. She had kind eyes and dark hair that dropped onto her shoulders. She smiled easily. But she looked frail, very thin.

They sat at the kitchen table of the home she had shared with John Washburn for twenty years. She had prepared coffee for her visitors.

"We are both opposites and soul mates," she said. "I was the bookworm growing up here in Placer. I was lonely. I didn't have anyone to share my books with. I went to college in Fort Collins and when I graduated and moved back, Johnny had moved here.

"He was worldly and loved to read. He was classy and incredibly handsome. I was only twenty, but we married after only knowing each other for five months."

"It sounds like the books, and the intelligent conversation were the 'soul mate' part," JC said. "But you said you are opposites too?"

"I love to snowboard," she said. Her January tan had already given her away. "Johnny wanted nothing to do with skiing or snowboarding. But that's okay. I was happy to come home to him every night and he was kind enough to listen while I told him about all my adventures."

"So, where is he?" JC asked. Bip had started rolling his camera.

Charlie exhaled and said nothing for a moment, and then she started to cry.

"I don't know," she squeaked.

Given time to compose herself, Charlie continued to talk.

"He is a good man, kind almost to a fault," she said. "He takes flowers to the cemetery to place on graves of people he hardly knew. He plants flowers on the graves of friends, but he also brings flowers for graves that he knows never get visits. He doesn't want them to be alone."

She started crying again.

"'He who fears he will suffer already suffers from his fear,'" she said, sniffling and wiping her eyes. "That's Montaigne. That was Johnny's way of saying 'Suck it up.' So, I'm trying to be strong."

"You have already spoken to the sheriff's office?" JC asked.

"Yes," she said. "They were here yesterday."

With the end of the interview, Bip turned his attention to shooting video of some pictures of John Washburn that Charlie had put out on the table for them.

51

JC could see the man Charlie was describing. He had a full head of gray hair and was quite good-looking. In most of the pictures, he was wearing a business suit or sport coat. Sometimes, he even wore an ascot. He looked very French.

"Could I ask you to let me know if you hear anything?" Charlie asked JC. "I know the police will be busy."

"Of course," JC told her. "And if anything else occurs to you…" He left the sentenced unfinished as he slid one of his cards across the table in front of her and thanked her for the coffee.

JC helped Bip carry his lights out to the car. The sun was bouncing off the snow-covered high peaks now.

It was easy to see why the ski resort had been named "The Craters." Cameron Pass was surrounded by ancient volcanos. They stopped belching fire and smoke millions of years ago and only shards of the volcanos remained. But many of the deep mountain lakes and valleys filled the left-behind craters.

John Washburn's disappearance was now the topic of discussion in the small community. Every permanent resident in Cameron County was at least acquainted with each other. And Washburn was a public servant; the man they paid their taxes to.

JC looked out on the ice covering Joe Wright Reservoir. Many locals called it a lake. There were ice fishers dotting the surface of the frozen water. Following a road to a boat launch, JC and Bip walked out on the ice to gather some man-on-the-street interviews.

Few of the local residents wanted to speculate on camera, about the fate of someone they knew personally. But those who weren't local, who just came to fish, suggested that Washburn probably drove off the road and froze to death. Others suspected that the county treasurer stole money and moved to the Caribbean.

"It is funny," one ice fisher said. "You can put decent law-abiding citizens next to a lot of money, and they just can't help themselves. They steal it. Treasurers for the little-league baseball team do it, treasurers for the school-parent association do it. It's human nature, I guess."

JC found that men and women fishing through a hole in the ice were a good-natured group, and patient. There was a frosty breeze blowing across the ice. The fishing fanatics explained that sometimes at Joe Wright, the ice was so thick that it was hard to drill a hole.

Returning to their car, Bip turned up his app so they could listen to the police-scanner frequency. So far, it had just been a mash of pulling over cars driving above the speed limit and an oversized truck coming over the pass.

"Do you think he's dead?" Bip asked while he watched the road.

"Washburn?" JC answered. "I don't know. But there's a reason he hasn't come home."

They were interrupted by a new conversation coming over the sheriff's frequency.

"The old Indian trail," one voice said. "I'll meet you there."

"Roger," another voice said.

"Any clue where the old Indian road is?" JC asked Bip.

"I have as good a clue as you do," Bip responded. "But with three feet of snow presently lining the roads, I can't imagine there are many to choose from up here. Make a guess and tell me which way to turn."

"East," JC said with uncertainty.

Their curiosity was soon rewarded. Less than two miles east of Placer, a short distance from the access road to The Craters, two sheriff's patrol cars were pulled over. Bip parked behind them.

He pulled his camera out from the back seat, where he'd protected it from the cold. He quickly began taping. If a deputy told them to get lost, adequate news footage would already be in the can.

The law officers' attention seemed to focus on a narrow, unmarked road. It was covered in snow. The path headed north off Highway 14. At a bend, it disappeared into the pines.

One deputy was Aaron Aguayo, the same one who was first on the scene when Loretta Sopris' body was discovered. The other was the captain of investigations, Rock Bush. They seemed to be waiting near tracks left by two or more snowmobiles.

The next vehicle to arrive carried Sheriff Brush. He climbed out of his 4x4 and approached his captain and Aguayo. The sheriff held out a hand to stop JC's advance.

"Let me speak with my deputies," the sheriff said. "I'll talk to you in a minute or two."

The law officers spoke in hushed tones. Sometimes, Aguayo would gesture up the path left by the snowmobiles.

While he waited, JC surveyed the peaks around him. Even covered in snow, he could see the damage left by the Cameron Pass wildfire a few years ago. It had cleared a lot of forest off the hillside. Blackened stumps and charred trunks poked through the snow. In the spring, new growth would sprout. Eventually, a new collection of trees would take the place of the old ones.

Another sheriff's vehicle pulled up, a marked pickup truck. Two men got out, dressed to explore the outdoors. They carried snowshoes. The larger of the two men led the way.

The sheriff approached JC and Bip. The news photographer threw his camera on his shoulder and began to roll.

"We're going to take a look at these snowmobile tracks," the sheriff said. "We think, because there isn't a vehicle with a trailer parked here, that the snowmobilers are gone. This is an old Indian path. We just want to see what's around the bend."

"This is part of the search for the county treasurer?" JC asked.

The sheriff gave the question some thought before deciding what he was willing to say.

"The effort to make contact with Mr. Washburn is ongoing," the sheriff finally commented. "We're following every lead we come across. Again, if anyone knows something about the whereabouts of John Washburn, please contact us."

"Do you think Mr. Washburn is alive?" JC asked.

"We sure hope so," the sheriff answered.

The interview over, Bip shot footage of the two deputies on snowshoes as they walked out of view around the bend.

"Why not bring out a couple of snowmobiles of your own?" JC asked the sheriff.

"We can still do that," Sheriff Brush answered. "But snowmobiles can be like a bull in a china shop. We want to employ a little finesse for starters."

"Is this a strong lead?" JC asked. Being off camera, he hoped the sheriff might be more candid."

"Not particularly," Brush answered. "But you have to follow every lead. You never know."

"Do you think he's still alive?" JC asked again, this time off camera.

"You never know," Brush responded.

JC and Bip waited in their car, keeping warm, for about an hour. The sheriff departed in his vehicle. Aguayo and the captain waited at the head of the snowmobile trail, staying warm in a patrol car.

Then, the two snowshoers reappeared. They were coming back empty-handed.

Bip got out of the car and shot more footage. The two deputies removed their snowshoes as they spoke with their captain. JC approached.

"Did you find anything?" JC asked when the captain was done talking to the deputies.

"No," Captain Bush said as he climbed into his patrol car. Deputy Aguayo did the same and both patrol cars drove away.

That left the black pickup truck with "Sheriff" written across the side in gold block letters. The two deputies were placing their snowshoes in the bed of the truck. One climbed into the cab and turned the heat on. The larger man remained behind and leaned his arm against the truck bed, looking at JC.

"We followed the snowmobile tracks until it looks like one of them had an oil leak or something," the deputy explained. "It looks like they turned around and came back. No snow was disturbed, other than the sled tracks. I don't think anything happened here."

The deputy rarely made eye contact with JC. He probably thought that he shouldn't be talking with the news media. Only, he was.

"I see you on TV all the time," the deputy then said, tugging on his knit cap with "Sheriff" written across the front. The deputy had a name tag on the breast of his jacket that said "Monk."

"Thanks," JC said as he held out his hand. "Deputy Monk?"

"Hank Monk," the deputy smiled and shook his hand. "Don't use my name when you report this, but I really don't think this is where Mr. Washburn is."

"We just came from talking with his wife," JC said, just to keep the conversation going.

"What did you think?" Deputy Monk asked.

"She seems upset," JC answered.

"I'll bet," Monk responded. "Did you sense that there was any marriage trouble? That's one of the theories, that it wasn't a good marriage. But don't quote me."

"I won't," JC told him. "Thanks, Deputy. And here's my card, in case you want to reach me."

They exchanged a nod and JC climbed into the news car as Bip pulled up. Deputy Monk climbed into the passenger seat of the sheriff's truck.

"I think he's dead," Bip said.

"Washburn? If they're searching old roads in the snow," JC said, "they think he's dead too."

9

"How are we going to cover this story if we're going back to Denver?" Bip asked JC.

"Well, you've shot a lot of footage of the area, and of John Washburn's office, and the photographs his wife provided for us," JC said. "If they find him, dead or alive, the anchor will read a story that they'll probably ask me to write, and we'll show the beautiful pictures you took."

"They *are* beautiful," Bip said of his video, smiling. "They're always beautiful."

"It's a money issue, the news director's call," JC said. "I get it. It's not a story that's worth spending what it would cost to cover. Not without a body. And there are missing persons that *never* turn up, ever."

Agreeing to grab dinner before making the drive back to Denver in the dark, JC and Bip headed back to the ski village and a restaurant they had spotted called "The Cache La Poudre and North Park Toll Road Company."

"It's a steak-and-spareribs place," Bip said. "Man food."

"Before we return to our women and they make us eat grass and tofu," JC agreed.

"The things we do for women," Bip said.

"The things that women do for us that make us want to do the things we do for women," JC pointed out.

"True," Bip agreed.

The Cache La Poudre and North Park Toll Road Company Restaurant had wood-paneled walls covered with old photographs of men and women wearing work clothes and holding still for the camera.

There were also photos of old wagons hooked to teams of horses. And there was a small building with the head and shoulders of a man protruding from an open door. Other men leaned against the shack. JC surmised that this was a toll booth.

The Cache La Poudre and North Park Toll Road was built over Cameron Pass in 1880. It was a wagon road cleared through the trees to make travel far easier. Users paid a toll.

JC ate his food and talked with Bip over dinner, but his eyes kept returning to a man sitting a few tables away. The face was familiar, but he hadn't coupled a name with it yet.

Then he did. He suspected that he was mistaken, but the face and physique matched a boy he knew when they were both in high school in Upstate New York.

The man's eyes met JC's. He stood and approached JC's table.

"Are you JC Snow?" the man said.

"Tommy Halvorson?" JC responded in an uncertain tone.

The man laughed and gripped JC's hand to shake it.

"How are you?" the man laughed. "You were a member of the Yellow Streaks." He laughed some more.

"The Blue Streaks," JC corrected him. "Our high school teams were called the Blue Streaks. But I think you're well aware of that."

The man laughed again. JC introduced Tommy Halvorson to Bip.

"JC was a pain in my ass," Tommy said. "He played football and skied for Saratoga High School, and I played football and skied for Shenendehowa High School. We were maybe thirty minutes away from each other, and big rivals.

"You were a better football player than I was," JC said. "But I got my licks in when we went ski racing. You were a good ski racer."

"I can't argue with any of that," Tommy said with a smile. "You were a better ski racer than I was."

Halvorson turned back to a woman at his table and held a finger up, suggesting he'd be back in a minute or two.

"Can I ask you something strange," JC asked.

"You can try," Tommy answered. "I've seen a lot of strange in my adult life."

"I thought you were dead," JC told him.

"A lot of people did," Tommy said, smiling. "I was working down in Puerto Rico when Hurricane Maria hit. It was bad. A lot of people died. There were mudslides, there was flooding, roads were washed out. I was in a town where the bridge was washed away and all the towers for cell phones were knocked down. I couldn't get word out to anyone. We were cut off from civilization for over a month. Some people assumed I was dead, and the story grew from there."

"My mom told me you had died," JC said.

"Yeah, it's not her fault," Tommy replied. "Someone must have told her that. That story spread through our hometown. It's no one's fault."

"Wow," JC said. "I'm glad they were mistaken."

"Yeah, me too," Tommy answered. "Listen, I'd better get back to my date. It's great to see you. Are you going to be here for a while? Are you skiing? It would be great to take some turns together."

JC explained why he and Bip were at The Craters and why they had to return to Denver.

Tommy laid cash on the bar and got the attention of the bartender, telling him that he was paying for JC and Bip's dinner.

"By the way," Tommy said. "Everyone here calls me Scooter. I'm not sure why. But if you want to find me up here, ask for Scooter."

"Alright, Scooter," JC said, laughing. JC gave him a card, writing his personal cell phone number on it, and they agreed to stay in touch. "Thanks for dinner."

"Was he a good friend of yours?" Bip asked in the car as they began to head down Highway 14 and back to Denver.

"He was and he wasn't," JC recalled. "He was a great athlete. The only thing I was better than him at was ski racing. Half the time, he was friendly and half the time he was an annoying trash talker. He liked to try to get inside your head right before a race."

"We were all kids back then," Bip advised. "Besides, did you behave any better?

"No, I didn't. You're right," JC laughed. "I would do a lot of things differently if I was back in high school. Sometimes I feel like I should offer a blanket apology to the world."

"Not me," Bip giggled. "I was cute and perfect."

"Wow," JC responded. "When did that change? It must have come as a terrible shock."

JC's phone rang. He didn't recognize the number of the caller. There were spots in Poudre Canyon where it was difficult to get a phone signal at all.

They happened to be in a tiny community of wooden cabins called Rustic. It was an old summer resort. He asked Bip to pull over.

"JC," the voice said. "This is Hank Monk. I didn't make this call, if anyone asks. But they just found John Washburn's body."

"Holy crap," JC blurted. "Where?"

"An old ghost town," the off-duty deputy said. "Hell, even the ghosts have moved out. It's hard to get to. Where are you, I'll try to give you directions."

"We're in Rustic," JC said.

"That's perfect," he said. "There's a road in Rustic, on the left. It's called Red Feather Lakes Road. Take that up some switchbacks and all the way to a T-intersection. Take a left and follow the fence until it ends. You'll see Larimer County sheriff's vehicles and some of ours. You're in Larimer County now. And be careful. There are some nasty switchbacks before you get here."

"What's Washburn doing there?" JC asked.

"Good question," the deputy answered. "He's just lying in the open. But it's lucky he was found at all. There are only a handful of houses up here. Not many people drive this road. And one more snow would have covered him up until May."

"What's the name of the town?" JC asked.

"It was called Manhattan," Monk said. "There's nothing left of it, except a few rotting logs. There's no sign or anything. If our cop cars weren't here, you'd never find it. And remember, I didn't tell you any of this. Not a word, okay?"

"I won't say a word," JC assured him.

"We must make a stop on our way home," JC said to Bip. "Take the next left."

JC's phone rang again. It was Rocky Bauman, the assignment editor. Bip had only just begun to pull his car onto Red Feather Lakes Road, and he pulled off again.

"Turn around," Bauman said.

"I don't think that's a good idea," JC told him.

"JC, they just found John Washburn's body," Bauman said urgently.

"I know, we're almost there," JC said triumphantly.

"Seriously? You already knew?" Bauman said, sounding a bit defeated. "How did you know?"

"I gave my card to the Grim Reaper," JC replied. "He does quite a business, you know."

"Alright. The cops are still there," Rocky said. "I'll call the Clark Hotel and extend your reservations. I'll tell Jem to keep the satellite truck there. Can you do a live shot for us at ten?"

"I wouldn't have it any other way," JC said and smiled. "The public can't get enough of me."

Disconnecting the call with Rocky, JC briefed Bip on the new plan.

"What am I going to do for fresh underwear in the morning?" Bip mocked.

"Seriously?" JC said to him. "You picked tomorrow to start wearing clean underwear?"

Bip steered their SUV up the switchbacks and proceeded on County Road 68C/162. Taking a left at the T-intersection, they followed the fenceposts on the left until they saw a collection of patrol cars parked to the side. Some were stamped with the Larimer County sheriff's logo, some with Cameron County.

Getting out of their car, JC zipped up his jacket and pulled the collar higher onto his neck. The sun was down, and the cold air adhered to his skin.

Bright lights were set up under a tent and aimed down at the snow. Presumedly, a body was on the other end of all that light.

"Don't come any further, fellas," a deputy said to JC and Bip as the deputy held out his hand like he was stopping traffic. "We don't want to add any more footprints to this scene."

Bip shot footage from where he stood. Under the tent, an official photographer for the sheriff was taking pictures of the body and the surroundings. Men in uniform gathered in small groups to talk. Deputy Monk was among them, avoiding eye contact with the two journalists. A forensic specialist kneeled next to the body.

The light set up by law enforcement made everything around the crime scene look darker. JC's eyes swept across the location. All he could make out was a hillside of young trees. He couldn't see anything that marked its past as a busy mining town. No saloon, no barbershop, no hotel.

"If you're looking for the town of Manhattan, you're wasting your time," Sheriff Brush said as he approached. "It was considered a fire hazard in the 1930s and the Forest Service burned the empty buildings down."

"They had no sense of history?" JC asked, but it was really a criticism.

"Not in those days," the sheriff said. "And what little was left after that was burned up by the Cameron Peak wildfire a few years ago. There's a cemetery somewhere around here. But you're not going to find it in the dark."

"What's he doing here?"

"The dead guy? Your guess is as good as mine," Sheriff Brush responded. "Maybe they couldn't find the cemetery."

JC's phone rang again.

"I'll be there tomorrow night." It was Robin's voice. "I'll pack you a bag. Sunny is going to pack Bip a bag. I'll bring them both."

"Make sure Sunny packs him some clean underwear," JC said. "He's choosing *now* to get picky about that."

"You're a jerk," Bip interrupted.

"Sunny is going to try to come too," Robin said. "She has to talk to her workplace. It might not work out."

"And how long are *you* staying?" JC asked.

"I'm working on that," she told him. He could hear her smile.

10

"Personally, I'm sorry to see you go, Badass," the man said as he hoisted a dram of whisky to face level. "I know I don't speak for everyone, in that regard. But you always treated me square."

Former state police trooper Bob Andrews nodded his head in appreciation and raised his own glass of straight Oban Scottish single malt. They both downed the entire glass. The other man wouldn't have ordered the good stuff, the Oban, but Andrews was buying.

The other man was named Bernie Watch. He was one of the few who had stood by Andrews' side during his darkest days. Andrews had a nickname for Bernie Watch.

He called him Tick Tock. Andrews had a nickname for nearly everyone.

They stood at the bar. The sun was shining outside, but it was dark in the Pioneer Saloon in Ketchum, Idaho. The Pioneer was a favorite watering hole for locals and visitors alike.

If anyone had ever turned up the lights inside the Pioneer, the building might be exposed as a worn hovel. But when lit like there was a full moon, it had a beauty that only one hundred years of beer, brawls, T-bone steak and friendship could form.

The manly author, Ernest Hemingway, used to drink at the Pioneer. His body was buried just down the road.

"Gotta go," Andrews said. "This town gives me a bad taste in my mouth."

Andrews, the former state cop, had close-cropped hair, thick arms and a thick chest. He was strong and gnarled. His hands had been broken; his face had been gouged. He looked like an old oak tree, knots and all.

"They'd forget, you know," the man said to Andrews. "'Time heals all wounds' and all that."

"I don't want to give them the time, Tick Tock," Andrews scowled. "I don't want to waste my time waiting for them to apologize. Fuck them."

Bob Andrews had once been known by his initials, B.A. But as his reputation grew for being a tough cop and a fist fighter, the B.A. came to stand for Badass.

It was a mantle of honor, he thought. That is, until his career as a law officer was dragged through the mud and he was banished.

The newspapers said that "Trooper Andrews was found to be in possession of heroin and cocaine. The veteran law officer who is well known for his aggressive patrols was arrested during a drug investigation that was not focusing on or even aware of his participation."

Trooper Andrews, during his career of fighting crime, had received awards for his conduct as a member of the state police. But the drugs and cash were found when a search warrant was issued for an apartment not previously connected to him. And there he was, Andrews, when law officers raided the address. It resulted in drug and weapons charges. Andrews was suspended and ultimately dismissed.

His agreement not to fight his exile from the force came in exchange for reduced charges to a single misdemeanor and a probationary jail sentence instead of any time behind bars. He was free to go. The state police force simply did not want him back in uniform.

"The fuckers," Badass repeated as he shot another dram of Oban.

"Stay for one more," the other man pleaded. "I'm buying."

"Fair enough," Badass said as a smile creased his leathery face. As he sat back down, he fingered some brass plates screwed into the bar. They bore the names of the bar's regulars. He had hoped to have his own name on one of those plates, someday.

They ordered Sawtooth Lager, brewed nearby in Hailey, Idaho. They eyeballed some new faces that walked into the bar, tan and just finished with a day of skiing at the Sun Valley Ski Resort that was only minutes away.

"You got enough money?" the other man inquired.

"They didn't take my pension away," B.A. answered. "And I've got a guy who owes me money. It's time I pay him a visit."

"Where you going?" the man asked.

"I got my eye on a place up in the mountains where no one will bother me," Andrews responded. He didn't say exactly where that was, and the man knew better than to pry.

After one more drink, Bob Andrews walked out the door of the Pioneer Saloon. Climbing into his car, he drove north on Main Street instead of south.

After only a mile, he pulled into Ketchum Cemetery and stopped by a plot located between two pine trees. It was littered—or decorated, depending on how you saw things— with empty bottles of whiskey, wine and French Armagnac.

The adventurous outdoorsman and author, Ernest Hemingway, had been buried there after his suicide.

Andrews never shut off the engine of his car. After a few wordless minutes, he pulled back onto Main Street. He headed south, out of Ketchum and onto the Sawtooth Scenic Byway. He had no intention of ever coming back. He looked behind him only once, in his rearview mirror.

"Fuckers," he said.

"Hello, Jean Claude," the voice said behind JC. He was sitting at the bar of Chambers' Revenge, in The Craters Ski Resort village.

JC swung his barstool around and saw the most beautiful woman he had ever laid eyes on. Her red hair dropped over her shoulders. She wore a waist-length winter coat with a hood and faux-fur trim. Taking it all in, he thought his chest was going to explode.

"Hey, babe," he said and gave Robin a kiss.

And he barely had to turn his head to see a black-haired beauty climbing on top of Bip.

"Hi, Sunny," JC said. "I'm glad you could make it."

"Hi, JC," she said, without taking her hungry eyes off Bip.

"We may have to call it a night," Bip said suddenly.

"I've got the tab," JC said to him, doubting he could break their momentum at any rate. He thought it was better that they got to their room.

Robin climbed onto the barstool that Bip had just vacated.

"Prosecco," she said to JC before he could ask.

JC ordered her drink and added a Soulcraft All-Mountain Amber for himself. The beer was brewed in Salida. The can had a picture of an SUV carrying skis, a bike and a kayak.

"So, he was found in a ghost town?" Robin asked.

"Washburn? Yeah," JC answered. "If you can call it that. I didn't see any ghosts. In fact, I didn't see any town."

"How did he die?" she asked.

"Stabbed," he told her.

"Who did it?"

"Haven't a clue," he said.

The décor of the bar was early tent-camping. The Chambers Lake theme could have gone two ways. Either the owners could decorate the restaurant with pictures and relics recalling the killing spree young Robert Chambers went on after finding his father murdered, or the décor could reflect the joys of camping on the shores of Chambers Lake, a century-long pastime. The restaurant owners decided on the latter.

There were lots of black and white pictures of men and women camping when cameras and photography were still in their infancy. There were dogs in a lot of the pictures.

The older photos required people posing for them to refrain from smiling and to remain absolutely still, to accommodate the long exposure. Dogs didn't take direction from photographers very well. The dogs in the pictures were usually blurred, especially the tail.

"I like this place," Robin said. She looked straight up and saw an old tent affixed upside down on the ceiling.

JC's phone rang. He recognized the number and pushed the green button to accept.

"Really?" JC said into the phone.

Robin watched him and sipped her Prosecco from a tall flute.

"What would it be doing there?" JC asked.

It was too loud in the bar for Robin to hear the voice on the other line. Not concerned, she knew JC would fill her in.

"Any blood or something that would suggest foul play?" JC inquired and waited. "Not talking about that at this time, huh?"

The bar was still filling up with the Friday-night crowd. There were out-of-towners who had just arrived, and plenty of skiers and snowboarders who had just showered after a day on the snow.

It was always a mixed crowd at ski-town bars. There were old friends who lived locally and greeted other locals with a smile and a handshake or hug. They behaved like they shared the secret to a great life.

And there were the visitors, the happy out-of-towners who were grateful to ski a big mountain and the great terrain before having to return home to their jobs and the daily grind.

"That was a sheriff's deputy, who is becoming a very good friend," JC told Robin when he got off the phone.

"Those are good friends to have," she said. "What's up?"

"They found the car belonging to the guy who got stabbed, John Washburn," he said.

"They arrest anyone?" she asked.

"Nope. The odd thing is where they found the car," he responded.

"Where?"

"At the airport in Hailey, Idaho," JC said. "It's right down the road from Ketchum. And Sun Valley."

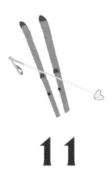

11

The next morning, the wind was blowing outside. It came with such force that it found its way indoors. There was a chill, inside and out.

"They may not be able to open the chairlifts if the wind doesn't die down," their server at breakfast told JC and Robin.

They were seated in a breakfast place in the ski resort village. It was called "Ute Susan's." The menu explained that Ute Susan was a Native American who was taken from her village during a raid by the Arapaho.

After some time, an Arapaho chief tried to trade her to a white farmer for a mirror and a hat, but the deal fell through. Sometime later, Susan was rescued and returned to her Ute family.

"Are we really going skiing?" Robin asked. "It's freezing. I don't think I brought enough clothing."

"Then let's go get you another layer," JC resolved. Finishing breakfast, they pushed away from their table and walked outside.

They followed the pedestrian walkway of poured concrete framed by railroad ties.

It was the first time they had a chance to look at the resort village in the daylight. It was built to replicate an old mining town. All the structures looked like simple flat-board buildings. A couple of store entrances resembled the entrance to old gold mines.

They entered a ski shop named "Ping." A salesperson told them that was the Indian nickname for an earlier settler named George Pingree.

"I hear the wind is dying down," the salesperson said. "They're going to open the lifts."

"It might not be windy but it's cold," Robin said. Her arms were wrapped around her like a fur coat.

"Let's get her another layer," JC told the salesman.

"Uppers or lowers?" they were asked.

JC looked to Robin for guidance, but she was gone. He found her rummaging through racks of ski pants, sweaters and jackets.

"Ski pants are a good place to start," the man said. "Do you know that stores across the country sold nearly four hundred million dollars' worth of ski pants last year. That's more than one pair for every man, woman and child in the United States. And since every man, woman and child doesn't ski or snowboard, that means a lot of us bought *two* pair."

A sign hung in the store. It said *Carpe Ski 'em*.

They pushed back out into the cold outdoors, Robin wearing a new pair of insulated bib overall ski pants and a sweatshirt saying, "Dig The Craters."

"Pretty sweet!" she exclaimed, happy with her purchase.

"You should have let me buy them for you," he said.

"I have a job too, you know," she told him with a smile. "The TV station actually pays me to spend time with you."

"Well, that explains a lot," he said.

They headed for the base chairlift where they agreed to meet Bip and Sunny. It was Saturday. After JC and Bip provided a live shot to Denver for the morning news, they had the rest of the weekend to play.

Waiting by the lift, JC and Robin studied the trail map. The east side of the ski area was steep. The west side provided easier terrain.

JC and Robin marveled at the high peaks surrounding them, stabbing the lower clouds. Some of the mountains were covered by charred timber from the Cameron Pass fire.

Above timberline, skiers and snowboarders at The Craters were above the trees. There were open bowls where they could carve their own path.

But there was nothing to block the wind. It could get fierce and frigid. And the snow could move around. There was avalanche danger.

The Medicine Bow Range had its share of legends. One said that the Indians would come there to find good ash timber to make their bows with. They called it "Good medicine," meaning it was good wood.

On the other side of Cameron Pass, you could eventually take a right-hand turn on Route 40 and arrive at the ski town of Steamboat Springs. A couple of hours past that, in the remote northwest corner of Colorado, you could ski at Minnie's Gap.

Minnie's Gap is where Bip met Sunny Shavano, when he was on assignment with JC.

JC and Robin saw the pair emerge from the crowd, approaching the chairlift carrying their snowboards.

"I'm stoked! Let's rip it!" Bip said with his characteristic enthusiasm. Sunny had a big smile on her face.

"Let's kill the hill," JC declared.

The four of them climbed on a gondola to take them away from the busy base of the mountain. From there, they hopped on a chairlift to get them to the top.

"Holy shit!" Bip exclaimed. The others were thinking the same thing. The chairlift they were riding climbed high above the ground.

"They call it HAGL when you're flying an aircraft," Bip said. "It stands for 'height above ground level.'"

"I *feel* like I'm riding in a plane," JC told them. "Do we get mid-flight meals on this chair?"

"I hope they show us a movie!" Robin added.

The extreme HAGL was necessary to get the chair to the top of a peak about two thousand feet above the base lodge.

"This is where she jumped?" Bip asked, still impressed with the height of the chair ride.

"I couldn't do it," Robin said. "I'd be too afraid of dying, to kill myself up here."

"Well, if the chairlift ride doesn't kill you," JC told them. "We're headed for a ski run called 'Heart Attack.'"

Sunny pointed at the side of the mountain. There was an opening.

"Look. It's an old mine," she said.

The opening in the side of the mountain was a gaping wound above the ski run called Heart Attack. The hole was nearly square and too dark to peer into. A steep slope of tailings cascaded from the old mine entrance. The broken rock fell all the way to the edge of the slope.

"I wonder what they called it," Robin stated.

"I'm reading about that," JC told them, already on his cell phone.

"What a shock," Bip and Robin both said.

"The state bureau of mines didn't start to keep records of all these mines until about 1895. So, many of the mine names or even their locations are uncertain."

As the chairlift arrived at the peak, JC stowed his phone in a zippered pocket inside his jacket. He was glad to pull his mittens back onto his cold hands.

It was windy at the top and even colder. Light snow began to fall.

"Is this really supposed to be fun?" Robin screamed over the wind as she pulled herself deeper into her outer gear.

"You look like a turtle," Bip laughed. "Pulling your head into your shell."

"It's freezing and windy," Robin replied. "And we're about to ski down something called 'Heart Attack?'"

"Pereunt et imputantur," JC declared.

"What the heck are you talking about?" Bip asked.

"It's some of his Scottish gibberish. Latin really," Robin answered, over the howl of the wind. "They perish and are reckoned."

"Oh, like Carpe Ski 'em," he said with a smile. "Cool."

With that, they pushed off and down the run called Heart Attack. JC chose the left side of the run, Robin the right.

He carved turns in powder piled even higher by the wind. *She* was looking for moguls.

Bip and Sunny cut paths down the middle, their snowboards looking graceful and in rhythm.

The wind died down considerably as they dropped below the peak, and the sun was starting to rise above the mountaintops.

"You guys looked good up there," a friendly voice said to them when they reached the lift line.

They turned to see the smiling sunburned face of a man leaning on his ski poles. He had a large sticker on the front of his helmet that said, "The Craters." JC guessed that he was an employee of the mountain, maybe a ski ambassador.

"Trigger Fischer," the man said as he extended a gloved hand to share a fist bump with them.

"Now I recognize you!" JC blurted. "You're the ski racer. It's a pleasure to meet you."

JC explained to his friends that Trigger Fischer was a star on the U.S. Ski Team a decade ago. He won a few World Cup races and a silver medal at the World Championships.

"Missed by that much," Trigger said of missing the gold medal. He held his thumb and index finger only a hair-width apart. He was amused. He didn't mind hearing a glowing review of his accomplishments.

"Is this where you live, now?" JC asked.

"Yes, if you can believe it. They pay me to ski every day and take runs with gunners like you," Trigger said with a smile. "So, how about it. Take a run with me?"

"Hell yes!" Bip pronounced, laughing.

As they rode the lift, Trigger took an interest in Sunny. Maybe it was because she was the quiet one. Maybe it was because she was quite attractive.

"Where are you from, Sunny?" the ski ambassador asked.

"Near here," she said. "In Utah."

"You are of the Ute people?" he inquired.

"Yes."

"This all belonged to your ancestors?" he asked. "The deeper into the mountains, the more likely it belonged to the Utes."

"Most of it," she said with a smile.

"Well, thank you," Trigger said to her. "For taking such good care of it."

"It should still be ours," Sunny said quietly.

"You'll get no argument from me," Trigger agreed. "I'll treat it with respect until it is returned to you. Thank you for letting me visit."

Sunny gave him a shy smile. He had won a friend. And he had demonstrated that he had a way with women.

On the remainder of the lift ride, Trigger pointed out peaks and chutes and couloirs that were out of bounds.

"Backcountry skiers really found all these trails," he told them. "They deserve a lot of credit for what is now this ski resort."

He pointed out runs that were out-of-bounds that backcountry skiers preferred. They'd even given them names, like Ptarmigan, The Wave and Pap Smear.

He drew their attention to nearby Montgomery Pass and runs called the Hot Dog Bowls and Hamburger Trees.

"Whether you're in-bounds, skiing The Craters, or out-of-bounds skiing the backcountry, it is really great skiing here. You just have to look out for the avalanches."

It was still snowing when they reached the top of the lift. Trigger waited until the group was together and then pushed over the top of Heart Attack. JC and the others were surprised by the speed that the former ski racer carried. The hill was steep and intimidating, but Trigger Fischer didn't seem to notice.

"Want to ski in some trees?" he asked after stopping halfway down the run and waiting for the others to catch up. "Or are you DDS?"

"We're not dentists," Robin told him.

"No," he smiled at her. "DDS is short for 'Don't Destroy My Skis.' Let's skip the trees and just rip to the bottom of the chair." And he took off without waiting for a response.

At the bottom of the chairlift, Trigger was recognized by a family vacationing at The Craters. They had been given a time to be at that spot to ensure they could ski with the former champion.

"Duty calls," Trigger said quietly to JC and the bunch with a smile. "You guys really rip. Look for me and we'll take some runs together again."

And he was off, patting a little boy and a little girl on the top of their helmets, charming their mother and fist bumping their dad.

"He is a good skier!" Robin pronounced.

"I think he's faster than you, JC," said Bip. It was sort of a friendly dig.

"Thanks, Captain Obvious," JC answered.

"He's very charming," Sunny said with a melody in her voice.

12

The icicles in JC's mustache began to melt. The four of them had kicked out of their skis and boards, pulled off their boots and stashed them at the Clark Hotel.

They walked past jewelry stores, restaurants and gift shops in the ski village that resembled a mining town.

At the end of the pedestrian walk, they saw a larger, more exclusive hotel towering over the village. It was called "Home." That had been the name of a long-gone town that was once at the base of Chambers Pass.

The architecture of the resort's most expensive hotel did not match the mine-camp theme. It was like a "before and after" picture. The mine camp was for those who hoped to get rich. The Home Hotel was for those who had already succeeded in doing so.

The building's design and accoutrements oozed money. The structure was mostly glass, offering the best views in every direction. There were timbers worked into the façade, machined to look like railroad ties.

The doormen at Home wore uniforms and pulled shiny gold baggage carts. Valets were available to carry your skis to the lift and check them in a secure pen to await your arrival.

It was the very luxury hotel where Loretta Sopris spent her last day on earth. Her suicide note was written on the hotel's stationery.

A long shadow was cast by the Home Hotel as the ski day was coming to an end. Skiers and snowboarders who had endured the freezing temperatures and overcast skies felt they had permission to declare victory and remove themselves from the mountain.

JC, Robin, Bip and Sunny ducked out of the cold and into Chambers' Revenge. They grabbed a booth in the back, away from the draft.

"JC!" a voice by the door rang out. "It's really cold out!"

JC looked at the man but didn't recognize him. He said "Hi" anyway. JC was used to being greeted by people who knew him from television.

"Hi, what?" the man replied.

"You called out my name," JC said, confused. "I just answered you.'"

"What, JC?" the man replied. "You look like a nice fella, but you think mighty highly of yourself if you think you're Jesus Christ."

"Please accept my apologies," JC said. "I thought you called out 'JC.'"

"I did," the man replied. "That's what my wife allows me to get away with, the initials. If I take the whole name in vain, I've got to say Hail Marys during the entire drive home."

"Sorry," JC said to the man. "My name is Jean Claude. Everyone calls me JC."

"Well, S," the man said as he laughed. "See, that's another one. If I just say 'S,' my wife thinks it is funny. If I say the whole word, I'm in trouble again. So, if I hit my thumb with a hammer, I just holler 'S'! And my wife even giggles a bit. I think she enjoys my pain."

The man moved on. Like everyone who had just emerged from outside, there was a frigid contrail following them.

JC and the others sat at the bar. A Denver Broncos playoff game had just kicked off. The crowd in the bar was energized.

They ordered warm food, soup and chili. JC and Bip ordered a beer brewed in Longmont by Left Hand called Milk Stout Nitro. Robin took sips.

"So, how long are you here, anyway?" JC asked Robin.

"I can't believe it took you this long to ask," she said, mildly disgusted. "I got here last night."

"Yeah, don't you two talk?" Bip needled them. "She's been here since last night!"

"Some nights don't require much talk," JC scowled at Bip, who laughed.

"I'm here on assignment," Robin announced.

"Are you replacing JC?" Bip asked. "They finally figured out that you're the brains of the operation?"

"I am," she agreed. "But I have my own work to do. He's going to have to struggle with his own workload."

"What is your assignment?" JC asked.

"Pat and Rocky want me to look into the suicide of that woman, Loretta Sopris," she told them. "The one who slipped or jumped off the chairlift."

"Since when do we cover suicides of people who aren't famous?" JC asked.

"Since Loretta's sister, the one you went to CSU with, camped out in the lobby of our television station and insisted that we take a closer look."

"Does she think her sister was murdered?" Bip asked.

"No," Robin said. "That's the unusual thing. She can accept that Loretta killed herself. But she wants to know why."

"Only rocks don't die," Sunny said quietly. "But her reason for dying may tell why she lived."

The other three stopped what they were doing and stared at her.

"That is incredibly deep," Robin finally said. "Somehow, I think you've told me where to start."

"Don't let her get away," JC said, looking at Bip. "You look smarter just sitting next to her."

"Look who's talking," Bip said, looking at Robin.

After warming up on food and drink, they walked back outside. They had decided to watch the rest of the football game at their hotel.

Night had fallen and the wind was dying down. JC was drawn toward music being played by a band on a large outdoor stage.

"These sticks are made for skiing!" the female vocalist half-screamed and half-sang. "And that is what they'll do. One of these days, these sticks are going to ski all over you!"

The woman at the microphone was sexy and abrasive. The band was called Kat and the Death Doula. The crowd screamed its approval.

"Let's take a detour. I want you to meet someone," JC said to Robin, pulling her toward the stage.

"Come on, you fuckers!" the lead singer screamed into her microphone, trying to raise the "room temperature." "Are your little panties starting to droop, just 'cuz you been skiing and snowboarding all day?"

Some parents with children in the crowd squirmed at the foul language, but the vast majority in the crowd roared with delight and began to jump in place as she started another tune.

"You think you're so damn smart!" Kat sang/screamed. "You think you broke my heart! You think you give me chills! I get that taking pills!"

The lead singer was wearing short cutoff blue jeans under an open, floor-length coat lined in thick fur. She was in control of the audience. She was charismatic and seductive.

Kat scanned the crowd, and her eyes reached JC. She winked and stuck her tongue out.

"I've got to take a break," she hollered into the microphone at the end of the song. "You guys wear me out. But I'm only taking a five-minute break!" she screamed. "Go get a beer and come right back. Or I'LL FIND YOU AND KICK YOUR ASS!"

The crowd screamed in delight. The singer pulled off her guitar and marched off the stage.

"Come on," JC told Robin and grabbed her hand. He pulled her to the side of the stage. Bip and Sunny followed.

The lead singer emerged from a door at the side of the temporary concert stage. She walked up to JC, put her arms around his neck and pressed her lips against his. It was not a short kiss, and it did not exclude her tongue.

Robin watched, eyes wide, more in shock than disapproval.

Released, JC took a step back. There was a surprised look on his face, but it quickly turned into a grin.

"Robin," he said. "Meet Kat Martinez, the greatest musical talent in the Rocky Mountains."

"How do you do?" Robin said, still confused.

"Who is Robin?" Kat asked with an evil grin as she studied Robin from head to toe. Her finger dragged a line across Robin's breasts.

"Kat, you procrastinated, and you'll regret it for your entire life," JC said to the woman. "Robin is my fiancé. The only woman I love more than you."

"You bitch," Kat said, then moved in to give Robin a long kiss on her lips too.

When Kat released her latest conquest, Robin took a step back and gave JC a confused look. He was laughing.

"How can you not love this woman!" JC said to Robin.

Kat Martinez was becoming a wildly popular entertainer in clubs around Denver and the Rockies. She met JC when he was investigating an old boyfriend of hers, back from a time when she preferred boys to girls.

And when Kat's own brother was murdered, JC played a role in catching the killer. Kat felt indebted to JC. He was one of the few people she trusted.

JC introduced his friend to Bip and Sunny. Kat shook their hands.

"What, no kiss?" Bip complained. But Kat was already eyeing Sunny.

"*You* gotta pay," Kat said to Bip. "You *are* pretty, but your friend is more my taste."

Sunny smiled, amused. Kat dialed it down a peg and rested an arm on JC's shoulder.

"What brings you to my lair," Kat asked. "Or should I ask, who died?"

"We're skiing for the moment," JC told her. "But a couple of people have died and yes, that's what brings us here."

"What is a death doula?" Bip asked. "That's the name of your band?"

"It is a spiritual guide who assists the dying and their loved ones," Sunny explained. "A midwife guides you into life. A doula helps you leave."

"You hang around with smart chicks," Kat said to JC.

There was a Black woman standing next to Kat. She had taken in the whole performance like she'd seen it before, often. But she still found it entertaining.

"This is my drummer and my girlfriend," Kat said, introducing the woman. "Meet Latoya. Her stage name is Sojourner *The* Truth!"

Kat looked around and saw the crowd pushing toward the stage again. It might have been even larger than when she began her break.

"Word of mouth," Kat speculated about the growing crowd. "Listen, sweetie," she said to JC. "I've gotta pack my bags and get out of here as soon as the show is over. But we're playing at Mishawaka, soon. Come see us play. We'll have more time to talk."

"We'll do our best," JC told her. "It's great to see you again, Kat. And thanks for leaving me with a lot of explaining to do," he said as he looked at Robin.

Kat looked at Robin and then looked at JC.

"She looks familiar," the musician said with mischief. "Red hair, beautiful. She reminds me of someone." She bit her lip and disappeared behind the side door leading to the outdoor stage.

Bip and Sunny decided to stay and watch Kat's second set. JC and Robin walked back toward the Clark Hotel.

"You think you'll do *it!*" Kat screamed/sang into the microphone as she began her next song. "You think I'll sub...*mit!*"

13

"Are you watching videos of cats doing cute things?" JC asked as he opened his eyes and saw Robin beside him with a computer resting on her legs.

"No," Robin answered. "I'm looking for clues."

They had watched the Broncos' game and gone to sleep. The next morning, they were still in bed at the Clark Hotel. A gas fireplace was burning at the foot of the bed. They had a view of the ski mountain out their window.

The walls of their room had a mahogany finish. The bedroom was on one side of a fireplace and there was a living room on the other side. Out a door, in the living room, there was an outdoor porch.

"This is a nice room," Robin smiled.

"The TV station must have found extra money," JC responded. "So, how are you going to go about your assignment?"

"First of all, I'm looking her up on social media," she told him. "I've found an article about her, and I've got her Facebook page."

"An article about her?"

"It's really an article about her husband, when they were married," she explained. "They got a divorce. They lived in Texas. He was a pharmacist. Eventually, Loretta moved to Fort Collins where she had gone to college."

"That's a lot of progress before getting out of bed on your day off," JC complimented her.

"Yes, but let's not work all day," she said. "It's Sunday. Let's do a little skiing and get some lunch and maybe shop a little."

"That sounds like a good day," JC agreed. "So, that's the end of your report on Loretta Sopris?"

"Not entirely. I spoke with the sheriff on the phone while I was driving up here Friday," Robin informed JC. "He says that she checked into the Home Hotel here on Saturday night. That's the most expensive place to stay here. She wrote her suicide note on their stationery. Then, she went shopping and bought a very expensive one-piece ski suit made by Obermeyer."

"Do you think she was preparing to end her life?" JC asked. "I've seen that kind of behavior by suicide victims before. Or did she do all these nice things for herself and find out they didn't cheer her up?"

"I've got to find one or two people who knew her," Robin said, and looked up from her computer. "It's surprising that Loretta's sister, Agnes, knows so little about her. She says they are a close family. But I also called Agnes as I was driving up here on Friday. She was unable to tell me that much about Loretta."

"Maybe she was able," JC said. "Maybe she just wasn't willing."

It was much warmer than the prior day. JC and Robin skied runs that they hadn't tried on Saturday. They started on the west side, on a cruiser named Laura's Lover that poured into a run called Handsome Peter.

They skied off the peak, down Colby's Couloir and then bounced over a challenging mogul run called Blair's Bumps. Robin excelled on the moguls. Halfway down, JC pulled aside and watched her in admiration.

The chairlift rides were magnificent. They were surrounded by spires that reached for the sky. Some rock features were crumbling, their debris slowly rolling down to a creek.

"You are visitors here?" a man asked as they rode the chairlift together.

"We are," Robin said. "We really like it. It's beautiful."

"I grew up here," the man said. "We were the only Black family that came and stayed."

JC introduced himself and Robin.

"Frank Steen," the man introduced himself. "I was on the high school ski team. I was good. Everyone liked me. Now, I'm the district attorney in Cameron County." He laughed. "Now, half of those people despise me."

JC told Steen that they were in town to look into John Washburn's murder.

"Well, I can't comment on that, of course," Steen told them. "But they've got a long way to go on that investigation. A long way to go."

JC was ready to seize the opportunity to further discuss the Washburn murder with the D.A. But Steen adroitly steered the conversation in another direction.

"Do you know where Cameron Pass got its name?" Steen asked. "It is named after a Union general in the Civil War, Robert Cameron. He founded the agricultural colony that has become Fort Collins."

The district attorney had made his point. He wasn't going to discuss business.

"Now, look to the west above that parking lot on Highway 14," Steen told them. "That is a ski run the backcountry skiers call Outhouse Gully, because it takes them to the parking lot and an outhouse that is placed there for them."

They reached the top of the chairlift, and the district attorney pushed away.

"Enjoy your stay here," he said in parting. "I hope only to see you here on the mountain, rather than see you at the defense table wearing handcuffs."

"That's a disturbing thought," Robin said as the D.A. disappeared down a catwalk.

"He makes it sound like there's a fifty-fifty chance," JC added.

JC and Robin called it a day early in the afternoon and ducked into Chambers' Revenge for lunch. They chose a table near the window.

"We should start reserving a table for four," a customer at the next table said. "We tend to show up at the same time."

The voice belonged to Mad Marv. He was with his girlfriend, Mercy.

They exchanged greetings, JC introducing Robin to the couple.

JC took the opportunity to examine Marv's wristwatch; the one Bip told him cost eighteen thousand dollars.

"You like my watch?" Marv said when he caught JC's eyes locked on it. "I bought it in a moment of weakness."

"That's beautiful," Robin exclaimed. "What kind of metal is that?"

"It's rose gold," he said, fingering the vintage brown leather strap. "It's Swiss-made. It's called a Breitling Aviator 8. They only made two hundred fifty-three of them. I'm a little embarrassed to be wearing something so pretentious."

"It's really pretty," Robin told him.

"I love your name," Mercy said. "I love Robins."

Marv suggested they try the New England clam chowder.

"Mary loves it," Marv said. His girlfriend nodded in agreement.

"Wait a minute," JC said, "I thought your name is Mercy. Did I get it wrong?"

"No," Mercy said, laughing. "My real name is Mary Mercy LaJeunesse. But I have a sister named Mary Madeleine LaJeunesse, and another sister named Mary Miracle LaJeunesse."

"Wait," Robin interrupted. "You are one of three sisters, all named Mary LaJeunesse?"

"Yes!" laughed Mary Mercy. "Our father was a minister and mother was devout. So, she named us all Mary M. LaJeunesse. The only way to tell us apart is to go by our middle names."

"So, you're Mercy," JC said.

"Yes, my sister, Madeleine, is a public defender here in Cameron County. My sister, Miracle, lives in Texas."

The conversation was interrupted by a disturbance at the other side of the room.

"I'm off-duty! Do I walk up to your table and interrupt *your* lunch?" yelled a man who threw his spoon into his bread bowl of chili. They recognized the man as Trigger Fischer, the mountain ambassador and former ski racing champion.

A father and son who appeared to have been asking Fischer for an autograph walked away. The boy looked chastised. The father looked angry.

"What is that about?" Robin asked.

"Trigger has his moments," Mercy said, sadly. "Being famous isn't all that it's cracked up to be. He's a nice guy. He just doesn't always come across that way."

Customers in the bar turned back to what they were doing after the outburst. Trigger Fischer, looking both embarrassed and angry, picked up his jacket and moved from his table to an open seat at the bar, taking his chili with him. The man he sat down next to at the bar put a comforting hand on his shoulder.

"Did you know the woman who died on the chairlift last week?" Robin asked, turning her attention back to their new friends.

"No, but what a shame," Mercy said. "I don't think she was a local. I heard that she was visiting from Fort Collins."

Marv didn't add anything. He just watched Mercy.

"Have you heard anything about her?" Robin asked.

"We met her sister. She thinks there's more to the story."

"Does she think she was murdered or something?" Mercy asked, somewhat shocked.

"Not necessarily," Robin told her.

JC and Robin had finished their clam chowder.

"Will you come shopping with me?" Robin asked JC.

"Of course. Maybe I'll find a tee-shirt," he told her.

"He loves tee-shirts," Robin told the other couple. "I think we're going to go shopping."

"It was good to see you again, JC. Nice to meet you Robin," Marv said. "We're going to stay and finish lunch."

JC held the door open for Robin as they left the bar.

"He really seems to adore her," Robin said to JC.

"Mad Marv is mad about Mary Mercy?" JC asked.

"Yes, couldn't you tell? The way he just watched Mercy and let her do all the talking. He seemed happy just to be in her presence," Robin said. "I wonder if they have plans to get married."

"It's good to see you again, Bob," Trigger said.

"Nice to be seen, Flicka," Bob Andrews said.

Flicka was Andrews' nickname for Trigger Fischer. It was due to the fact that Trigger was the name of a horse ridden by television cowboy Roy Rogers in his popular 1950s TV series. Flicka was the name of another horse, on a 1950s television series called *My Friend Flicka*. This was the way Bob Andrews' mind worked.

Bob "Badass" Andrews was the man Trigger sat next to at the bar after his outburst.

"I just lost it," Trigger explained the outburst with remorse. "I only feel worse about myself when I do that."

"How's your leg?" Badass asked.

Trigger answered without saying a word. He was past complaining and past denying the pain he endured on a regular basis. It was the pain that led to the outbursts. But he was tired of explaining that, too.

Trigger and Badass shared a friendship going back before Andrews' fall from grace. They met back when Badass was still a cop and Trigger was still a ski racer. Andrews had provided police protection for the skiing celebrity on a couple of occasions.

Now, it wasn't as easy as it used to be for Trigger to score the kind of painkillers that worked. When Trigger called on his old friend, Badass had a way of acquiring the medications that Trigger found to be salvation.

Sitting at the bar of Chambers' Revenge, Trigger was sipping a Fat Tire beer, brewed in Fort Collings by New Belgium. Badass was drinking a single-malt scotch.

"How are you feeling?" the former Idaho state trooper asked the former ski racer.

"When it doesn't feel like I'm being stabbed, it only throbs," Trigger acknowledged. "But it's felt that way for so long, I've forgotten how it is supposed to feel."

Trigger didn't look the part of a drug addict. He was long and lean and muscular. He had an easy smile.

"You look good," Andrews told him, surprised that someone hooked on meds could look so healthy.

"I try," Trigger responded. "Some days are better than others."

"Well, I'll be living here for a while," Andrews told him. "I'll be able to take care of you."

CARPE Ski 'em: a Murder on Skis Mystery

"Thanks, Bob," Trigger said. "I don't know what I'd do without you."

Trigger Fischer saw an acquaintance across the room and waved.

"Who is that?" Andrews asked.

"That's what I do for a living. I wave in a friendly manner at people," Trigger told him. "I go skiing with some of them, make people feel like a former ski racer is their best friend. In return, the ski resort gives me some money and a slope-side condo to live in. It's how heroes who become drug addicts survive."

"But who is he?" Andrews persisted. "The man you waved at."

"His name is Marvin," Trigger informed him. "He invented that quirky GPS system. It cracks jokes while giving you directions. I think he invented some video games too. They call him Mad Marv."

Andrews sipped his scotch, but his eyes kept following Mad Marv.

14

"It was an unhappy marriage, that's what I hear," Scooter told JC.

Tommy "Scooter" Halvorson had spotted JC and Robin sitting on a wooden, high-backed bench by a fire in the outdoor town square of the resort village. Across the square, resort employees had picked up debris after last night's Kat Martinez concert. The area was spotless.

The village was emptying out. It was the last night for out-of-town visitors. Week-long vacations and weekend visits were ending. It was almost time for all of those skiers and snowboarders to go home and get ready for work Monday morning.

It was the best part of the week for some locals. They liked it when the crowd disappeared each week. Dinner or social outings with friends on Sunday night allowed the locals to take a breath. Skiing on Monday was close to a "locals only" holiday. But already, a new wave of vacationers would be arriving. By Tuesday, the adrenaline-induced activity would again be at full tilt.

Scooter Halvorson grabbed three hot chocolates, took a seat next to JC and Robin and distributed the warm drinks.

"This is perfect," Robin said, sipping out of her paper cup.

"So, you're here investigating the murder of the county treasurer, John Washburn?" Scooter asked JC.

"You're a local," JC said after acknowledging that was the purpose of his visit. "Did you know him?"

"Everyone knows a local politician to an extent," Scooter pointed out. "I went into the treasurer's office to pay my taxes, like everyone else. He seemed pleasant enough. I'll say this, there was no one else like him around here. Some people called him 'Frenchy' behind his back. He dressed in nice suits and wore one of those things around his neck."

"A tie?" JC asked, amused.

"Well, yeah," Scooter laughed. "That's pretty unusual, too. But I'm thinking of that thing French men wear around their neck. It's like handkerchief."

"An ascot?" JC offered.

"Yeah! An ascot," Scooter agreed. "He wore an ascot, cufflinks, a hanky in his coat pocket. No one dresses like that up here. He had to go down to Denver or Fort Collins to find clothing like that. None of the stores up here sell that stuff. That about says it."

"I doubt he was killed because he dressed nice. Do you know anyone who would like to kill a 'pleasant enough' man?" JC asked.

"I have a couple of friends who are deputies," Scooter said. "Everybody knows everybody in a small place like this. It sounds like they think it was an unhappy marriage. That's what I hear."

"So, his wife killed him?" JC asked, without committing to the theory.

"Or had him killed," Scooter stated. "She's a little thing. Maybe she hired someone to kill him. He was old as dust. She's like forty years old, and still pretty hot."

"That sounds like grounds for divorce, not murder," JC offered.

"There aren't many divorces up here," Scooter observed. "People just seem to tolerate each other."

"There aren't many murders up here, either," JC suggested.

"No, that's true," his old high school friend agreed. "But I only know what I'm told. And I'm told they're taking a close look at the wife."

A man had quietly slipped into the chair next to Scooter Halvorson. He had been so quiet, it startled the others when he spoke.

"'Sup Scooter?" the man said.

"Hey, Horace!" Scooter responded "'What's up?"

"I'm just looking for loose change sitting on the ground," Horace said, laughing.

"You should head closer to the Home," Scooter told him, laughing. "People drop five-dollar bills over there."

Both men laughed and Scooter introduced Horace Emerson to JC and Robin.

"Reporters!" Horace exclaimed. "I didn't kill anybody!" Horace and Scooter shared another laugh.

"Can you think of anybody who *did* kill John Washburn?" JC asked.

"Him!" Horace said, pointing his thumb at Scooter as they laughed hysterically.

"As productive as this interrogation has been, gentlemen, I think we will take our leave," JC said to the laughing pair.

"It was nice to meet you, Horace," Robin said. "Nice to see you again, Scooter."

"Yeah, man," Horace said to the two of them. "We'll catch you on the flip side."

JC and Robin strolled down the pedestrian walk of the village, going into a few shops and peeping through the windows of others.

A small creek ran down the middle of the village. There was a statue of an old miner on his knees, panning in the creek for gold.

The creek separated people walking north from people walking south. There were elegant bridges spaced out for those who wanted to cross the creek.

JC noticed a man with a familiar face walking toward them. It was Sheriff Jerry Brush, out of uniform and off duty, but still wearing his cowboy hat. Then JC realized he recognized the woman, too. The couple was holding hands, and their walk was leisurely.

"Hi, Sheriff," JC said when they neared each other. JC and Robin didn't know what to say to the woman. They were a bit confused by the sight.

"Hi, Robin and JC," Mary Mercy LaJeunesse said, with both her hands now wrapped around the sheriff's arm.

"You've already met my wife?" the sheriff asked after saying hello.

"Marv and I bumped into them," Mercy said without remorse. "We were at Chambers' Revenge."

JC and Robin didn't know what to say. The woman introduced to them as Mad Marv's girlfriend was also the wife of the county sheriff.

"This is the only time we come down to the resort village, unless Jerry is on official business," Mercy said, filling the awkward silence. "Most vacationers have gone home, and the new vacationers are just unpacking or won't get here for a day or two."

"May I come by your office tomorrow, Sheriff, and talk about Loretta Sopris?" Robin asked. "The woman who killed herself?"

"Is there something that I don't know?" the sheriff asked. "I didn't think the news media covered suicides, unless it was someone famous."

"Normally, that is true," Robin said to him. "But her family is pressing for a closer look."

"Oh, I've spoken to the family," the sheriff said, sounding like they were wearing him out on the subject. "It was a suicide. It was not a murder."

"I have no reason to doubt you," Robin said in a conciliatory way. "I just want to talk over some things."

"Sure, talk to my secretary in the morning," the sheriff told her. "She'll arrange something."

The two couples bid each other farewell. JC and Robin were both anxious to extricate themselves from the unusual pairing.

"What the heck was that?" JC asked, once they were out of earshot from Mr. and Mrs. Brush.

"Mercy was matter of fact when she told the sheriff that we saw her with Mad Marv at the bar," Robin said, puzzled.

"It's one thing to have an affair behind your husband's back," JC added, "but is she having an extramarital affair that her husband and the whole town is aware of?"

"Pretty weird, right?" a third voice aid.

They turned and saw Horace Emerson behind them. He caught up and walked with them.

"I was watching your faces while the whole encounter was going down," Horace said. "I do that a lot. It's always pretty funny to watch people try to figure out that threesome."

"Is that what that is?" Robin asked. "A threesome?"

"Not really," Horace laughed. "It's like a couple and then another couple, but the woman plays the same role in each couple."

"And the sheriff and Mad Marv are aware of each other?" Robin asked.

"Oh yeah," Horace told them. "They're pretty civil about it. Sometimes, out at a bar, you can see all three of them sitting together. But at the end of the night, she goes home with one or the other of them. I'm not sure how that works, how she picks who she is going home with that night."

Robin looked at JC.

"Don't look at me," he said. "I don't understand it, either. The sheriff is her husband, but Marv is her boyfriend?"

"That about sums it up," Horace said, giggling.

"They don't get jealous?" JC asked.

"The two men?" Horace asked. "I don't know, but I've never known them to fight over it in public. I've never heard either of them say a bad word about the other man, or Mercy. I guess the three of them have an understanding."

"What about vacations?" Robin asked.

"Mercy is the winner there," Horace told her. "She gets to go on vacation with both of them, one at a time. She gets twice the slice of apple pie."

"Do the three of them ever go on vacation together? The three of them?" Robin asked.

"I do not ever remember seeing them do that," Horace acknowledged.

They looked in the direction of the couple as Sheriff Brush and Mercy walked away. They were walking hand in hand, strolling across one of the ornamental bridges crossing the creek.

"She's pretty good at this," Horace said. "I'll give her that. If someone has a funeral to go to, she goes with him. If one of the men is being honored at a conference, she is there too, sitting at the table and beaming with pride."

"How does she explain it?" Robin asked.

"She doesn't," Horace replied. "She doesn't discuss it. I guess she thinks it's nobody's business."

"This is a wonderful world," JC said. "But it's got a weird cast."

15

It always hurt. The pain began in his knee, and as the day wore on, it ran down his lower leg like a waterfall.

His ankle got swollen, and his foot. It always happened the same way, and it never skipped a day.

Because of the pain, Trigger Fischer never got a full night of sleep. And it was impossible to nap. Sometimes, because of the pain and sleep deprivation, he'd lose his temper in public. Tourists who did not know him, but caught him in that moment, judged him to be ill-mannered and entitled.

And that is the story those tourists would take back home to Iowa and Illinois and Georgia and tell their friends. He began to become weighed down with the reputation of a sullen brat, an angry has-been. It cost him goodwill and job opportunities.

But friends who knew him before the last few ski racing accidents said that he had changed. His energetic persona had lost a lot of its wattage. His sharp wit had been dulled. He was clinically depressed. Life had lost some of its joy.

At The Craters, his old friends mostly remained his friends. They tried to work around his affliction. The Craters and Cameron County became the only place where Trigger Fischer dared exist. It was a bubble of kindness, but it could feel like a prison.

After multiple surgeries to make the pain go away, it persisted. Doctors acknowledged that something was wrong. It was out of the ordinary. Some wondered if it was in his head. He sometimes wondered the same thing.

But the pain wasn't imaginary. It was sometimes blinding. More often, it was a five on the scale of ten. It was endurable, but it never stopped. There was never a break in the pain, never a day off. The days became weeks, and the weeks had become years.

After having retirement forced upon him by injury, Trigger worked a long time to lose the limp. In the morning, he walked normally enough. And he skied better than he walked. But in the evening, his leg stiffened, and the limp returned.

Trigger used to have the alarm on his iPhone set for eight times a day. That was to remind him to take his medication. The alarm was set to play a bouncing British ditty called "By the Seaside."

But the uplifting melody eventually became the theme for his life's tragedy. The alarms began to mark the event when he would take pills that didn't help much anymore. He needed to find something that worked better. And eventually he did: heroin.

Acquiring the narcotic wasn't that difficult, at first. He was still a star in ski country. His face was on magazine covers and prominently displayed on social media. But after a while, the doctors who enjoyed rubbing shoulders with a celebrity became nervous and stopped supplying his dangerous addiction. They advised him to seek help.

"Don't you think that's the very first thing I did?" he raged. "Whatever they advised, whatever they prescribed, it didn't work! They quit trying. But the pain didn't quit. Seeking help didn't make me feel better—those doctors quit!"

Hiding his addiction, he made his living as a ski ambassador. The Craters management felt it gave their mountain credibility. They thought that if a world-class ski racer everyone had seen winning championships on television preferred to ski at The Craters, then it must be as good as Zermatt and Val d'Isère.

There were more good days than bad, Trigger thought. He would take ski runs with tourists, he would appear at some corporate events, and there was always a ski bunny on vacation who wanted to bed a celebrity.

Walking to the Lady Moon Café for breakfast in the town of Placer, JC and Robin ran into Charlie Washburn, who was just leaving.

"How are you holding up?" JC asked, politely.

"It's a lot to bear," the newly widowed woman answered. "Right now, I have arrangements to make. The funeral is tomorrow. I'm almost afraid of what happens when I don't have these distractions. Then, I'll just be in an empty home without Johnny."

"Does the sheriff have any idea who is responsible?" JC asked, trying to avoid the word "murder" with the widow of the murdered man.

"They don't...no," she finally uttered.

"Do you?" JC asked.

Charlie Washburn looked at him. Her eyes were piercing. Was it anger or was it something else? He couldn't tell.

"I have a lot to do," the woman said tersely. "I have to go."

Anger, JC supposed. He and Robin watched the woman walk away from them down the sidewalk.

"Can't blame her," Robin said.

"No," JC agreed as he held the door open for her at the Lady Moon. "I guess we can't."

JC placed a phone call while he and Robin waited for their breakfast order to arrive.

"I have nothing to say at this time," the sheriff told him over the phone. "But maybe you'll want to check back with me at the end of the day."

"So, you're close to an arrest?" JC asked.

"Check back in at the end of the day," Sheriff Brush answered. "And could you do me a favor? Can you ask your colleague, Robin Smith, to wait a day before she comes in to discuss Loretta Sopris? Things are kind of busy today."

The sheriff ended the call. JC relayed the message to Robin.

"That doesn't leave either of us with much to do today," JC told Robin. "What else is on your plate?"

"I want to go to Fort Collins," she said.

"Why?" he asked.

"That's where Loretta Sopris lived," Robin asserted. "Everyone here says that they didn't know her. Someone will know her in Fort Collins."

"Give Rocky a call," JC suggested. "You don't need his permission, but as the assignment editor and the conduit to our news director, he likes to stay in the loop."

"Why don't all three of you go," Rocky suggested, when Robin called him. "You, Bip and JC. Why don't you all go?"

"I don't have any problem with that," Robin told him. "But why JC?"

"I'm sitting with Pat in his office," Rocky told her. "You know, the one with 'News Director' written on the door? He thinks it's a good idea to keep you and JC together. He says that viewers enjoy seeing the two of you together. You've become a celebrity couple, now. Viewers feel it's like watching an episode of *The Crown*, and you're the royal couple."

"Do we move the needle?" Robin asked, quoting her news director's penchant for justifying his actions by making their TV ratings go up.

"He says, 'It moves the needle,'" Rocky laughed, apparently being instructed by the news director how to respond.

"Alright," Robin said before hanging up. "We'll duck down to Fort Collins for the day."

While eating breakfast, they contacted Bip and told him to prepare for the brief road trip. Sunny elected to go with them.

Leaving the Lady Moon, JC and Robin eyed the county courthouse down the street. The tall pillars made an impressive façade in front.

But they would have been more interested if they had seen what was going on in back of the courthouse.

With her head down to avoid attention, and in the presence of an attorney, Charlie Washburn walked down the steps to the back entrance of the sheriff's office.

16

Rocky Mountain sheep hugged an impossible cliffside above Colorado State Highway 14 as Bip drove the news car underneath the herd. It was a collection of ewes and lambs with only one male bighorn visible.

JC, Robin and Sunny craned their necks to look out the car and up at the wildlife.

"I never get tired of seeing them," JC said. The others agreed.

The travelers were following the length of Cache La Poudre Canyon. It would take them downhill all the way to Fort Collins.

Their trip passed Poudre River Falls and the old Sportsman's Lodge. There was a general store there and cabins for rent.

They passed a rock formation that looked like a sleeping elephant and was known by that name.

Seasonal campgrounds were placed on both ends of the Narrows. But they were marked by signs saying they were closed for the winter.

JC pointed out a spot past the fish hatchery where a mountain man's cabin used to be visible.

"It wasn't a real mountain man's cabin, though. It was a movie set for a television epic back in 1978 called *Centennial*. It looked just like a mountain man's log cabin. But when you touched it, you realized it was made of spongy material. It was just movie magic."

They passed a spot where legend said that a mountain man named Dutch George had been mauled to death by a grizzly bear. The spot was taken by a campground now. There had not been a confirmed grizzly bear sighting in Colorado in the last forty-some years.

Further down the canyon, they passed the Mishawaka Inn, where Kat Martinez said she had a performance coming.

Exiting Cache La Poudre Canyon, they turned right at Ted's Place, a gas station where a beloved diner used to stand.

"Horace Greeley," JC said. "He was a New York newspaperman who visited the Cache La Poudre in 1859."

"He's the guy who said, 'Go West, young man,'" Bip added.

"Yep," JC concurred. "Greeley said the Poudre was the biggest river between Denver and Laramie, Wyoming. It was so wild, they were afraid to cross it. The mountaineer who was taking Greeley all the way to California studied the river for hours. He said he'd already seen too many men drown."

"So, they turned around?" Robin asked.

"No, they finally made the crossing," JC told them. "It was a near-disaster, but they made it."

JC directed Bip to follow Overland Trail Road. It was a more scenic route, in his mind. Traveling south, Horsetooth Reservoir was on their right.

"Fort Collins was named after a cavalry commander," JC told them. "His son, Caspar, was a cavalry officer too. He was killed in a battle with the Indians. They named Casper, Wyoming, after him."

"So, Fort Collins was really a fort?" Bip asked.

"Yep," JC said. "The original Camp Collins was washed away when the Poudre River flooded. It wasn't the last time that was going to happen, so they moved it closer to where the town is now. And when the fort was shut down by the U.S. government, the civilians who were left behind made Fort Collins an official town in its own right."

"Look at the bison!" Robin said, pointing to the west. "That must be the herd that CSU is breeding."

"Bip, Sunny, that's CSU's Foothills Campus," JC said. "The Arapaho said these fields used to be black with buffalo, as far as the eye could see."

Bip turned the car up LaPorte Avenue, took a right and a left and ventured east on East Mountain Avenue.

He pulled up in front of a small house with a "For Rent" sign outside.

"That's where Loretta Sopris lived," Robin said, checking her notes. "So, Johanna Forbes lives next door."

This stretch of East Mountain Avenue was almost fully transitioned from a residential neighborhood to a commercial one. A new hotel had just opened down the street.

The house where Johanna Forbes lived was modest. It was painted gray and was one level. There was no lawn in the front, just concrete. An insurance office was next door. There was some old snow pushed aside in the shadow of the home.

"Come on in," the woman said when she opened the door. "This is quite a crowd. Does it take this many people to photograph an interview?"

Robin and Bip would be conducting the interview. JC could interject if he cared to. Otherwise, he was just another pair of ears. And Sunny was excited to see Bip at work.

"I'm sorry," Robin said. "We can kick a couple of them out, if it makes you uncomfortable."

"No, it don't matter," the woman said. "I've got a big pot of coffee on. There's plenty for everyone."

Bip set up his tripod and lights in the front room, a living room. Johanna Forbes served the coffee as she explained that she was renting the house.

"I suspect that my landlord is just waiting for the right offer from some commercial developer and he'll sell it," Forbes said. "He owns the one next door too. That's where Loretta lived. Poor thing."

"How did you know Loretta?" Robin asked. The interview commenced and Bip began taping.

"We lived next door to each other," the woman said. "I'm a little younger than her, but not a lot. We were both divorced, and we went out at night together sometimes. You know, we kept an eye out for each other. And some days we'd go to Horsetooth Reservoir and sit in the sun. We'd go hiking. I think she won some free tickets, and we went to a CSU football game once."

"You know that she took her own life?" Robin asked.

"I do," Forbes said. "But I can't say I've ever been more shocked in my life. I didn't see her as the type. I didn't really see her unhappy that much. Of course, we both were pissed off at our ex-husbands. We'd talk about that sometimes."

Johanna Forbes was thin and pale but had an attractive body and a nice smile. She had some tattoos on her arms. Her brown hair was pulled back and she wasn't wearing makeup.

"Is there something besides her divorce that she was unhappy about?" Robin asked. "She had been divorced for about two years?"

"Yes, and she wanted the divorce," Forbes told her. "She wasn't dumped. She wanted to end the marriage."

"Tell me what you know about her past?" Robin asked.

"Well, she graduated from CSU," she began. "She studied accounting, I think. That's where she met her husband. The firm she worked for did the accounting for a string of pharmacies. Her husband was a pharmacist."

"Did you ever meet him?" Robin inquired.

"No. I saw him out the window when he stopped by once. But they didn't live in Fort Collins when they were married. I think they lived in Texas."

"You said that you'd go out at night together?" Robin asked. "Where would you go?"

"We'd usually walk downtown, go to dinner and maybe a bar," Johanna remembered. "Sometimes we'd go to classy places like Social or Blue Agave. Once or twice, we went to the New Belgium brewery on the edge of town. The boys liked her. I mean, I do okay. But she really attracted some nice-looking men."

"I don't mean to be blunt, but would she go home with them?" Robin asked.

"Not really," Johanna responded. "She liked to have a good time. She'd dance with them. We would drive out to Bruce's sometimes. You know, the cowboy bar with the good Rocky Mountain oysters. We'd both dance up a storm, but we'd come home together."

Johanna laughed at the memory of two girls holding their own in the cowboy bar between Fort Collins and Greeley.

"I thought she had a boyfriend up at The Craters," Johanna recalled. "She and her husband used to go skiing there. I think they rented a condo once or twice. Anyway, after the divorce, I think she took up with some famous guy there. A ski racer."

"Trigger Fischer?" Robin asked.

"I think that was it! I remember because he had the same name as Roy Rogers' horse," Johanna laughed. "They were together for about two years. I mean, I think they were still together."

"Could that be what she was upset about? Her relationship with Trigger?" Robin queried.

"Anything is possible," Johanna agreed. "But I really don't know."

"When is the last time you saw Loretta?" Robin asked.

"A couple of weeks ago, not even," Johanna told her. "We went out for drinks at Ace Gillett's, downtown."

"So, the last week she was alive?" Robin pressed.

"Yes. It's kind of creepy when you put it that way," Johanna sighed. "But yes, I guess it was a few days before she died. Poor thing."

"Do you have a picture of Loretta? One you could spare?" JC asked, speaking up for the first time.

"You're in luck," Johanna told him. "I'm old-school. I still like to keep photo albums. I have a few of Loretta and me. I'll give you one."

Robin left Johanna with her card and took the picture of Loretta Sopris. As they exited the house, JC walked next door to peer into the window of Sopris' home. It was a gray single-story house much like the one Johanna Forbes lived in.

One house used to be the office, and the other was the workshop for a tombstone-carving business. The owners sought a more dignified name and called it a "Monument Shop."

Through the front window, it looked like everything in the living room was boxed up. It was scrubbed clean, the wooden floors were bare, and nothing was left hanging on the walls. The furniture looked like it was staying for the next renter.

The bright sun was getting low as they stood outside. Temperatures had warmed into the fifties. The front range of Colorado was notorious for spring-like temperatures while snow was still piled high in the mountains.

"So, this is NoCo?" Sunny asked, never having visited Northern Colorado before.

"That's what the trendy set calls it," Bip told her.

"And if you want to be more specific," JC added, "They call this FoCo. Fort Collins."

"Where to now?" Bip asked as he placed his equipment in the back of the car.

"We have her picture now," Robin said. "Let's see if we can find anyone else who knew her."

"Cocktail hour is approaching," JC announced.

"You read my mind," Robin told him.

"You have a live shot to prepare for," JC reminded her. "Why don't Sunny and I hit some bars while you and Bip prepare your story. We'll see if we can find anyone else who knows something about Loretta. I promise we won't drink the town dry, without you."

JC and Sunny walked west on East Mountain Avenue and crossed traffic at Linden. Facing north, the street had been closed, years ago, and turned into a pedestrian mall. String lights came on overhead. Down the block, there was a small ice-skating rink.

To gain entry to the bar named Social, you had to win the favor of a doorman guarding a stairwell that led down to the basement. He told JC and Sunny to wait, and he spoke into a microphone clipped to the cuff on the left sleeve of his jacket. A line of other customers hoping to gain entry quickly formed behind them.

When a couple walked up the stairwell and departed, JC and Sunny were told they were free to descend the stairs and enter the business.

"We're just going to look for a seat at the bar," JC told the woman at the bottom of the stairs.

The big room was dark. There were modern tables placed close together, some on a raised level. There were a lot of mirrors, and the crowd was energetic and young, dressed for a night on the town.

Taking a seat at the bar, Sunny ordered a drink called a Sgt. Pepper. It mixed tequila with lemon, pineapple juice, vanilla bean, black pepper and pink peppercorn on the rim. JC ordered a drink called an Old Stogie. It contained rye whiskey, citrus bitters and brown sugar. The bartender presented the glass, turned upside down over a modest lump of peach Earl Grey tea leaves.

"Turn it over and smell it," the bartender said with a smile.

JC picked up the glass and turned it over. Sniffing the aroma, it smelled just like a cigar. The bartender poured the whiskey and the other contents into the glass.

"This is really good," JC told the bartender.

"It's my favorite drink here," the bartender said agreeably.

JC pulled out the photograph of Loretta Sopris and held it up so the bartender could see it.

"Does this woman look familiar to you?" JC asked. "Was she a customer?"

"Do you want to guess how many women we get in here each week?" the bartender asked. "And they're all demanding a drink and they're all demanding it right away. I work fast."

"I can imagine," JC and Sunny sat at the bar to give the bartender a little time to think about it. The picture of Loretta Sopris sat beside his drink, facing the bartender. He glanced at it a couple of times when he walked by to serve another customer.

JC and Sunny realized it was a rare moment when they were alone together. No Bip, no Robin.

"How are you adjusting to being away from home?" JC asked.

119

"It's an adjustment," she agreed. "Denver is very nice. The apartment Bip and I share is much nicer than where I lived in Utah. But it's different too. My mother doesn't live downstairs. My aunt and uncle don't live next door. I haven't known the woman behind the counter at the corner store for my entire life, like I have at home."

"Are you and Bip happy with each other?" he asked.

"Oh, Bip is wonderful," she said. "He's very understanding. And we have fun together."

"He's a good guy," JC agreed.

With their drinks done, JC gave the bartender a look.

"Sorry," the bartender told him. "I just don't place her. She was probably in here, but like I say, a lot of customers come and go."

JC voiced his thanks, picked up Loretta's picture and slipped it into his pocket. He left his business card in its place.

They walked to South College Avenue and took a left. The sun had gone down, and an abundance of fairy lights sparkled in the trees lining the sidewalk.

They decided to move on to another bar Johanna Forbes had mentioned, Blue Agave.

The entrance was in Oak Street Plaza Park. A crowd of young people stood where there was a splash pad in the summer. They were talking over plans for the evening. Some of them hopped from one foot to the other to keep warm. When the sun dropped, the temperature dropped.

Blue Agave was in the basement of the old post office. Mexican guitar music greeted them as they entered. Again, they told the hostess that they'd find seats at the bar.

Sunny ordered a Mexico City sour, more tequila. JC asked the bartender for a Horse and Dragon Sad Panda; another beer brewed in Fort Collins.

"So, where does Northern Colorado begin?" Sunny asked. "Where is the line where it is not Northern Colorado?"

"That is a good question," JC told her. "And it's not something there is a lot of agreement on."

He asked the two bartenders. One said, "North of Boulder." The other said, "No, it's further up than that. Longmont."

A man next to them at the bar said, "It depends which way you're coming from," and laughed. "If you're coming from Wyoming, it begins at the state line."

JC produced the picture of Loretta Sopris. He asked the two bartenders if they had ever seen the woman in the picture. Both told him that they couldn't separate her from any of the other hundreds of visitors they served on a weekly basis.

He was disappointed that there wasn't reason to delay their departure. He saw mango tacos and blue-corn enchiladas on the menu.

JC and Sunny walked back outside, and JC's phone rang. Robin and Bip had finished their live shot and asked where they should meet. JC suggested Ace Gillett's, further down the block.

Making their way down South College Avenue, JC and Sunny stopped to look over a hardware store with more non-hardware items in their substantial display window than most department stores.

"Are you thinking of buying me a snowblower?" Robin asked as she crept up behind her fiancé.

121

"Nope, just a long-handled brush," he told her as he turned around and slipped his hands around her waist. "So, you can get all the snow off my car while I sit in it and pick a good radio station."

She gave him a small kiss, and they continued down the street to the Armstrong Hotel, at the corner of South College and West Olive. They had reserved rooms for the night.

The Armstrong Hotel had evolved from low-cost rooms for hard-luck unfortunates in the 1970s, to luxury boutique lodging with the best location in town. They checked in and went upstairs to change their clothes.

Walking back down the stairs, they were watched by faces in a dozen oil paintings of various Hollywood celebrities. The art hung over a sofa and some chairs placed around a coffee table.

Next to the check-in desk there was a bar that was open for cocktail hour. It did a brisk business, with tables and chairs set up next to the Armstrong's large windows looking out on South College. It was a comfortable place to watch people walk by.

They walked down another flight of stairs to Ace Gillett's. It was designed to resemble an old speakeasy.

The lights were low, and a long bar stretched across the length of one wall. There was neon lettering on a small wall of exposed brick. It read, "Good Vibes Only." Next to it was a wall of vinyl record albums and a turntable.

"We'll play one for you, if you want," a man said after emerging from behind the bar. He said his name was Bobby.

Robin picked a classic album she saw on the wall, *The Temptations Greatest Hits*.

They told the bartender that they'd be staying for dinner and were escorted to a table against the wall.

"I'm your bartender and your waiter," Bobby said. "What can I start you with?"

Robin and Sunny ordered a drink called Crimson Fever. It was a blend of cognac, aged rum, brown butter, vanilla and orange cream.

JC and Bip ordered a Boulevardier, with cork-strength whiskey and sweet vermouth with an orange twist.

Bobby returned to his post behind the bar and began mixing their drinks. When he returned to their table with their order, JC pulled out the picture of Loretta Sopris and showed it to Bobby.

"Ah, Sweet Loretta," Bobby said. "She is a regular. I probably saw her two weekends ago. She leaves town sometimes. I saw her on a Friday. I remember because we had live music that night and she really liked the guy's music."

"And you're sure it was this woman?" JC asked.

"Loretta has been coming in for a couple of years," Bobby said. "She's a beautiful woman. Classy. She had no interest in me, beyond being her bartender, but..."

Bobby was a man of twenty-five years. He had handsome boyish looks with a pierced ear and a congenial manner.

"I saw her with another woman," Bobby told them. "They seemed to be friends. They looked like they had some heavy stuff to talk about. But yeah, I definitely saw her, two Fridays ago."

"So, if you knew Loretta, do you know Johanna Forbes?" Robin asked.

"I don't think so. But that must have been her," the bartender replied. "Do I hear you talking in past tense? Did something happen to Loretta?"

"She died last weekend," Robin informed him. "The sheriff thinks it was a suicide."

The bartender's gentle eyes widened with surprise. He didn't say anything for a moment.

"Well, that is sad news," the bartender finally uttered. "That is really sad news."

"Any idea why she would do that?" Robin asked.

"I don't," the bartender responded. "I really don't."

They placed their food order. Their appetizer was called Devil on Horsetooth, dates wrapped in bacon and cream cheese. JC ordered a roast half chicken for dinner. Sunny and Bip had elk burgers. Robin enjoyed red snapper.

Following dinner, they moved into one of several adjoining rooms with comfortable chairs set around coffee tables. A fireplace warmed their room.

They ordered more drinks and sifted through the day's discoveries.

"Bobby's story seems to confirm what Johanna told us," Robin said. "It turned out to be the last time Johanna saw her. Loretta must have left the next morning for The Craters."

"So, there's something here in Fort Collins that we haven't found," JC offered. "Or the answer is back up at The Craters. What drew her there?"

Calling it a night, JC and Robin climbed into bed in their second-floor room. It had a cast-iron radiator to keep them warm. But they left the window open a crack to enjoy the cold fresh air.

A freight train blew its whistle as it slowly passed through town on South Mason Street.

"Are you any closer to understanding why she's dead?" JC asked as he rolled toward her. "What did Johanna tell you after Sunny and I left?"

"Mostly the same thing she said when you were there," Robin answered, facing him with her head in the pillow. "She said the New Belgium brewery was really fun." She had a silly smile on her face.

17

"I might be eating his grandson," Robin said, looking up at the taxidermized head of an elk while eating her elk steak with some eggs.

"Yeah, he doesn't look happy with you," Bip agreed.

"We ate here a few years ago, didn't we?" Robin asked JC. "I like this place."

JC nodded in agreement. They were eating at Vern's, north of Fort Collins. He told them that if they kept driving north on 287, you could be in Laramie, Wyoming, before lunch and Yellowstone National Park for dinner.

"Great," Robin reacted. "More angry elk."

They planned to return to Placer and The Craters Ski Resort after breakfast. JC wasn't sure that the trip to Fort Collins had paid for itself.

"What did we learn here?" he asked as they ate breakfast.

"That she went barhopping and people liked her," Bip offered.

"And that New Belgium's brewery is really fun," Robin said with a grin.

"But she didn't go home with men," Sunny added.

"That may be important," JC acknowledged. "Johanna said that men hit on Loretta, but she didn't go home with them."

"Maybe she was being loyal to one particular man," Robin suggested. "Was it Trigger?"

"I guess we have to find out," JC said. "Did he break her heart? Could that have sent her spiraling into depression?"

The taxidermized heads of bison, elk and pronghorn antelope stared down on them as JC and the others ate huevos rancheros and veggie omelets. Country music played in the background, and the server kept their coffee cups full.

Vern's was a landmark in the Poudre Valley. There were diners who had been coming there for breakfast since its opening, just after World War Two.

"When I read that Horace Greeley book and the chapter about this area," JC said as he sipped the remains of his coffee, "he said the mountain men that were with him spoke about their favorite foods. They liked to eat antelope, deer and buffalo. And if it was prepared right, they'd all enjoyed dog."

"Oh, please stop," Robin begged. "Why do they have to eat their dogs?"

"Sorry. I guess they were hungry," JC apologized. "They didn't think bear tasted very good, nor wolf or mountain goat."

"But they liked dog? Tell me more," Bip said, just to annoy Robin. "Did they have favorite breeds?"

Robin gave JC a look that declared, "Don't you dare say one more word about eating dogs."

"You had better sleep with one eye open," Robin sneered at Bip. "I am going to punish you."

Laughing and finished with their breakfast, they paid their server and emerged from Vern's. Its big, wood-plank awning was held up by thick posts with bark left on the wood. A sprawling false front towered above the roof.

It was a crisp morning. The breeze had a bite to it. The sun was just peeking over the eastern plains.

"The Arapaho used to camp near this spot," JC said. "There was an Arapaho leader called Chief Friday. He was educated in St. Louis. He liked white people, but he also knew that, in time, Indians would be at the mercy of the whites. He tried to get along, and it worked for a long time. During the Indian attacks on white settlers, Chief Friday and his people camped at Fort Collins and sat out the violence."

Sunny paid particular interest. The Utes that came before her lived to the west, up in the mountains.

"But the Arapaho were bitter enemies of the Pawnee," JC continued. "The last big fight between the two tribes unfolded just north of here. Many warriors on both sides lost their lives. I read that it lasted for three days. The Pawnee finally slipped away during a stormy night. And the Arapaho held onto their favorite hunting grounds."

"You're lucky you already have a girlfriend," Bip said. "Because being a history nerd is not sexy."

"But you have to admit, it's interesting," JC asserted.

"I do admit that" Bip said.

With one more scan of the historic plains outside Fort Collins, they climbed into their car and headed up Highway 287.

JC looked north toward the site of a proposed new reservoir in the foothills. It had been the source of dispute for decades. A few more farms were going to be submerged, and the water would be diverted from the Cache La Poudre.

JC pointed north and told his friends about an old Indian buffalo jump he had visited when he was in college at Fort Collins. The elderly landowners allowed him on their pasture. They showed him boxes full of old bones and arrowheads.

He remembered seeing rocks that still marked teepee circles. And he recalled seeing deep ruts formed by wagons when they followed the Overland Trail well over a century ago.

Bip took a left off 287 at Ted's Place and ventured back up Poudre Canyon toward The Craters Ski Resort.

As they traveled back up Poudre Canyon past Mishawaka, they passed more ground scorched by wildfires in recent years. They passed homes still being rebuilt after being destroyed by flames.

And they looked for moose. There was no known moose population in Colorado in 1978, until twelve animals were introduced near Cameron Pass. Now, the moose population was estimated as high as one thousand.

Highway 14 faithfully followed the Poudre River until it delivered them back to Long Draw Road and The Craters.

JC's phone rang. They were just pulling up to the parking lot behind the Clark Hotel.

"Where are you?" the voice asked.

"We were out of town," JC answered. "We just got back."

"Well, you might want to get down to the courthouse," Deputy Hank Monk told him. "They've arrested Charlie Washburn. They're bringing her to the courthouse to charge her with her husband's murder."

JC informed Bip that they needed to get to the courthouse quickly. Robin exited the car, saying she had work to do. Sunny decided to stay with JC and Bip.

"This is exciting," she said.

They rushed to Placer. Cameras would not be allowed in the courtroom. So, upon arriving in the parking lot of the courthouse, Bip pulled his camera out of the car and positioned himself where he had learned that prisoners were walked into the building. Sunny served as an extra pair of eyes.

Old courthouse facilities usually provided a good opportunity for news photographers to get pictures of the suspects. Deputies were in the habit of pulling up to the curb and walking the accused perpetrator into the courthouse. Cops and camera ops called it "The perp walk."

Newer courthouses were built with garages. The garage doors would be closed before the defendant was ushered out of the car. No perp walk.

JC hurried into the building and ran up the stairs to the second floor. A guard steered him toward the courtroom where Mrs. John Washburn would be arraigned.

JC walked in discreetly. Judges demanded decorum in their courtrooms. Court hadn't convened. Charlie Washburn hadn't yet made her appearance. JC took a seat in the front row of the area provided for the public.

Captain Rock Bush, the sheriff's right-hand man, was standing by a side door in the front of the room, speaking with the bailiff.

Seated over JC's left shoulder, he noticed the county's deputy treasurer, and his co-worker named Jed. They were sitting a few rows behind him.

Over JC's right shoulder, he noticed his old high school acquaintance, Tommy Halvorson.

"What are you doing here, Tommy?" JC asked as he slid onto the bench beside him.

"Shh, Scooter, remember? Call me Scooter," Tommy said in a whisper.

"Okay, what is your interest in this case, Scooter?" JC inquired.

"I knew John. I mean, I know Charlie too," Scooter responded. "But I used to work in the financial sector. It paid well enough that now I can be a ski bum. John Washburn and I used to talk over the financial markets and money. It was just something we enjoyed chatting about over an occasional beer."

"I thought you said you only knew him from the times you paid your taxes," JC challenged.

"I didn't feel like saying more," Scooter explained. "They were looking for the guy who killed him. I didn't feel like drawing any suspicion on myself. Now, they've caught the killer."

The conversation was interrupted by the opening of the side door. Charlie Washburn was walked in. She had her head down and she was handcuffed.

JC quietly returned to his front-row seat, to hear the discussion about to ensue.

"All rise!" the bailiff commanded. The judge entered the courtroom by a back door and sat behind his bench.

"Your Honor," District Attorney Frank Steen addressed the judge. "We are charging the defendant, Charlene Washburn, with second-degree murder in the death of John W. Washburn. We are asking the defendant be held on a bail of one million dollars."

JC recognized the district attorney. They had taken a ride together on a chairlift the other day.

Charlene "Charlie" Washburn never raised her head. Her handcuffs had been removed for the proceeding, but her hands remained clasped together in her lap.

Washburn's defense attorney introduced herself to the judge as a formality, though he knew who she was. Her name was Mary Madeleine LaJeunesse. JC recognized her name and thought she must be the sister of Mercy LaJeunesse. Madeleine was a public defender.

"Your Honor," the public defender stated before the bench. "The prosecution has presented no evidence, at this point, to determine my client's guilt. In fact, I don't even know what she's doing here. We would ask the court to release her without bail."

"Your Honor," the district attorney pounced. "We are early in this investigation. But we have an eyewitness who says she saw a woman at the scene where Mr. Washburn's body was later found. Our witness was driving up County Route 68C and 162, which goes right by the spot where the victim was discovered. She also says she saw an unusual automobile parked there on the side of the road. We have since identified that car as John Washburn's Citroën, the most unusual automobile in the county. Our witness says she thought nothing of what she saw at the time, but after hearing news accounts of the murder of Mr. Washburn, she realized that she had seen something important."

"Your Honor," Madeleine LaJeunesse argued. "That wouldn't convict a scarecrow of standing in a cornfield. Mrs. Washburn was born and raised in this community. This is her home. And we are pleading, by the way, not guilty!"

"Well, Ms. LaJeunesse," the old judge said in a firm voice. "We *have* done things in a bit of a backwards manner, this morning. Is that your plea, Mrs. Washburn?"

"Yes, Your Honor," Charlie Washburn said in barely more than a whisper. She raised her eyes when she said it, but not her head.

The judge paused for a moment to think.

"I will set bail at one hundred thousand dollars," the judge declared. "Mr. Steen, Ms. LaJeunesse, please make your availability known to my court by the end of the day and we will set a date to proceed."

"All rise!" the bailiff shouted as soon at the judge dropped his gavel.

With that, the judge rose and exited the court through the same back door from which he had entered.

A deputy stood guard by the door in the back of the courtroom. It was Aaron Aguayo. Sunny pulled on the door and walked past him as she entered the courtroom.

"Bip told me to tell you that he got footage of Mrs. Washburn," she whispered to JC as she slid onto the bench next to him. "And he will be waiting for you outside, if you want to do any interviews."

Charlie Washburn's head remained lowered as she waited for her exit from the courtroom. She almost appeared to be in a trance. She extended her arms, and they were shackled again. With the assistance of a jail guard, she stood and was led from the room.

Sunny accompanied JC to the door in the back of the courtroom. Next to the door, Deputy Aguayo eyed her.

"Ahnah ne̅/gut?" the deputy said quietly, only for her ears. His thumbs were tucked into his belt buckle. He made no effort to approach her.

Sunny stopped next to him and stared at the man for a moment.

"Noo̅√ ni ne̅ah Sunny Shavano," she responded in her Ute language. Also speaking Ute, he had asked her name.

"Noo̅√ ni ne̅ah Aaron Aguayo," the deputy said as he smiled. "Uh voo̅ sah rah." It was a friendly greeting of farewell.

"You are of the Ute people?" Sunny asked.

"My mother," Aguayo told her.

"You speak our language?" Sunny asked with a smile.

"Uh me̅ch," he said, smiling back. "A little," he said.

Sunny gave him a warm look and walked out of the courtroom. But she looked over her shoulder at him before scurrying to catch up with JC.

"Ms. LaJeunesse," JC blurted as she briskly walked past him and out the courtroom doors. JC walked at a fast clip to keep up with her.

"I don't have anything to say," the defender told him. "I was only assigned this case moments before court. I don't feel I should comment before speaking to my client. That being said, you heard my client say in the courtroom that she is not guilty."

"Does your client have an alibi for the time that Mr. Washburn went missing?" JC asked quickly.

"I told you, I don't have anything to say," Madeleine LaJeunesse replied with an even voice. "Maybe another time."

You should probably come up with something, JC said to himself.

18

Employees at Sawtooth Funeral Home—its full-time staff numbering two—found themselves in a quandary. They were on untracked snow, so to speak. They had neither a body nor a grieving widow for the memorial service scheduled for that afternoon.

The body of John Washburn hadn't been released by the sheriff's office, as the corpse still might provide more clues once investigators knew precisely what they were looking for.

And the grieving widow, upon her arrival at the funeral home in downtown Placer, had been scooped up by uniformed deputies and escorted in handcuffs to the courthouse.

But it was important to keep things at the mortuary tranquil. No one wanted to visit a funeral home where the hosts were tearing their hair out.

Uncertain what else to do, the staff at the funeral home calmly changed the message on the felt letter board in their lobby. It now read, "Service for John W. Washburn postponed until further notice."

Things were far less serene at the small county jail. Madeleine LaJeunesse sat in an old cell with a client she had met less than an hour earlier. Her client, who had said exactly three words while in court, said even less while they sat in her new home with cracked paint on the walls and a stainless-steel combination toilet and sink.

Charlie Washburn sat in a trance on a cot and stared at the floor.

Mary Madeleine LaJeunesse was known to friends and family as "Maddie." She was statuesque. Her brown hair was teased blonde. She wore a business suit with a skirt. Everything was "button-down" for business in the courtroom.

The appointed defender sat on the one chair in the cell and rested her briefcase on her lap, somewhat afraid of picking up bedbugs if she laid it on the cot.

Opening the briefcase, that day's mail rested on top. She had opened it waiting for her new client to be escorted from the jail and for court to convene. The papers on top consisted of two love letters from inmates LaJeunesse had represented. "Love" was a stretch, she thought. Rather, they were solicitations to enjoy conjugal visits while her former customers were incarcerated.

She pushed those aside and reached for a folder labeled "Washburn." It contained what little information she was able to obtain before her first meeting with her new disciple.

"'Unhappy marriage,'" Maddie LaJeunesse blurted. "Where do they get this shit? Were you sleeping with another man?"

"No," Charlie whispered. The defender noted that her client had uttered a word. They were making progress.

"A woman driving by the scene at sunset thinks she saw a woman," Maddie sneered. "Was she driving or was she sightseeing? You take your eyes off that road for a second and you end up in a ditch or driving off a cliff!"

Charlie said nothing.

"Small footprints in the snow were found near the body," Maddie read off the document in her hand. "That doesn't even mean it was a woman. It could have been a small man! And how many tourists visited that ghost town before the body was placed there? There could be twenty sets of prints!"

Maddie looked at her client. Charlie's vacant stare was still aimed at the sticky floor badly in need of a paint job.

"Any time you want to jump in," Maddie said. "Feel free."

Sheriff Jerry Brush was poring over a set of entirely different documents. He sat at his desk scratching the red hair on his head.

He hated math. He did everything to avoid it. It didn't make sense to him even when it was perfect. But this didn't look perfect. He needed to call in an expert. Jerry Brush knew he wasn't qualified to say the books taken from the county treasurer's office didn't make sense. Maybe there was a reasonable explanation for whatever an "allowance" was.

Outside, the weather was pleasant. Skiers and snowboarders at The Craters felt blessed, basking in the sunshine and warm temperatures. Lift operators, usually frozen in place during the winter, peeled off layers and smiled at customers as they helped them onto their chairs. One lift house was playing music from The Beach Boys.

But dark clouds were climbing over the mountains. It began to sprinkle. It was only expected to drop into the low forties overnight. This might last awhile.

It began to rain heavier. Stunned customers who had been skiing under the warm sun actually heard thunder. They fled for the indoors. With the threat of lightning, the gondola and chairlifts stopped. It was officially a mid-winter meltdown.

Nightfall descended and it continued to rain. JC and Bip found a porch with a roof to hide under and delivered a live report to Denver regarding the arrest of Charlie Washburn.

But the rain was big news in Placer too. It was going to wash away much of the snow on the slopes of the county's largest employer. Tourists were going to cancel their reservations and go home.

Restaurants during peak season would be only a quarter full. Inventory on the shelves of stores would go untouched. It would take some time and some effort to replace the snow they would lose over the next twelve hours.

Their workday done, the rain was still coming down. Soft light glowed from the windows of homes and hotels where people had taken cover.

JC and Bip dashed into another tavern at the resort village. It was called Zimmerman's Cabin.

The décor blended a log cabin interior covered in ski and snowboard memorabilia. Lots of skis and snowboards were screwed into the walls. An old chair from a lift hung from the ceiling in a corner. There was a large fake ski hill in another corner. It was left over from an old beer promotion.

Robin and Sunny, their hair tucked into hats to hide from the rain, joined the men at a table and they ordered dinner.

The crowd inside Zimmerman's heard more thunder rumble outside. Skiers in the bar applied an inexact formula, saying one inch of rain would have brought ten inches of fresh snow. They felt robbed.

Scooter stopped by the table. His ski jacket and pants were wet.

"I got caught on the other side of the mountain when it began to pour," he said with a smile. It would be his adventure story for the evening. He'd repeat it every time he started a conversation with a new set of ears.

Scooter had short blond hair. The sides were going gray. He had a large jaw. He clenched it as he ran some paper towels over his head to dry his hair.

He ordered the same beer JC and Bip were drinking. It was called Snow Day, a winter seasonal brewed by New Belgium.

"Those raindrops felt like BBs when I skied through them," Scooter said as he pulled an empty chair over from the next table. His blue eyes were flashing as he told the story. "I got soaked. Of course, most of the way down, the rain froze on my goggles. So, I had to choose between skiing blind or stopping and scraping off my goggles, only to have them ice up again."

Scooter paid cash for the round when his drink was delivered. But only a moment later, he said he was meeting someone and rose to move across the room. He literally bumped into Mad Marv as he was walking away. The exchange between the two men was not cordial.

Marv, with Mercy in tow, pulled up a second chair and joined JC and his friends. Marv grabbed their waitress to order food.

"Is there a problem between you and Scooter?" Robin asked.

"Scooter isn't everything he pretends to be," Marv told her.

Mercy, meanwhile, was looking at the dinner menu. She was making sounds that resembled a bird chirping. She caught Sunny staring at her.

"I'm chirping," Mercy said. "That's my field of study. I was saying, 'I'm hungry' in the language of a robin."

"Are you serious?" Robin asked. "That would be really cool, if you really understood the language of a bird."

"It really is my field of study!" Mercy insisted. "That's why I like your name, Robin. I'm getting my degree online. 'I'm hungry' is something that robins say a lot.

"They also say, 'Look out,' a lot. 'Look out, here comes a man,' or 'Look out, here comes a fox,' or 'Look out, here comes a hawk.' That's called the Peek-and-Tut. As you can imagine, they're afraid of a lot of predators."

JC, Robin and Bip exchanged glances, still wondering if Mercy was pulling their leg. But Sunny, who grew up with a closer relationship to nature, was drawn in.

"Once you understand their language, you appreciate that they're pretty much on the defense all of the time," Mercy told them. "There are really a lot of animals who want to eat them. Do you know why they chirp so much in the morning?"

"Are they talking to each other?" Robin asked.

"They are," Mercy responded. "They're very happy. They're saying, 'I survived the night! I'm alive! It is going to be a beautiful day!' That's called the Dawn Song. Oh, they also chat a lot during March and April about mating."

Their food was delivered, hot meals to warm the damp chill in the room.

"There are over one thousand species of birds in the United States," Mercy continued. "The most common is the American robin. So, wanting to make my study as practical as possible, I chose the robin."

"I know that they rarely visit bird feeders," Sunny said. "They don't eat seeds. They eat worms and fruit and things."

"That's right!" Mercy applauded.

"I like their sky-blue eggs," Sunny told her.

Zimmerman's Cabin was getting crowded. Trigger Fischer stopped by the table to say hello. They invited him to pull up a chair. He did and ordered a red ale called 90 Shilling, brewed by Odell in Fort Collins.

"Did you get caught out in the rain?" JC asked.

"No," Trigger said, laughing. "But I saw Scooter hustling down the mountain. He was getting poured on."

"Who is that with Scooter at the bar?" JC asked, looking in the direction of his old acquaintance across the room.

"That's Bob Andrews," Trigger told him. "Nice guy. He's an ex-cop. His nickname is Badass. Watch out, though. If he meets you, he'll give *you* a nickname. And it might not be nice. You know Horace? He calls him 'Whore House.'"

That elicited a laugh from the table and Trigger excused himself as he stood up. They watched as he crossed the

room and approached an attractive blonde sitting by herself
at the bar.

"He is a professional," Marv said. "I've never seen a man
who can pick up women faster than Trigger."

"Is that part of his job as ski ambassador?" Robin asked
with a smile.

"If he sends them home happy," JC said. "Then I guess
he earned his money."

"I remember him with his tousled hair," Robin said.
"When he was famous, his hair was fantastic. It was blond
and always a little scruffy, like a little boy. What young lady
could resist?"

"His post-famous look is as good as when he was
famous," JC suggested. "Wait until you see *my* post-famous
look. I'll wear a dirty, sleeveless tee-shirt, won't shave and
I'll sit on the stoop of our apartment smoking a cigar and
holding a half bottle of beer while I play chess with a
neighbor."

"And I will wear a filthy, shapeless sundress, even in the
winter. It will get caught on my belly," Robin countered.
"My stretched-out support hose will be falling down to my
ankles, and I will rarely wear my false teeth."

"It makes me want to marry you even more!" JC said as
he wrapped his arm around her waist, and she laughed.

Finishing dinner, JC and Robin rose to return to their
hotel.

"It was all that hot talk about false teeth and support
hose," JC told them.

Bip and Sunny said that they were going to remain at the
tavern for a while longer.

Instead of heading for the door, though, Robin weaved
through the crowd toward Trigger. JC followed.

143

"I may not be the answer to your long-term problem," they heard Trigger tell the blonde woman with a smile. "But I sure can be a short-term solution." The woman beamed at him.

"Are you calling it a night?" Trigger asked JC and Robin when he saw them standing there.

"Yeah," Robin said. "But can I ask you something? Were you and Loretta Sopris a thing?"

"This is neither the time nor the place to have that discussion," Trigger said with a smile, glancing at the pretty blonde who was giving him a mischievous grin. "Can this wait for another time?"

And with that, Trigger rose, took the hand of the pretty blonde and headed for the exit.

19

No two raindrops are alike, just like snowflakes. The rain continued to come down the next morning. Folks in Cameron County stayed inside if they could.

The Craters Ski Resort was closed for the day. A river of water ran down the middle of a slope called Blizzard. The sound of raindrops pelted the ski lodge's wooden deck and windows.

Vacationers who hadn't cancelled their reservations played board games provided in recreation rooms off the lobby of the Clark Hotel. Children flocked to a small arcade room with video games. It was the same scene at the Home and other accommodations at the ski mountain.

Adults had lost looks on their faces, knowing how much effort and money it had taken to get there. Some curled up on comfortable sofas and read books. Many buried their heads in a laptop and caught up on work. Others reported to the bar earlier than usual.

The small movie theatre in downtown Placer had its best day of the winter. An action film that was family-friendly sold out both showings.

The forecast was constantly being checked. The rain was supposed to end that afternoon. But after nightfall, when temperatures dropped below freezing, the ski runs would be turned into glazed ice.

Overnight, an army of crews called "Guns and Hoses" would report to their snowblowers and begin covering the mountainside to provide a few soft inches between skis, snowboards and the ice. The resort would reopen in the morning.

Bip and JC had started their day at the base of the ski resort, shooting video of the rain running down the ski slopes. Their television station's weather department would use those images during the evening newscasts.

Aside from the movie theatre, there was little activity in downtown Placer. If anyone came to the county building to pay a bill, they would find the door to the treasurer's office locked. Inside, a pair of financial auditors was looking over books. They had been loaned to the sheriff by the state.

The sheriff's office had issued a brief news release announcing the closing of the treasurer's office for one day, saying there was an investigation underway into "financial irregularities."

Bip and JC stopped by the county building to take video of the treasurer's locked door and disjointed images of people who were barely visible on the other side of the frosted security glass.

"Maybe Charlie Washburn didn't kill her husband," JC suggested.

"You mean, *this* is why Washburn was killed? Something to do with his office?" Bip asked. He framed another shot of the shadows moving on the other side of the translucent door. "Something to do with those 'financial irregularities?'"

"Clearly, the sheriff thinks there was something wrong going on," JC agreed. "I wonder what Charlie Washburn knows about it."

JC and Bip walked down the stairs to the sheriff's office. The small jail occupied one hallway, behind a locked steel door, in the space allotted to the sheriff and his department.

"She has refused to see you," a jailer said after JC made an official request to visit Charlie.

"I've got to get to the bottom of this," JC told Bip as they walked back up the dark stairs to the lobby of the county building. "Here's a theory: one or more employees in the treasurer's office was stealing money. Washburn caught wind of it and the thieves killed Washburn in order to cover their tracks."

"It wouldn't be the first time someone decided money was more important than a human life," Bip agreed as they pushed the door open and walked back out into the rain.

"Charlie has to know something," JC muttered in frustration. "But since she isn't in the mood to talk today, I have another idea."

Bip and JC positioned their car in the parking lot behind the courthouse to see anyone entering or exiting the sheriff's office.

"If there is even a suspicion of a theft in the treasurer's office, the sheriff is going to have to question the treasurer's employees," JC suggested. "And the sheriff isn't going to procrastinate. He's going to want to speak with them today."

So, the two journalists waited. Rain spotted the windshield of their parked car, requiring Bip to activate the wipers at annoying intervals.

"So, do you want to talk about auto racing?" JC asked Bip.

"I can't believe it's come to this," Bip sighed. "Sure."

Keeping an eye on the entrance to the sheriff's office, JC and Bip discussed Formula One auto racing, IndyCar racing, and JC's insistence that the late Scotsman, Jimmy Clark, was the greatest race car driver of all time.

"Then why does Lewis Hamilton have so many more Formula One wins?" Bip challenged.

"Because they didn't have as many championship races when Clark was alive. And it was back when crashes killed you. Clark was only thirty-two when he died in a racing crash."

The backseat door of the SUV opened. Robin climbed in with a bag of sandwiches and coffee.

"You are the answer to my prayers," Bip told her.

"Yeah, sorry it took so long," she said as she settled in and pulled down the hood on her jacket. "You must be famished."

"Yeah," Bip replied. "But your arrival means I don't have to discuss auto racing with him anymore. You are an angel."

"He can talk your ear off, can't he?" Robin agreed, smiling at JC.

"I'm sorry, I can't hear you," Bip told her. "My ears fell off about an hour ago."

"I don't mean to interrupt this slanderous rant about my character by you two," JC said, "but look who just got out of his car and is walking to the entrance of the sheriff's office."

Bip jumped out of the car, grabbing his camera from the backseat and started recording video. The county treasurer's employee they knew only as Jed was working his way toward the county building, accompanied by a man who very much looked like an attorney. Their heads were down to avoid the rain and, more so, the camera.

Less than an hour later, the man known to JC and Bip as the deputy treasurer emerged from a car and followed the same path to the rear entrance to the sheriff's office. Again, there was a man in tow who looked suspiciously like a lawyer.

"The plot thickens," JC muttered.

"Yes," Robin agreed. "But are they the suspects or the witnesses?"

"That's a fair point," JC responded. "We can go with the theory that they were stealing the money and killed Washburn when he found out. Or we can go with a theory that Washburn was stealing the money and.... I don't know. Why would he be murdered if he was also the guy stealing the money?"

"So, you don't think Charlie killed her husband?" Robin asked.

"I don't really know," JC told her. "But it *is* a bit of a coincidence that the treasurer may have been committing a significant felony *and* he happened to get himself killed for a reason that is in no way connected."

149

"How about a partner?" Robin offered. "What if Washburn had a partner in the theft and the partner killed him?"

"That's good theory," JC reacted. "Again, Jed or the deputy treasurer, or both, could have been the partner and they killed Washburn to cover up their participation in the crime. Then it would all be blamed on Washburn."

"Have we thought of self-defense?" Bip added. "Maybe Washburn wanted to kill his partner but died trying?"

JC pulled out his phone and called Sheriff Brush. The sheriff's secretary answered and said that the sheriff was unavailable.

"And considering that you've been parked in your car outside our office for half the day," the sheriff's secretary said, "I think you know why the sheriff isn't available right now."

"I also wanted to ask about the murder weapon," JC told Robin when the call ended. "As far as I know, they still haven't found the murder weapon, presumably a knife. Do they even know *where* he was killed? They might only know where he was *found*."

"And that all gives you a lot of reasons to wonder if Charlie is innocent," Robin surmised.

The rain began to let up. JC and Bip remained in the car, waiting for the two treasurer's office employees to emerge from the sheriff's basement. Robin drove her car back to the hotel to work on leads regarding the death of Loretta Sopris.

After more waiting, JC nudged Bip as he eyed a woman approaching the back entrance to the courthouse. Bip and JC both jumped out of the car. Bip grabbed his camera; JC made a straight line to the woman.

Public defender Maddie LaJeunesse carried a briefcase and walked with determination. She eyed JC as he approached.

"You met my sister and her husband and her boyfriend," Maddie said without breaking stride. "If you've got that one figured out, please enlighten me."

JC walked alongside the attorney, matching her stride.

"I'm still running the algorithms on that one," JC said. Maddie gave a small smile. A blonde strand of LaJeunesse's hair fell into her eyes. She let it be. JC thought she looked more approachable, less military.

"Will you ask your client to speak with me?" JC asked, referring to Charlie Washburn.

"What makes you think she'll talk with *me?*" Maddie responded.

"If she's innocent, it might help if she said so," JC told her.

"You heard her in court," Maddie said to him. "She pleaded 'not guilty.'"

"Actually, I heard *you* plead 'not guilty,'" JC replied, still walking to keep up with the attorney. "All I heard her say was 'Yes, Your Honor.' She could say the same thing if he asked if she wanted some ice cream."

"What flavor?" the attorney said.

JC considered this just long enough for them to reach a door marked "County Employees Only." Maddie LaJeunesse pointed at the sign and disappeared behind the door.

20

JC had enough ammo to intrigue viewers during his live shot to Denver that night. Attention was now *shared* by the murder of John Washburn and suspicions that he was another crooked politician stealing money from the taxpayers.

The rain had picked up again and the satellite truck engineer, Jem Norvell, had set them up in the ski village under cover on a stone porch with a wooden awning above.

After the live report back to Denver, JC was still restless. He didn't know why Charlie Washburn had been arrested so quickly.

While Bip called Sunny and Robin, telling them to meet for dinner at the North Park Toll Road Company, JC telephoned Scooter Halvorson with the same message.

Walking toward the restaurant, JC spotted Hank Monk, the sheriff's deputy. Both men had their heads down, trying to keep the rain out of their faces. But JC's eyes were always scanning his surroundings.

Monk stood out. He was larger than most men in Placer. His face was rugged and pockmarked. Despite that, he was handsome. His dark hair was covered by a cowboy hat. He was off duty and appeared to be on his way somewhere. He had a bottle of wine in his hand.

"Do you have a minute?" JC asked Monk after exchanging greetings. They ducked under the protection of a canvas awning. Monk looked over both shoulders, as if he wanted to be sure he wasn't being watched.

"Do you guys know *where* Washburn was killed?" JC asked. "Do you have much physical evidence?"

"By 'us guys,' do you mean the sheriff's office investigating the crime?" Monk asked.

"Yep," JC responded. And he looked at Monk, searching for answers.

"Not really," Monk replied after giving it some thought. "I'm more of their guy for outdoor duty. I'm kind of the mountain man for the sheriff's 'to-do' list, so I'm not on the inside of this investigation. But no, they haven't found blood splatter on the carpet of the Washburn home, if that's what you're asking."

Monk looked both ways again. Then he said that he needed to be going.

"How come you said you didn't know John Washburn?" JC asked his old high school friend. JC and Scooter sat at a separate table from Robin, Bip and Sunny at the North Park Toll Road Company Restaurant. "Then you admitted that you used to drink beer with him and talk about finance."

A server came to the table and delivered them two beers, a sour by a Fort Collins brewery called Funkwerks. Scooter gave her a twenty and told her to keep the change.

"I told you," Scooter reminded the journalist. "I didn't want to get involved in the murder investigation. It had nothing to do with me and I didn't want to get involved."

"And why did Marv say that you're not all you pretend to be?" JC asked. "What's he talking about?"

"Ha!" Scooter bellowed. "*He* said that about *me*? Do you want to hear the truth about *that* parasite?"

"I'm all ears," JC told him.

Scooter shifted in his seat. JC thought he was considering what or how much he wanted to tell.

"He ruined people," Scooter stated in a quiet voice as he leaned forward. "He conned them out of their life savings with a cryptocurrency scam he based out of Puerto Rico."

"I read a short newspaper article about this," JC recalled. "But I didn't hear anything about it again."

"It was covered by the news in Puerto Rico," Scooter insisted. "That's where I was living. You remember I told you that's when Hurricane Maria hit. Mad Marv was down there too. But his arrest wasn't big enough to make the national news on the mainland. It all happened in the closing weeks of the U.S. presidential election. He was lucky. There was hardly room in the national newscasts for *anything* that didn't involve politics. A story had to be huge to get on the air, like maybe the moon blowing up."

"So, what happened?" JC asked.

"Here was Marv's scam. Cryptocurrency is pretty volatile," Scooter explained. "Marv made his move during a downturn in crypto values. There have been some pretty steep falls. So, he started dipping into the funds of his customers during those plunges and assigning what he stole to the loss column of their investment portfolio. It appeared that every penny was accounted for. No one suspected a thing."

"And when he got caught?" JC asked.

"The federal investigators had a hard time understanding crypto," Scooter explained. "It's not easy for a newcomer to get an accurate understanding of how much crypto money there is, where it came from and where it has gone to. Marv led them through the whole process, like they were puppies on a leash. He took a plea agreement and agreed to pay a fine in the millions of dollars. The feds counted it as a victory."

"But you're saying they missed a lot," JC stated.

"*A lot*," Scooter emphasized. "When it was all over, he still had millions of dollars in stolen assets."

"And he wasn't sent to prison?" JC asked.

"No. And now," Scooter said while shaking his head, "he is free to live at a luxury ski resort in God's country."

JC was thinking it over, sipping his beer and stroking the search app on his phone.

"He had good lawyers," Scooter added. "He has officially paid his debt to society. But he's essentially *hiding* up here because there are some pissed-off people looking for him."

JC's phone now was producing images of Mad Marv and stories from Puerto Rico related to his prosecution for carrying out a cryptocurrency scam.

"Are you one of his victims?" JC looked up and asked Scooter.

"No, I can honestly tell you that I was not victimized by Mad Marv," Scooter said with a grin.

"That's not why I told you to meet me here, anyway," JC said. "In fact, I almost feel like you were throwing me off the trail."

"Who, me?" Scooter asked, smugly.

"Tell me what you know about John Washburn," JC insisted. "Was *he* a thief, too?"

"I don't know," Scooter said.

"Is someone else in that treasurer's office stealing?"

"I don't know," Scooter insisted.

"Did he ever say anything to you, while you were sipping beer together discussing money?" JC prodded.

"I can't say that he did," Scooter maintained. But he was tiring of the third-degree grilling he was receiving. "I came here as a friend. I told you all about Mad Marv. And you seem to have a bug up your ass about me. You're still kind of an asshole, did you know that?"

"I'm just getting started," JC grumbled and got up and left Scooter sitting alone.

JC took his beer to the table where Robin, Bip and Sunny awaited. They ordered dinner and talked over what they had learned.

"Why isn't Charlie out on bail?" JC asked. "There are just so many things wrong with her arrest."

"We are in the Wild West," Bip said. "Maybe they're just going to hang her in the morning."

"Hank Monk told me they don't have any blood evidence from the Washburn house," JC continued. "I don't think they can even prove where it happened. And where is the knife? This arrest just bugs me. It doesn't pass the smell test. Not yet, anyway."

Bip and Robin swayed at mention of the smell test. JC's smell test, whether or not he was actually smelling something, usually proved to be accurate. And that meant they were all going to have to follow him swimming upstream for a while.

"Mr. Snow?"

JC looked up and saw the man he had been told was a former police officer.

"Bob Andrews, right?" JC said, extending his hand.

"How do you know me?" Andrews asked, as though his cover had been blown.

"I think I saw you talking with Scooter Halvorson," JC told him.

"Donut? Yeah, he's a good guy."

"Donut?" JC asked.

"Yeah, that's what I call him," Badass responded. "Don't mind me. I give everyone a nickname. It reminds me who they are. Halvorson is Danish. Donuts and Danish are my favorite breakfast treats."

"It's nice to meet you, Bob," JC said and introduced the others at the table.

"You in town covering Frenchy's murder?" Andrews asked.

"Yep," JC responded.

"What about the skydiver?" Badass inquired.

"Loretta Sopris?" JC asked, after giving some thought to who Andrews might call "skydiver."

157

"You learn fast," Andrews said, smiling.

"We're interested, but it's been taking a back seat to Washburn," JC said.

"You think Chuck did it?" the former law officer asked.

JC was stumped again. Trigger was not wrong. Andrews liked to assign nicknames to just about everyone. "Chuck," JC realized, was Charlie Washburn, the woman accused of killing her husband.

"You used to be a cop," JC said. "What do you think?"

"Sometimes, cops get it right and sometimes they get it wrong," Andrews stated.

"What about this time?" JC inquired. Badass just shrugged.

"You're friends with Mad Marv?" Andrews asked.

"We're acquainted," JC said. "He seems alright."

"Don't fool yourself," Andrews replied. "Do yourself a favor and keep him at an arm's distance."

JC noted the former police officer's size and girth. It seemed like he was used to throwing it around.

"I appreciate the advice," JC said, pleasant but without commitment.

"Nice to meet you, Snowman," Badass said, shaking JC's hand and giving the others a nod. Then he walked back to the bar.

"I guess you have a nickname, Snowman," Bip grinned.

"Everyone seems to have a nickname," JC said. "You need an instruction manual to follow him in a conversation."

"I don't think I'd like to tangle with him," Bip said.

"That can be your nickname: 'Scaredy Cat,'" JC grinned. "But you do get the feeling that he likes to tangle with people," JC responded.

Scooter Halvorson walked past the table without stopping or saying anything. Robin saw him as he passed and looked at JC for an explanation.

"I probably owe Donut an apology," JC said, looking at Scooter as he left the bar.

Maddie LaJeunesse climbed out of the shower and dried herself off. She toweled off her hair but didn't pull a brush through it. She kept it wild, tossing it into place with her hands as she looked in the mirror. It was her "off-duty" look.

She pulled on a pair of blue jeans and a soft button-down sweater. She didn't wear a bra and left a few buttons at the top of her sweater unclasped.

She emerged from the bedroom and climbed on the couch, tucking her legs beneath her as only women can do. Hank Monk clasped her waist and pulled her closer. Some of his dark hair fell over his forehead.

"Am I in trouble, Deputy?" Maddie purred. Monk glanced at the unbuttoned top of her sweater.

"I believe you have given me probable cause to search you," he said softly.

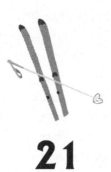

21

"Seriously," JC pleaded with Maddie LaJeunesse. "I need to speak with your client."

It was JC's first visit of the new day. The public defender was in her office early. She was preparing for her day in court. These cases had nothing to do with her biggest case, Charlie Washburn, but her other clients still deserved attention.

JC brought her coffee. He was on a mission. He knew he was close to something.

"And what, do tell?" asked the public defender. "What would you ask my client?"

"I think John Washburn was stealing money from the county taxpayers," JC explained. "I want to ask Charlie if she knew he was stealing from the treasury and if she knows what he did with the money."

"Did it occur to you that providing that information might incriminate my client?" Maddie inquired.

"It did," JC told her.

"And did you think I was just going to stand by and let my client incriminate herself?" Maddie asked.

"I hoped you would," JC answered. "I think it could help her. Maybe she *didn't* know he was stealing the money, but she might know where he put it."

"Mr. Snow," Maddie began. "My client has a public defender representing her only because she won't speak. She hasn't said anything since she said, 'Yes, Your Honor,' in court. Oh, no, wait. She once told me 'no.' So that's it, four words. She can afford a more prominent attorney to represent her. But she won't even ask for one. That would require speaking. But she's lucky, because I am not just out of law school and I am not an idiot. I am a damn good defense attorney. And in that role of said attorney, I am not going to let you ask my client if she knows where the stolen money is!"

JC gave her answer some thought. Her reasoning seemed flawless.

"Is there any wiggle room?" he asked anyway.

"What do you think?" the public defender responded.

JC walked out of the courthouse with Bip at his side.

"Maybe she'll change her mind," Bip said.

JC turned to the photographer, looking at him like he was crazy. But Bip was laughing.

"Okay, let's do this the hard way," JC told him. "First, let's stop at the ski shop."

The rain had finally stopped. JC thought this was time to test his theory or they'd have to wait until spring.

They walked down the sidewalk from the courthouse to the Tie Hack ski shop and work-clothing store.

There were wet spots on the sidewalk. The rain and melted snow had spilled onto the walkways and roads. Water pooled on exposed lawns.

"This may be an unusual request, but I'm from out of town," JC told the first salesperson he saw inside Tie Hack. "Could we borrow an old ski pole without a basket? I'm guessing that you have one in the back. We'll even return it."

The clerk was a young woman with dyed maroon hair. She looked at JC like she had a long list of more important things to do, even though it had been raining outside in January and the two journalists were the only non-employees in the store.

"Wait here," she said and walked down an aisle that had work boots on both sides.

Within minutes, she returned carrying an old composite pole without a basket.

"The matching pole snapped," she explained. "We already salvaged the basket."

"I've snapped a few of those myself," JC said with a smile. The feeling of joviality was not returned by the salesperson.

"What are we up to?" Bip asked as they walked to the car.

"We're going on a treasure hunt," JC told him.

Bip was instructed to drive toward the cemetery. Steam rose thick over puddles of standing water on Joe Wright Reservoir. The ice was still too thick to melt.

Before arriving at the cemetery, the news car stopped at a hardware store where JC purchased a narrow shovel.

The cemetery was up a one-way, one-lane paved road and on a hill. It wasn't large and some of the graves were quite old. The names and dates of the oldest monuments were no longer readable. Their soft marble had been worn away by the weather and acid rain.

"Let's start in the newer section," JC suggested. "Charlie and some of Washburn's friends have told us he was such a nice guy that he'd plant flowers at the graves of acquaintances who had passed on."

They walked up and down rows of graves. There were some with U.S. flags and some with plastic flowers. But JC didn't see what he was looking for.

"I know it's not the time to plant flowers," he said. "But I hoped there would be some sign of flowers from last summer. And after this warm weather, we're in the unique position of being able to push a ski pole into the soil in January."

Then, JC's eyes landed on a mourner kneeling in front of a grave a few rows away.

"Is that Horace Emerson?" JC asked.

"It sure looks like him," Bip said.

The two men walked slowly in that direction. Horace seemed to be lost in a private conversation. JC and Bip stopped at a respectful distance and waited.

"They were good people," Horace finally said in a loud voice, intending for JC and Bip to hear him. They walked toward him.

"Your parents?" JC asked.

"Yes," Horace said. "They adopted me. I know they wouldn't like the path I'm on. I probably wouldn't be doing what I do if they hadn't died. They were good people."

"You come here a lot?" JC asked in a somber tone.

"I do," Horace said. "I come and talk things over with them. I should probably come more often. I should probably have them buried in my backyard, so I can talk to them every night before I go out."

"Did you ever see John Washburn here?" JC asked.

"I did," Horace said. "He used to bring flowers and plant them at graves of his friends, or even people he knew wouldn't get any visitors."

"Anyone in particular?" JC asked. "I mean, can you point out some of the graves where Washburn would plant flowers? I know it's a weird request. It's part of the story we're working on."

"Sort of a tribute, huh?" Horace said. And he pointed out a grave a few rows away that was under three aspen trees. He pointed out another that was next to a new mausoleum.

"Thanks," JC said to Horace. "I think your parents would still be proud of you. We all make mistakes, but your spirit is good. I think they knew that."

"Thank you, man," Horace said quietly.

JC and Bip slowly walked in the direction of the graves that Horace had singled out for them. JC carried the ski pole in his hand.

"I'd rather not have an audience for this," JC said as he scanned the cemetery. There was only Horace, in the distance to their back. "We might look like grave robbers, probing the ground with a sharp instrument."

"What exactly are you looking for?" Bip asked.

"Something that Washburn could place a good deal of money in," JC told him. "Why don't you get your camera and record this. But if anyone sees it and we're wrong, we're going to be in a lot of trouble."

"You mean, 'not-going-to-heaven' trouble?" Bip asked.

"Desecrating a grave? Yeah, that might fall under the definition of sacrilege," JC answered.

Bip hurried to get his camera out of the car. JC stopped at the grave under the oak tree. A spot of dirt pointed out the probable place that Washburn planted flowers. They had been removed for the winter season.

Glancing at their only witness, JC eyed Horace and then turned his back toward him. JC's body would block Horace from actually seeing him plunge the ski pole into the dirt.

The pole slipped into the soil without much resistance. JC tried a second gravesite and again the ski pole just pushed deeper into the ground. A third attempt also failed to hit anything.

"Those are promising spots," JC said in a whisper. "We're looking for something that is buried shallower than a body."

"What are you going to do if you do find a steel box with money inside?" Bip asked. "Are you going to take out your shovel and dig it up? Here in a cemetery?"

"That wouldn't be well received by witnesses, would it?" JC said.

He was relieved to see Horace stand and walk down the hill and out of the cemetery. Now, they were alone.

And the ski pole hit something solid. JC and Bip looked at each other. JC ran to the car and returned with the shovel.

"Do you want me to capture, on camera, the moment you commit this unforgiveable sin?" Bip asked, snickering.

"Maybe not," JC said, leaning on the shovel. "I can imagine how that would make me look in the eyes of worshippers."

Bip put the camera down and JC got to work, digging a small hole about the width and length of the dirt where the flowers were planted.

It didn't take long to reach the box. It wasn't buried very deep.

JC pulled out a metal box that was not locked but was securely fastened. It didn't look like it had been in the ground for very long.

Bip powered up his camera and began to roll again as JC brushed dirt off the box and opened it up. Inside, he quickly counted fifty-one-hundred dollar bills.

"Five thousand dollars," JC said to Bip.

They walked over to the other grave that Horace pointed out, next to the mausoleum.

JC poked the ski pole into the ground. On the second chance, he hit something.

"Let's leave it alone," JC said. "Let's give the sheriff a chance to see that we're not yanking his chain. I'd better give him a call."

The secretary at the sheriff's office told JC that the sheriff was not available.

JC told her it was important.

The secretary repeated for JC her description of the sheriff's unavailability.

"I think I found where Washburn was hiding the money," JC said into the phone.

"Please hold," the secretary said.

"This better not be a joke," Sheriff Brush said brusquely.

"It's not, Sheriff," JC assured him and suggested he come to the cemetery.

22

For Cameron County, it was a significant police presence. Four patrol cars, with "Sheriff" printed on the side, sat at the bottom of the road into the cemetery. They sealed it off from visitors. Another vehicle belonging to the sheriff was up in the cemetery, a short distance from the mausoleum and the two small holes near a gravestone caused by JC's ski pole.

Deputy Aaron Aguayo placed one foot on the shovel and pushed it into the dirt. In very short time, he pulled out a metal box that was not locked but was securely fastened.

"Will you look at that," the sheriff said as he opened the lid to the box and saw thousands of dollars in cash. He was wearing gloves and ordered Aguayo to close the box and place it inside an evidence bag.

"Okay, this is a crime scene now," the sheriff said. "You have to leave." He was looking at JC and Bip.

"But I found it," JC said.

"Yes, thank you," Jerry Brush said. "Now, you have to leave. We can't have you or anyone else trampling a crime scene. Go stand with your photographer over by your car."

That was a disguised gesture of gratitude by the sheriff. He could have ordered JC to go down the hill and leave the cemetery grounds. Instead, Bip's long camera lens could continue to record the investigation, out of earshot, from the spot where they parked their news car.

When they had what they needed, including an interview with Sheriff Brush, Bip and JC drove down the hill and out of the cemetery. It was time to edit their story and report live to their audience in Denver.

Bip pulled the car up to the curb when they saw Horace standing.

"Was that you up there?" Horace asked. "Did you find the money?"

"Yep," JC said.

"Did you find it in those graves I told you about?" Horace asked them.

"Yep," JC said with a smile.

"Damn. I told you Washburn was a nice guy," Horace said. "He left those dead people flowers. He even gave them money."

JC and Bip laughed as they pulled away.

"I can't believe you figured that out," Bip said. "You found the money. Do you think there might be fingerprints to tell them who killed him?"

"That's a good question," JC replied. "By the way, let's stop by the ski shop on the way to meet the satellite truck. I told them I'd return their ski pole."

The news anchors back in Denver read their introduction to JC, comparing him to the man who discovered King Tut's tomb. JC was standing by live *in* the cemetery.

JC, Bip and the satellite truck were allowed by the sheriff to come back up the hill to the burial ground and do their live shot, as long as they kept their distance from where investigators were still examining the scene.

In the mind of the newsroom's management, a live shot with gravestones and sheriff's deputies behind him was worthy of an Emmy Award. It was great television, and the story was about their own reporter finding the stolen money.

"JC, you're magic," the news director, Pat Perilla, told him after the live shot.

"Can we bring you back to Denver now?" the assignment editor, Rocky Bauman, asked, his eye on the budget.

"The party is just getting started," JC said. "This is no time to leave. We've got to figure out who murdered Washburn. And you have Robin working on the story about the death of Loretta Sopris."

"Tomorrow is Friday. Then we have the weekend to think about what we do next," the news director stated. "The possibilities include bringing you home, JC. I just want you to understand that. You are an expensive habit."

"That wasn't a bad piece of investigative reporting," Maddie LaJeunesse said when she stopped by JC's table at Ute Susan's. He was having breakfast with Robin, Bip and Sunny.

"Did it shake any cobwebs in your client's mind?" JC asked.

"She didn't say," Maddie told him. "I informed her of your find, and she looked up with quizzical eyes. I swear she almost spoke to me. It was kind of exciting."

Then, Maddie gave them a sarcastic grin and moved on to find a table.

The evening news broadcast of JC's television station reached Placer and the ski resort via cable. So, a lot of people had their eye on JC that morning, after seeing his live shot the night before.

"You would have been a good cop," Bob Andrews told JC as he stopped at the table.

"Thank you, Trooper," JC answered.

"I'm not a trooper anymore," Andrews said, stating the obvious. "Call me B.A. Or you can call me what everyone else calls me, Badass."

They all shared a chuckle and Andrews moved on to order his breakfast.

"So, how do we use your steaming-hot celebrity to get what we want?" Bip asked.

"Wow, you are my soulmate," JC said to Bip. "I was thinking the exact same thing."

"Great," Robin said. "I think JC is jilting me for his photographer." She eyed the two men and then her engagement ring. "Hey Sunny, you want to marry me? JC seems to be taken and I've already got the dress."

JC pulled his fiancée closer to him and gave her a kiss on the cheek.

"We're just saying we've got their attention," JC told her. "How do we use it to our advantage? The benefactors of our working vacation are starting to feel the pinch in their wallet. We need to do something big to keep the money tree shaking."

"You mean, we aren't doing this all for the good of mankind?" Bip asked with mock naïveté.

"In fact, we do," JC said. "But that goes only a short way with the masters of our fate. They like money."

"You know the next story you should do?" The interruption came from a familiar voice. JC looked up and saw Horace Emerson.

"Hi, Horace. Thanks again for your help," JC said. "Did you say you have another story for us?"

"I sure do," Horace said. "And I can be your guide. You ought to do a story asking why The Craters is even here. They took prime terrain away from us backcountry skiers. We didn't love that land for the money. We loved it for the wicked skiing and boarding. The owners of The Craters just love it for the money it makes them. It's all about greed."

"Don't you ski at The Craters?" JC asked.

"Hardly ever," Horace told them. "I stay in the backcountry. It's better skiing, anyway."

"Do a lot of people feel this way?" JC asked. "Is there local resentment aimed at The Craters?"

"No man, there's just a select few of us," Horace answered. "Everyone else is happy making their money, too."

"Is there room for both of you?" JC asked. "Is there enough terrain for backcountry skiers and those who want to ski inbounds?"

"I guess so," Horace told him. "I just like it the way it was before."

"You mean, before The Craters opened?" JC inquired.

"Yeah," Horace agreed. "Before then."

"You said you'll be our guide?" JC asked.

"Yeah," Horace told him. "I know every inch of the backcountry here."

"We don't have any skins," JC said. "I think we'd have to rent backcountry skis."

"Do it," Horace said. "You won't regret it. Tomorrow?"

"Tomorrow," JC said, shrugging his shoulders.

Horace had a huge grin on his face as he walked away.

"How did I get us talked into this?" JC asked.

"What do you mean, us?" Robin asked.

But, after some discussion, all four of them agreed to go backcountry skiing with Horace as their guide. They set off for Tie Hack to rent their equipment.

Mad Marv had planned to sleep in late, alone. Mercy was sleeping in her husband's bed.

Marv had gone to sleep after drinking some Old Standard Rye Whiskey, a tasty product of Old Town Distillers in Fort Collins.

Maybe he'd had a bit too much. But he was burdened by thoughts that it might be time to leave Cameron County. Maybe too many people had arrived who knew who he was.

He wondered if Mercy would come with him. It would mean leaving her husband and leaving the only place she'd ever called home. He had his doubts.

He wondered where he could go. He'd burned his bridges in Puerto Rico. He could go to the Silicon Valley in California, he supposed. Money earned in a vague manner would just blend in there.

Montana was inviting. People seemed to let things alone there. Alaska? He'd be left alone there too, he thought. But it was too remote.

He noted background noise that he'd been listening to for a few minutes. There was nothing unusual about the sound of the whirr and the chugging coming from his printer.

But he hadn't printed anything. He was still in bed.

He raised his head so that he might hear more clearly. He knew then that he wasn't mistaken. His printer was printing.

Confused and curious, Marv climbed carefully out of bed, wearing boxers and a blue tee-shirt with "Ping" printed in white letters. It had come from the ski shop at the resort.

It was still dark out. He gripped the railing as he walked down the circular staircase. He paused to turn on the coffee maker. He had prepped it before going to bed. Then he advanced on the room where he kept a printer, a desk and a laptop. It was off the living room with large windows overlooking the Medicine Bow Range. With the sundown, he only saw a scant number of lights coming from other mountain homes.

Entering the room, he flipped on a light switch, heard the printer chugging and saw a piece of paper advance into the paper tray.

He was puzzled. He deliberately chose not to allow his printer to receive dispatches from the outside world.

The chugging stopped. The message had been delivered. He reached for the piece of paper and pulled it out of the tray.

"Time's Up," the message said.

Marv felt a chill crawl up his spine. He turned to look over his shoulder. No one was there. He turned off the light and slowly walked the circumference of his house, peeking out the windows. No one was there, either.

But then, where were they?

23

"Insane!" JC shouted with a smile as he came to a stop at the bottom of a backcountry ski run called "The Gash."

You wouldn't find the run on any official trail map. It came down the side of South Diamond Peak, which wasn't an official ski area. Backcountry skiers had found the run and gave it that name.

JC tried to catch his breath as he watched Robin come down behind him.

"She's a good skier," Horace said with a grin as he watched her.

"That was scary," she said, laughing, when she reached them. "That top is steep!"

175

"I told you it was cool," Horace said, laughing. "It's Saturday, and you'll still never wait in a lift line."

Sunny was the next one down. She slid down on the edge of her snowboard on the steepest parts.

"That's a lot to ask of a snowboard," she said when she stood among her friends.

Bip, on the other hand, straightened his line and headed down The Gash with courage. He caught air off two snow-covered rocks. His quickness made every move look preordained.

"You are nuts," JC proclaimed when Bip kicked up a cloud of snow upon his arrival. Bip's smile indicated that he wanted more.

They skinned back to the top of the peak and took an easier cruiser down to Highway 14 and a car they had ferried to that spot on Cameron Pass.

"That is a lot of walking uphill to get to some magnificent skiing," Robin said to Horace. "You must be in amazing shape."

Horace just smiled.

"I know you can't do anything about The Craters," Horace said to JC. "I just appreciate the fact that now you know."

Patrol cars from the sheriff's office continued to block the entrance to the cemetery in Placer. Deputies armed with shovels had unearthed more boxes buried at grave sites. The sum of the money inside the containers exceeded $100,000.

The employees who worked beneath John Washburn in the treasurer's office were brought back in for questioning by the sheriff. They swore they knew nothing about buried money. They also swore they didn't kill him.

Charlie Washburn's attorney also denied that her client knew anything about money buried in a graveyard. She did so because it was her duty. Her client still wasn't actually talking to her.

The sheriff was in the process of obtaining the bank records of John and Charlie Washburn.

After skiing, JC and the others returned to the Clark Hotel to get cleaned up. They had a couple of hours to relax before having dinner together.

When JC and Robin entered their room, they noticed a note had been slipped under the door. JC picked it up.

A seven-word message said, "Houston, we have a problem. Find me." The note was signed, "HM."

"Hank Monk, the sheriff's deputy, just sent me a rather cryptic note," JC told Robin. He read her the contents.

"Why so cryptic?" she asked.

"He doesn't want the sheriff catching him talking to a TV reporter," JC responded.

"I guess we'd better find him," she said.

JC called the sheriff's office, though not disclosing his name. He was told that Deputy Monk was not on duty. JC asked if she might know where Monk would be on a Saturday.

"It being Saturday," the deputy on the phone told him. "I would look for somewhere that is cold and where it is hard to stand up. He loves the outdoors."

"We just came from there," JC thought out loud. But they hadn't seen him.

JC remembered that Monk had called *him*. He found the number in his phone and reverse-dialed, but no one picked up.

"What do you want, JC?" Tommy "Scooter" Halvorson was the next call JC placed. Halvorson's tone sounded like he regretted picking up the phone. It reminded JC that his old school chum felt he had been mistreated by the journalist.

"Listen, Tommy," JC said. "I'm sorry about how I treated you last time. I was on the hunt for the money Washburn stole. I get tunnel vision when I'm close to getting answers. I apologize."

"Well, that was quite a get," Tommy said. "How did you know he was burying the money?"

"It's a long story," JC responded. "Listen, you said you know a lot of the deputies. I'm looking for Hank Monk. He's off-duty today. I know he's a big outdoorsman. Do you know where he is today?"

"Yeah, I know Hank," Tommy said, his spirits lifting. "But I don't know where he goes when he wants to get all 'Daniel Boone' on his days off. Sorry. I'd help you if I could."

"That's alright," JC said. "I'm grasping at straws."

"You know that he's dating Maddie LaJeunesse, don't you?" Tommy said.

"Hank Monk is dating the attorney for Charlie Washburn?" JC blurted.

"Yes, he is. See? I'm not so mean to you after all," Tommy said.

"No, you're not," JC said, laughing a little. "Again, I'm sorry about last time."

"Apology accepted," Tommy replied. "I'll see you around. And remember, out in public, call me Scooter."

"Gotcha," JC said, ending the call.

"Are you friends again?" Robin asked.

"Thick as thieves," JC smiled.

JC called Maddie LaJeunesse's phone number. She didn't answer.

"If you were nicer to people, they'd take your calls," Robin said with a smug smile. "They always take mine."

"That's because you're a stunning beauty," JC said. "No man is going to refuse your call."

"And I'm nice," Robin insisted in a sugary sweet voice.

"And you are nice," JC said, his voice deflating.

"It's almost dinnertime," Robin said. "Do you want to walk around in the resort village until we meet Bip and Sunny?"

"That means we're going shopping, doesn't it?" he said. She smiled.

JC took a quick shower and pulled on a zippered turtleneck with a Grizzly Mountain logo. Then, he put a fleece vest over that.

They headed for the shopping district in the resort village. For a while, they looked over listings of houses and condos for sale at The Craters. Pictures of the homes and the asking prices were posted in the window of a local realtor. JC and Robin couldn't decide if the cost of a home there was alarming or amusing. Almost all of them were unaffordable.

They saw Mercy LaJeunesse, and she made a straight line toward them.

"Have you seen Marv?" she asked with a sense of urgency. She had a worried look on her face. She was biting on her nails.

"No, we haven't," Robin said. "We've been skiing most of the day. Is something wrong?"

"I can't find him," Mercy answered. She turned as she said it, scanning the crowd in every direction.

"Did you call him?" JC asked.

"He isn't answering," Mercy said, almost frantic.

"Has this happened before?" Robin asked calmly. "Is this something that he does sometimes?"

"No, he doesn't," Mercy said, reflecting.

"When was the last time you saw him?" Robin asked.

"Yesterday afternoon, maybe?" Mercy replied, having difficulty concentrating. "I slept at Jerry's last night."

Jerry Brush, the sheriff, JC thought. It was odd that she didn't call that place "home." She was married to Sheriff Brush. But there didn't seem to be much about that relationship that didn't strain the seams of a normal marriage.

"We can keep an eye out for him," Robin said in a soothing manner. "I'm sure it will turn out alright."

"Thank you," Mercy said. She was still turning her head in every direction, hoping to see him.

As she walked away, Robin thought she could make out a whistling sound. It resembled a bird's distress call.

"What do you make of that?" Robin asked JC as they walked away.

"That relationship makes my head spin," JC replied. "It's hard to figure out what normal behavior is with them. Maybe he found another girlfriend who is married to another husband. He'll probably show up."

Robin peeked in the window of Ping, the ski shop, as they walked by.

"Oh, this you will want to see," she said to JC, smiling.

They entered the store. The ski equipment was in front; some clothing and souvenirs were in the back. Robin led JC by hand down an aisle where they saw Bip and Sunny looking at the merchandise and giggling.

Bip was trying on cowboy boots. He had also pulled on a buckskin jacket and was slipping on a ski helmet.

"Are you dressing to be *all* of the Village People at the same time?" JC asked.

A nervous store clerk walked down the aisle after hearing laughter. Bip quickly removed the store merchandise he was wearing.

"Sorry," Bip said as he and Sunny moved toward the door. That left JC and Robin on the receiving end of stares by the store employee.

"Kids," JC said to them, sheepishly.

JC and Robin caught up with Bip and Sunny at The Cache La Poudre and North Park Toll Road Company, where they planned to have dinner.

"Thank you so much for making us look like idiots back there," JC said.

A hostess showed them to a table.

"Mike t gooum," a man said as they passed his table. He was looking at Sunny.

"A gah rah u?" Sunny replied in their Ute language after searching the man's face.

"Too i e in," Deputy Aguayo replied.

Sunny paused and introduced her friends to the deputy.

"He is Ute," Sunny said smiling. Bip and JC shook his hand.

"We've seen each other around," JC said. "You don't know where Hank Monk is, do you?" JC asked.

"No, I'm sorry," Aguayo told them. "We both have the day off."

JC wouldn't be surprised if Aguayo had another phone number for Monk than the one he had given JC, the one that Monk wasn't answering. But JC also knew that Aguayo wasn't going to give Monk's number to a journalist.

Aguayo was sitting with a woman who looked like his date. He introduced her. But his eyes lingered on Sunny.

24

"Sheriff, we have got an unusual situation up here."

"Did you just hear that?" Bip asked JC. Bip had the police frequency app turned up on his phone. They were at the Lady Moon Café with Robin and Sunny. They had waited in line outside for a breakfast table.

Bip turned up the volume. "Let's listen to this."

"I don't even know how to describe it over a public frequency," Deputy Aguayo told the sheriff. "I tried to call you on the phone, but I'm not getting cell service at this spot."

"Okay, let's try 'animal, mineral or vegetable,'" the sheriff responded over the radio.

"Well, it is definitely animal," the deputy said. "Maybe animal versus animal."

"Where is he?" the sheriff asked his dispatcher and secretary.

"He is somewhere in or near that old mine at the top of The Craters," she told him. "Near the top. You can see the mine from that high chairlift."

"The lift the woman fell off?" the sheriff asked.

"Yes, sir," the secretary and dispatcher said.

The sheriff shook his head over the close proximity of the two spots.

"Can you find Hank Monk and get him up there?" the sheriff asked. "This is what we've got him for."

"Yes, sir," the secretary and dispatcher responded. "I can try. It's Sunday. It is his day off and I might not be able to find him."

But it didn't take long to find Deputy Monk. And it took him only an hour before he got to the top of the mountain and was sizing things up.

In a grove of pine trees, he saw that snow had been pushed aside and old boards had been pried up. It appeared to be an air shaft into the old mine.

Deputy Monk rappelled down into the darkness, wearing a headlamp. Once on firm footing, shards of natural light led him to the entrance that could be seen from the lift.

The square hole in the rock was on the side of a steep ridge. Wooden scaffolding or stairs had rotted away long ago.

Monk joined Deputy Aguayo, who first called in the potential "animal versus animal" incident.

"How did you get here?" Monk asked.

"I came in the front," Aguayo said. "It's all scree and tailings. I was slipping all the way. I thought I was going to die."

"Maybe you ought to come out my way," Monk said with a chuckle.

"Like a snake coming out of a hole?" Aguayo said. "No way, I'll take my chances on the scree, like a mountain goat."

"So, what do we have?" Monk asked.

"It's pretty sick," Deputy Aguayo told him. "You see that glove?"

There was a ski glove on the floor of the mine. The glove looked new.

"It's got a hand still in it," Aguayo stated. "Take a look."

Deputy Monk gave Aguayo a suspicious look. With friends on the weekends, maybe after a few beers, they would put a snake or big spider in the glove and get him to hold it up to his face.

But this was official business. Aguayo was a fellow professional and neither of them had been drinking.

Monk picked up the glove and peered inside. He pulled the loose glove away from some flesh.

"Wow," the big outdoorsy deputy said, his eyes big. "That looks like a human hand."

"I told you," Aguayo said.

"Where's the rest of him?" Monk asked, looking around.

"I don't know," the other deputy responded. He looked down the dark mineshaft. "We're going to need some lights to do a full search."

"Agreed. This is a good way to get killed," Deputy Monk surmised. "There are elevator shafts in a lot of these old mines. The elevators are gone. All that remains is a shaft going straight down for hundreds of feet. You'd be nuts to walk back there in the dark."

"Hey, by the way," Aguayo said. "That reporter is looking for you. Snow. The one with the pretty Ute assistant."

"What's he want?" Monk asked.

"He didn't say," Aguayo answered. "He asked for your private phone number, but I didn't give it to him."

"Thanks," Monk said.

Without phone service inside the mine, Monk climbed out the airshaft he had rappelled down.

"Are you sure it's a human hand?" Sheriff Brush asked when Deputy Monk phoned him at his office.

"I didn't try to pull it out," Monk told the sheriff. "I figured the evidence boys would want to get first crack at that. But it's a human glove and it looks like a good fit."

"How do you suppose it got there?" Brush asked his deputy.

"If it was summertime, I'd say a bear," Monk said. "But bears are hibernating right now."

"Wolves?" the sheriff pondered.

"Maybe," Monk answered.

"Yeah, maybe," the sheriff muttered. "But I have a feeling the predator is going to turn out to be human. The human savage."

In time, an evidence-gathering team from the sheriff's office got into the mine. They were lowered down the airshaft Deputy Monk had located.

The hand in the glove was indeed human. But a thorough search of the accessible areas in an unsafe mine failed to turn up any other body parts.

"Good thing there's a hand in that glove," the sheriff said. "At least we can get a fingerprint."

"Sheriff, there is a reporter on the phone, asking for you," his secretary and dispatcher said as she poked her head into his office.

"Who is it?" Brush asked.

"The one who found that money in the cemetery," she said.

"Snow? JC Snow?" the sheriff asked.

"Yes, sir. That's the name," she said.

"Sheriff, what do you have going on up on the mountain?" JC asked when he was put through.

"Well, this time, that's for me to know and you to find out," the sheriff responded.

The sheriff felt a sudden fondness for the present crime scene, if that is what it was going to become. It was remote and literally hanging off the side of a cliff. The news media and other such pests couldn't get near it.

"Can you give me a clue?" JC asked.

"Seriously," Brush told him. "It's too soon. We're just sorting it out. It may be nothing. We'll issue a press release when we have more to say. Do we have your email address?"

JC passed along his email address, unsatisfied with the entire exchange.

Bob Andrews grew up in Cheyenne, Wyoming. He was an offensive lineman for the Cheyenne East High School football team. In the winter, he was on the wrestling team. In the spring, he threw shot put for the track-and-field team.

He played hard, like most of the kids did. He just played a little harder. He was a bruiser.

Bob Andrews was called B.A. by his friends. He moved to Idaho because he liked to hunt and fish. And Idaho had a ridiculous amount of both.

He became a cop because someone suggested he become a cop. He was big and tough, just the way they liked their cops.

As a cop, B.A. became known as Badass. The run-of-the-mill criminals were afraid of him. An arrest could also come with a beating. And if you complained to the higher-ups or your defense attorney, a beating in your future was certain.

He skied sometimes, but he skied alone. He didn't even call his friend, Trigger Fischer. He couldn't keep up with the ski champion and he didn't feel like talking all day. In fact, he didn't feel like talking at all.

Badass rode the chairlift up in silence. His steel-gray eyes looked off in the distance at nothing at all.

"Let's play 'I spy.'"

Badass didn't respond. He didn't even hear the human voice coming from beside him.

"Let's play 'I spy.'"

Andrews ascertained there was a noise coming from his right. He looked in that direction and saw nothing. No one else was on the chairlift.

"You start."

Following the voice, barely more than a squeak, Badass looked down. There *was* someone on the chair.

"You start," said the little girl. She wore a red ski jacket and matching pants. Her helmet was adorned with pink ears adhered to the top, so they stuck up like a rabbit.

She looked up at Badass with innocent expectations. She had red cheeks and wisps of blonde hair sticking out of her helmet.

She was waiting for him to start. He considered jumping off the chairlift.

"I spy something red," the retired law officer finally said. He didn't smile and he didn't look at the little girl.

"Me!" the girl said excitedly.

"You're very good at this," Andrews said without emotion, still staring ahead. "I don't think I can beat you. We should stop."

"No, I think you can do better," the little girl said, giving him encouragement. "It's my turn now. I spy something white."

"The snow," Badass said without changing his expression.

"See?" the little girl said in an encouraging manner. "You got one! Okay, I'll go again. I spy something orange."

Her prompt was returned only with silence.

"I spy something orange," the little girl repeated after waiting patiently.

Still, there was only silence from the other side of the chairlift.

"Orange!" she said with more volume in her squeaky voice.

"I'm looking!" Andrews blurted impatiently as he anxiously searched the area below them.

The little girl giggled.

25

"It wasn't me," Deputy Monk said over the phone.

"The note that was slipped under my door at the Clark Hotel was signed, 'HM,'" JC informed him.

"I understand," Monk told him. "But I didn't slip a note under your door. What did it say again?"

"Houston, we have a problem. Find me," JC said, reciting the message on the piece of paper. He was sitting on the porch attached to the room he shared with Robin. He could look down on the hotel's heated swimming pool. The pool and lounges were surrounded by plexiglass, to hold the wind at bay.

"Why didn't he or she just knock?" the deputy asked. "Then whoever sent the note could speak with you face-to-face."

"I thought that maybe you didn't want to be seen with me and be identified as a mole," JC told him.

"I don't," Monk replied.

"Besides, we found the note when we came back to the room," JC said. "We'd been out skiing in the backcountry."

"Really? How did you like that?" asked the sheriff's outdoor deputy.

"It was great," JC answered. "Horace Emerson was our guide. He can really ski."

"Yes, he can," Monk agreed. "He could probably go to Chamonix and make good money as a backcountry guide. Instead, he steals fire trucks."

JC shook his head at the truth in that statement.

"Hey, what were you guys doing up on top of The Craters yesterday?" JC asked.

"I can't tell you that," the deputy told him. "I don't know what the sheriff wants to release, just yet. You'd better ask him."

"So, you didn't write the note, huh?" JC asked.

"No, I didn't," Monk told him. "If you find out who did, let me know."

Ending the call, JC watched the steam hover in the cold air over the warm swimming pool. The sun was shining. Children splashed in the pool and parents sat on lounges reading a book or napping.

JC pondered the note and the day ahead. He got back on the phone and called Sheriff Brush. The sheriff had just wrapped up his Monday morning meeting with Rock Bush, his second-in-command.

"Alright, here's what I can tell you," the sheriff informed JC. "We found a ski glove. A skier called 9-1-1. He just said it looked odd. It was in the mouth of that old mine that you see while you're going up the chairlift."

"We saw the mine from the chairlift," JC told him. "How does a ski glove get to the mouth of that mine? That would be a heck of a throw."

"Exactly," the sheriff agreed. "That's why the skier made the 9-1-1 call. He wondered how that glove would get there."

"That's it?" JC asked. "You sent deputies up to the mine for four hours to find a lost ski glove?"

"Well, that's not all," the sheriff acknowledged. "There was a hand in it."

"A hand?" JC repeated. "A human hand?"

"That's right," Brush confirmed. "We hope to get a fingerprint off of it and have an I.D. today."

"Did you only find a hand?" JC asked. "Not a body missing a hand?"

"Just the hand," the law officer confirmed. "Of course, we'll continue to look for the rest of the body. It's an old mine. The miners who dug it, over one hundred years ago, were looking for gold. They found a vein, but it wasn't a very long vein. They went broke pretty fast paying for labor to cut through all that rock. We're looking for a map or diagram of where the tunnels and shafts are, but we're not having any luck so far."

"Can we come by for an interview?" JC asked.

"Sure," the sheriff said, sounding resigned to the notion of being cooperative with the news media. "But I'm not telling you anything more. That's all I'm telling anyone right now."

192

"A human hand inside a ski glove is a good story," JC said. "By itself."

JC called Bip's room and told him to gather his snowboard and camera.

"I love this job," Bip said. "How many people get paid to snowboard?"

Robin and Sunny were invited to come along, but Robin felt she needed to make a breakthrough on the Loretta Sopris story, or she wasn't going to be able to justify her prolonged presence in Cameron County.

Pat Perilla, on the other hand, loved the storyline that JC pitched. The reporter called the newsroom with his plans for the day. The news director sounded like he was drooling when JC informed him of the discovery of a hand inside a ski glove.

Their stay at The Craters was extended for an undetermined amount of time. That night's live shot to viewers in Denver would revolve around the hand. There would be speculation that it was connected to the murder of John Washburn.

"We might know whose hand it is, by the time we go on the air," JC told his news director. "The sheriff is trying to get fingerprints."

"Twenty-seven and sunny!"

It was JC's battle cry when a winter day hit what he believed were perfect weather conditions to ski.

He and Bip had first stopped to interview the sheriff at the county courthouse. Then they advanced on the ski mountain.

They hopped on the gondola at the base and then took a chairlift to the top. Bip balanced the camera on his shoulder and shot images of the mine entrance while they rode the chair up alongside the ski run called Heart Attack.

"I'd bet there was scaffolding and ramps when the mine was open and being worked," JC said, sizing up the hole on the steep slope from his side of the chair. "That would have made it easier to get the miners in and out with their equipment."

After they shot the mine entrance from the chairlift, JC skied into the trees to find an airshaft to the mine that had been described to them. Bip followed on his snowboard.

The shaft was hidden from view by trees that were not there when the old mine was open and working. There was police tape around the hole. Boards that had sealed the shaft had been pulled up and tossed aside.

Bip shot footage of the shaft after they both climbed out of their bindings. The snow was firm enough to hold them.

JC took a moment to admire the view from the flat top of the mountain. He saw the Medicine Bow Range stretch west, the forested Laramie Range to the north, the Mummy Range to their east, and the northern peaks of the Never Summers.

"Do you want to go down there?" JC asked, peering down the shaft.

"Do you?" Bip asked. The tone of his voice made it known that he did not want to risk his life plunging into a decrepit, unlighted mineshaft.

JC lowered himself to his knees and looked down the shaft, offering some illumination from the app on his phone that provided a flashlight.

The walls of the shaft looked sheer, and he couldn't make out the bottom.

"I don't even know how we'd get down there," JC said. "Other than jump and hope it isn't more than ten feet deep. And I have no idea how we'd get out."

"I am against this," Bip said. "That is my vote."

"I hate being a chicken," JC said, trying to break the tentacles that pulled him toward that hole in the ground.

"I'd hate being dead," Bip told him. "We've got the footage that we need for tonight's live shot."

JC looked at Bip, knowing his caution was justified.

"Okay, let's go before I change my mind," JC said. He was still looking back at the hole as he snapped back into his skis.

"We have tracked the glove to a small company in Fort Collins," Deputy Aguayo reported to Sheriff Brush. "A professor at CSU designed it and manufactures them in his basement."

"Really? You can do that in your basement?" the sheriff asked.

"People are making skis in their basement these days," Aguayo told him.

"Wow," the sheriff said. "Alright, what does this professor tell us?"

"His name is Arthur Patterson. He started making gloves because his wife's hands got cold when she skied," Deputy Aguayo told him. "He thought he could do a better job of insulating her gloves. He uses the same materials that the other good gloves use, but he puts more air in them. He says that traps more body heat."

"And he sells them?" the sheriff asked.

"Yes, sir," Aguayo responded. "And this is where we got lucky. He sells almost all of them online. So, he has a list of his customers."

"Can we get the list?" Brush inquired.

"Yes, sir," Deputy Aguayo told him. "He says it may take a day or two. But I thought that if we're about to identify a fingerprint, we could match that name to the list Professor Patterson will be able to compile. It might be faster that way."

"That's good thinking, Deputy," Sheriff Brush said. "As soon as we get that fingerprint identified, get that name to the professor. Let's get that I.D. corroborated. At least we'll have a face that goes with the hand."

"Yes, sir," Aguayo said to the sheriff. "Do you want coffee? I thought I'd run down the street."

"Yeah, sure. Thanks," the sheriff responded, turning his attention to other matters on his desk.

With her friends performing their respective jobs, Sunny Shavano was left behind. She had decided to go to Ute Susan's for coffee. She brought along a book she could read while sitting alone.

It was cold again. A haze hung over the ski mountain as snow guns worked to replace everything the rain and warm temperatures had taken away.

She walked into the restaurant and chose an empty table. It was quiet, between lunch and dinner.

"May I join you?" a man asked, having approached her table.

Sunny looked up and saw Aaron Aguayo, the Ute sheriff's deputy.

"Mwe̅ vice," she said. "That is up to you."

"To we ŏck." He smiled and pulled out a chair to sit on. "Thank you."

26

"Human feet, still inside their shoes, have been washing up on the Pacific coast for years," JC told them, after receiving an update from Sheriff Brush.

"I've read about that," Robin added. "It's been a big mystery. There was some thought that the feet were all that remained of people killed by the Mafia and dumped in the ocean."

"Yep, Mafia torture or devil worshippers," JC said. "Another theory is that the feet belonged to victims of shark attacks. Or maybe the feet belonged to people whose boats sank and then sharks ate them."

"And the truth is?" Bip asked.

"Probably all of the above," JC told him. "But the key to the riddle was overlooked until recently. It was the shoes."

He received quizzical looks from the others as they ate breakfast at Ute Susan's. The topic of devoured human meat didn't bother them.

"The rest of the bodies might still be bouncing around in the current somewhere on the bottom of the ocean," JC said. "But scientists say all that banging around on the sea floor will detach the foot from the leg pretty quickly. The ankle is a relatively weak joint, I guess. Then, there's only a foot and a shoe. And a lot of the gym shoes we wear are pretty tough. Many of them are leather. They can take the beating, and the foot is pretty safe in there. But the exposed ankle is weak. Eventually, the foot washes up on shore."

"So, if I fall into the ocean, I should be wearing an outfit made out of gym shoes," Bip suggested, grinning. "I'd be shark-proof."

"You should try and see how that comes out. But let me finish," JC answered, though grinning at Bip's epiphany. "Good gym shoes or running shoes also have a lot of cushioning. And most of that cushioning is provided by compartments of trapped air."

"So, they're buoyant," Bip concluded. "They almost float."

"It's like bubble wrap," Robin added.

"Well, why all of a sudden?" Bip asked. "Why did these feet suddenly start showing up on the beach?"

"The scientists that solved the mystery say that sneaker design improved," JC answered. "It was 2007 when manufacturers began installing air pockets in shoes."

"Is this feature listed on the shoe box?" Bip asked, the grin having returned. "They could advertise that at least *some* of your body will be recovered, even if a shark eats you."

"I'm sure that would be a great selling point," JC stated. "That still doesn't tell you what happened to the rest of the body. It still might be someone killed by the Mob or who fell overboard or whose boat sank."

"And you're saying sharks ate the body belonging to the hand found in the gold mine on the ski mountain?" Bip said, still grinning.

"Probably not," JC said, grinning at Bip. "The similarity struck me, because this glove maker uses more air compartments in his gloves to keep his customers' hands warm. The unique gloves are going to help the sheriff get a fingerprint identification on the hand in the glove, if he hasn't already."

"There's Mercy!" Robin exclaimed, observing a woman as she walked in the restaurant. She looked tired. She stopped just inside the door and scanned the crowd of people having breakfast.

"Mercy!" Robin called, in a voice just loud enough for the woman to hear but not loud enough to disturb a majority of the customers in the restaurant.

Mercy gave Robin a look of recognition and approached the table. She looked like she needed sleep. Her hair wasn't entirely combed.

"Have you found Marv yet?" Robin asked in that empathetic tone she was so good at invoking.

"I don't know where he could be," Mercy said as she shook her head. She put her hand up to her mouth. Saying it out loud was difficult for her.

"Have you talked to the sheriff?" JC asked. He immediately felt stupid. The man who was missing was Mercy's boyfriend. But the sheriff was her husband and was fully aware of the relationship.

Mercy looked at JC as his face disclosed his mistake. She didn't answer. The answer was obvious.

"I have to go," Mercy said. "I just wanted to see if *you* had seen Marv."

"We haven't, honey," Robin said. "I'm sorry."

"How stupid am I?" JC muttered as they watched Mercy open the door to the restaurant and walk back outside.

"Don't say that" Robin told him. "It's such an unusual relationship between Mercy and Marv and the sheriff, any one of us could have said that."

"Yeah," Bip said, and started to chuckle. "I'm just glad it was you."

"You're not stupid," Sunny said. She had been sitting quietly, listening to the conversation and eating her breakfast.

"Thank you, Sunny," responded JC. "Bip, why can't you be more like Sunny?"

As the others talked, JC drank his coffee and sat in silence. He was thinking.

"The initials 'HM,'" he finally said. "I assumed they belonged to Hank Monk. I never thought of Mad Marv. But his real name is Henry Marvin, HM."

"You think that was *his* hand?" Bip said in surprise.

"Who else do we know here, with those initials, who would slip a note to me under my door?" JC asked.

"And Mercy can't find him," Sunny added.

JC called the sheriff's office. The secretary and dispatcher said that Sheriff Brush was unavailable.

At that very moment, Brush was on another phone line as he sat behind his desk in his office.

"Professor Patterson," the sheriff said. "We have a name that we got off a fingerprint. We want to see if that name is on your list of customers that you have sold ski gloves to."

"That's fine, Sheriff," the college professor said, sitting in his office on the CSU campus in Fort Collins. "As I told your deputy, almost all of my business is done online. So I have a record with the credit card of each those purchases."

"The name is Henry Marvin," the sheriff said.

"Let me look at my list," the educator said, sounding like he was already running his eyes over the list of names and records. "I put them in my briefcase this morning. I do this work at home in my basement, but I thought you would call today."

Sheriff Brush was patient, letting the man do what the sheriff had asked. Professor Patterson came across names that were similar. Out loud, he muttered names like Martin and Mason.

"You must be doing a good business if you have that many sales to look over," the sheriff said cordially.

"Yes and no," the professor laughed. "My manufacturing process is not as fast as real glove factories. But I can sell whatever I make."

More time passed. The sheriff waited in silence. He wondered that if it *isn't* Marv, then who *is* it? And where is Marv?

"Ah, here it is," Patterson finally proclaimed. "My filing system isn't really designed for this. But here he is. A Henry Marvin purchased my gloves, ordered on his computer this summer."

"Henry Marvin?" the sheriff repeated. "And what address did he have you send them to?"

Professor Patterson read off a shipping destination for a house with a Placer mailing address.

"That's his house," the sheriff declared. "Thank you, Professor Patterson, for all your help. We may need to be in further contact in the future. I hope that won't be a problem."

"Not at all, Sheriff," the educator said and then ended the call.

The sheriff's next call was placed to the district attorney.

"Hi, Frank," Brush said. "You asked me to call when we had a name on the victim."

"Is he local?" District Attorney Frank Steen asked.

"I'm afraid so," the sheriff responded. "It's Henry Marvin. We fingerprinted the hand and it's his. We also have identified the glove as one he purchased over the summer."

"I'm always more disturbed when it's a local resident," Frank said. "Marv didn't live here long, but we all knew him to some extent."

"I feel the same way," Brush said. "I like to think it's my job to protect the people who live here, who elected me."

"Do you know who did it?" the district attorney inquired.

"We're just getting started on that," the sheriff answered. "Now that we know who it is, we can look into who would want to take his hand off."

"You don't think Henry Marvin is still out there somewhere alive, missing a hand, do you?"

"I've seen crazier things," the sheriff told him. "But, no, I don't think so. But we still have to find the body."

"Probably thrown down a mineshaft," Steen suggested.

203

"Yes, and that won't make our job any easier," the sheriff answered.

"Jerry," the district attorney started. "Can you come by my office this afternoon?"

"Sure, Frank," the sheriff said. "What's it about?"

"We'll talk when you get here," the D.A. answered and ended the call.

27

"**D**amn it, Frank, don't do this," Sheriff Brush pleaded.

The two men stood in the second-floor office of the county building that was assigned to the district attorney. The room was lined with shelves that were lined with law books.

"I have to, Jerry," the district attorney, Frank Steen, argued. "Don't you see how it would look if I didn't?"

"It would look like you trust me to do my job," Sheriff Brush contended. "It's the job the people here elected me to do."

"You're too close, Jerry," the D.A. said.

"Do you think I killed Henry Marvin?" the sheriff asked.

"Of course not," Steen argued. His answer was more of a reflex than the whole truth. The district attorney was not one to rush to judgment, in either direction. "But it's an obvious conflict of interest."

"There are less than a thousand people who live in this county. We *all* know each other to some extent," Brush pushed. "If I give a waitress a good tip, I could be accused of trying to tamper with a future member of a jury."

"I know, Jerry," Steen acknowledged. "We live under unusual circumstances here."

"I know how it would look to an outsider," Brush continued to argue. "But these people know me. Cameron County knows me."

"Jerry, can I be frank?" the district attorney asked. That term always sounded a little silly when the D.A. said it, since his name *was* Frank.

But he continued, regardless of permission. "The people of Cameron County scratch their heads at what goes on in your household. What you really mean is, the people here try to stay out of your business. That's how the local people were raised."

"Damn right," the sheriff blurted.

"But it doesn't mean they don't think it's weird as hell, what's been going on between you and Mercy and Marv," Steen said. "You three are like seeing a three-headed dairy cow. It's strange as hell, but if it produces milk, who is to judge?"

"Right!" the sheriff plowed on. "They don't judge us! What we do is unusual, it's not against the law."

"But the understanding people of this county aren't making their decisions in a court of law," the district attorney reminded him. "And that's where the trial of Henry

Marvin's killer will take place, in a court of law. And you're too close."

"And the jury will be made up of the people of Cameron County," Brush reminded him. "That's why the judicial system is set up the way it is, so the whole thing is judged by a jury of peers."

"I know," Steen said, with some sympathy. "That's why they keep letting Horace Emerson walk out of court a free man. The people here have it in their head that he means no harm. He'd be doing ten years in prison if he did some of this stuff across the border in Larimer County."

"Frank," the sheriff said. His was the voice of a man who was pleading.

"Hell, I'd probably motion to move the trial to another county," the D.A. interrupted. "I couldn't seat a jury here without knowing some of them sympathize with you."

"Besides," the sheriff remarked. "We haven't even found a body. We've only found a hand."

"And has anyone seen Henry Marvin walking around with one hand?" Steen asked. "Does anyone in this room think Henry Marvin is out there, somewhere, alive?"

There was a pause. The sheriff took off his cowboy hat and placed it on the district attorney's desk. He was getting warm. His head felt like it had been lit aflame.

The district attorney was growing weary of dancing around the obvious. Jerry Brush was a friend and trusted colleague. They had worked together on a hundred prosecutions. Their relationship had always been cooperative, and they had long ago become friends outside of work.

"Jerry," the D.A. finally said. "You're a suspect."

"What?" the sheriff asked in a loud voice, incredulous to the notion.

"You're a suspect," the D.A. repeated. "At this moment, you're probably the *chief* suspect."

"Frank," the sheriff said, looking for understanding.

"Jerry, I know," Steen said, trying to lower the intensity of the conversation. "But look at this case. A man is sleeping with your wife. The man turns up dead, murdered. Who is suspect number one? Who is the first guy *you* would look at?"

"Frank," the sheriff repeated, looking at defeat in the face.

"Does the scenario sound familiar, Jerry?" Frank said, softening his tone. "It's a murder triangle. In your experience, Jerry, how many cases of murder between two men involve an argument over a woman?"

"About half of them," Brush mumbled. His shoulders sagged and he sat against the district attorney's desk.

"Yes, about forty-three percent, according to the FBI's Uniform Crime Report," Steen said.

"I can do this, Frank," the sheriff said. But his voice was weak. It struggled to find firm footing.

"How can you investigate yourself?" the D.A. asked. "What defense attorney couldn't overturn a conviction of someone else by simply using the argument that the sheriff ignored the number one suspect in the investigation, himself?"

The sheriff sat silently, staring at the floor.

"I didn't do it," Brush finally said, quietly. "We had an understanding. This was the way she wanted it. If I had put my foot down, I would have lost her. I couldn't do that. I couldn't live without her."

"I understand," Steen said. "We all kind of understood it was something like that. But I've already been in contact with the governor's office. I've asked the governor or the attorney general to appoint a special investigator."

"Frank," the sheriff pleaded in a soft voice.

"You'll not be removed as sheriff," the district attorney informed him. "You're not being accused of anything. You'll just be removed from this investigation and be expected to carry on your other duties."

"What did the governor's office say?" Brush asked, choking on the words but trying to return this conversation to one of protocol and official business.

"They're going to get back to me," the district attorney informed him. "But I think they see things the same way. It's just the prudent thing to do."

"So, who would be the special investigator?" the sheriff inquired. "Would one of my deputies take over? Rocky Bush?"

"That wasn't our thinking when I spoke on the phone with the governor's office," Steen said. "They were thinking about bringing in an outsider, letting an experienced homicide investigator from another jurisdiction come in and do the job. This is a highly unusual situation, Jerry. None of us could come up with anything quite like it. It's not a run-of-the-mill police-brutality case. This is entirely different."

"Is there any precedent?" Brush asked.

"We haven't found any yet," the D.A. conceded. "That would make things easier, wouldn't it? This might be the first of its kind in decades, maybe more."

"When?" the sheriff asked.

"The governor understands the urgency of this. It could come today or tomorrow," Steen informed him. And the district attorney exhaled. "How is Mercy?"

"Distraught," the sheriff told him. "She's leaning on me. That's the funny thing. That's what's different about this, Frank. She harbors no suspicion whatsoever that I killed Marv. She is clinging to me like we just lost a son."

"It's one for the books," Steen said. "I'll give you that."

"So, what do I do now?" Brush asked, picking his cowboy hat up off of the district attorney's desk. "I am arranging for a thorough search of the mine, to see if we can find the rest of Marv's body."

"Let it rest, Jerry," the D.A. advised. "Leave it alone, for the special investigator to proceed with. He'll be here in a day or two."

Frank Steen held out his hand and Jerry Brush shook it.

"We'll get through this, Jerry," the district attorney said. "It will all be over soon."

The sheriff nodded, put his cowboy hat back on his head, opened the door to the office and slowly walked out.

Instead of walking down two flights of stairs to his office in the sheriff's department, Brush decided to go for a walk outside to clear his head.

Walking down the front stairs of the courthouse, he thought he would stroll to the edge of town. There was less likelihood of running into someone who would expect a conversation out of him.

"Let me guess," a voice behind the sheriff said. Brush winced. Here was one of those conversations that he didn't want to get into. He turned and saw a man he had never met. But he knew his reputation.

210

"Bob Andrews," the man said, extending a hand to shake. The sheriff took it silently.

"Let me guess," Andrews repeated. "Frankenstein just took you off the Marvin murder investigation."

"Frankenstein?" the sheriff repeated.

"The district attorney," Andrews said. "His name is Frank Steen, right? I give everyone nicknames. It helps me remember who they are. Anyway, I call him Frankenstein."

"Cute," the sheriff said, without expression. He didn't think it was that cute.

"I'm an ex-cop," Andrews explained. "I was a trooper up in Idaho."

"I know you by reputation," the sheriff told him.

"Don't hold that against me," Badass said with a half grin, half sneer. "I just thought that if you ever needed a shoulder to cry on, I'd know where you're coming from."

"How did you know they took me off the Marvin murder case?" Brush asked.

"Standard operating procedure," Andrews told him. "How could they keep you on it? You're the most likely killer."

"I guess," the sheriff said quietly, rubbing his head. He began to realize that it was obvious to everyone except himself.

"What's your nickname for me?" Brush asked.

"Twig," Badass responded without hesitation. "It's because your name is Brush. Plus, if you *didn't* kill Marvin, I can't understand why not. Most men would have snapped."

"Twig, huh?" the sheriff said.

28

The governor asked the state attorney general to appoint a special investigator to the Marvin murder investigation. The governor wanted an announcement by the start of business the next day.

The first call was placed by the attorney general herself to the executive director of the Colorado Department of Public Safety. The executive director was a former county sheriff. He was sensitive to the position Jerry Brush was in.

"But we're up to our eyes in turkeyfoot grass," he said. "We can't spare anyone from the state police. We have a president of the United States who is a skiing president. He is coming to Colorado with his family in four days. He will ski here for a week and receive a few foreign dignitaries who also ski. In addition to the Secret Service, they will also need our protection. We'll have troopers skiing in front of them, behind them and beside them. We will have troopers guarding the ski chalet where they will be staying, the restaurants where they dine, the ski lodges where they will shake hands with voters and entertain the news media with impromptu news conferences. And that's just if nothing big happens on the global stage. If that happens, we may be asking the Secret Service for more bodies."

"I understand your problem," the attorney general told him. "But the governor wants a quick decision. What do you suggest?"

"I have the director of the Colorado Bureau of Investigation with me," the public-safety chief said. "He has someone in mind. He's not from the CBI, but he's highly recommended by CBI investigators who have worked alongside him. And his availability might not be an issue."

The decision was made in a matter of hours. The pay would amount to a pro-rated $65,877 annual salary, on top of paid leave from his normal duties. The governor appointed a Denver police detective to conduct the murder investigation in Cameron County, Steve Trujillo.

"Do you want to get this part over with?" Trujillo asked Sheriff Brush over the phone. "I'm right upstairs. I arrived overnight."

Detective Steve Trujillo, normally assigned to the District 2 police station in Denver, had told his wife that the sooner he got to Placer, the sooner he'd be able to return home. He packed a bag and left for Cameron County only hours after his appointment.

Driving up Poudre Canyon in the dark, his way was illuminated by a clear night and shining stars. He spotted some bighorn and elk by the side of the road.

He had asked for and received office space that was on a different floor in the county courthouse than the sheriff's office. He didn't want anyone who walked into his office to be seen by Sheriff Brush or the people who worked for him.

"I suspect that you're aware that I've been appointed special investigator in the case of a missing person by the name of Henry Marvin?" Trujillo asked the sheriff over the phone.

"Well, his hand has been found," the sheriff stated. "It's the rest of him that is missing."

Detective Trujillo smiled a small smile. He liked cop humor.

"Would you like to come up to my new office and have a talk?" the detective asked. "It would be on the record and involve what you know about the disappearance of the rest of Henry Marvin, minus the hand."

"Should I bring an attorney?" Brush asked.

"I'm not bringing one," Trujillo responded, off the cuff. Then he remembered that he was not speaking with a colleague in law enforcement under normal circumstances.

"Let me be to the point, Sheriff. I like to do that with people," the special investigator said. "As much as I want to like you and get to know you as a colleague, that's not why I was brought here.

"At this early stage in the investigation, everyone is a suspect. That includes you. If you see fit to bring a lawyer with you, that is well within your rights and probably not the worst idea you've ever had."

"Oh, hell," the sheriff said. "I'll be right up."

The interview took place in the special investigator's office. There wasn't an interrogation room available to Trujillo. He wouldn't have placed Sheriff Brush in one of those, anyway. His office would be fine, and a secretary loaned to the special investigator would be outside the door to stop anyone from interrupting him.

The four walls of the special investigator's office were mostly blank. There was a picture of the governor that had been hanging there when Trujillo walked in. But that was the only ornamentation, other than a picture of Trujillo's wife and children that sat on his temporary desk.

The interview proceeded as it would in any murder investigation, though it slowed down to allow Trujillo to understand exactly how the sheriff's wife was also the girlfriend of the missing man.

"And everybody knew this?" Trujillo asked the sheriff.

The sheriff nodded.

"This was out in the open?" the special investigator asked. "They were seen together out to dinner or walking together in a small town like this?"

"Yes," the sheriff nodded. "I guess you could say that the three of us had reached an agreement."

Trujillo used every muscle in his face to disguise his confusion over the arrangement between the husband, wife and boyfriend.

"Boy, do I have a story for you," the sheriff said.

"Your wife's name is Mary LaJeunesse?" Trujillo asked.

"Mercy," the sheriff answered. "She goes by Mercy. Her real name is Mary Mercy LaJeunesse. But she has two sisters who are also named Mary."

"There are three sisters named Mary LaJeunesse in this town?" Trujillo asked.

"Two live in this town," the sheriff clarified. "The third sister named Mary moved to Texas."

"And who is the other Mary LaJeunesse who lives in town?" Trujillo inquired.

"Maddie," the sheriff told him. "Mary Madeleine."

Trujillo again found himself trying not to show that he thought this was weird. He wrote down Mary Mercy LaJeunesse's name. He'd want to talk with her. He wrote down Maddie's name too. He'd want to see what, if anything, her sister said to her.

"Maddie is the public defender here," the sheriff advised. "If you arrest Mercy, she'll probably hire her sister, Maddie."

"Would that be wise?" Trujillo asked.

"In a small town like this, there aren't that many lawyers," Brush explained.

"Small town," Trujillo wrote in his notes, trying to wrap his head around what he had gotten himself into.

Steve Trujillo had a resplendent record as a detective on Denver's police force. He was stocky, with big hands. He had dark, thick hair and was a taller man than Jerry Brush.

Trujillo's father had been a farm foreman. Trujillo and his siblings grew up helping doing manual labor. That, as much as anything, inspired Steve to go to college. Being a cop was a tough job, but Trujillo thought that it was easier than being a farmer.

Trujillo asked the sheriff the names of his deputies. He wrote them down, planning to also interview them.

At the end of the interview, Trujillo stood and shook the sheriff's hand.

"Sorry we had to meet under these circumstances," the Denver detective said.

216

"You're just doing your job," the sheriff said, dismissing the awkward nature of the conversation.

"Anywhere you'd recommend for lunch?" Trujillo asked.

"There aren't a lot of choices," the sheriff stated. "But you could do worse than the Lady Moon Café. It's right up the street."

About five minutes after Sheriff Brush left the special investigator's office, Detective Trujillo emerged from behind the door.

"I'm going to take time to have some lunch," he told the secretary. "I haven't had much to eat since I left home last night."

Trujillo walked down the front steps of the county courthouse and walked where the sheriff had told him to walk. The detective was looking at the signs over storefronts in the small downtown, searching for the Lady Moon.

"Detective Trujillo?"

The special investigator turned his head to eye level and saw Bob Andrews.

Badass introduced himself, by name and as a former law officer.

"Uh-huh," Trujillo said. "I was told that I might run into you."

"Friend or foe?" Andrews asked. "Who told you?"

"It doesn't matter," Trujillo told him. "Have you broken any laws lately?"

"No, Detective," Badass said, trying to disguise his sneer. "I haven't."

"Well, then you and I are starting with a clean slate," Trujillo said.

"I thought I'd offer you my help," Andrews said. "Being an ex-cop, maybe you need someone to do a little legwork for you. The menial jobs that you don't have time for."

"You sound like an ex-cop who wants to be a cop again," Trujillo noted.

"I'm just a little bored in retirement," Andrews said.

"I'll keep it in mind," the special investigator said as he walked past Andrews and began again to search for the Lady Moon. In Trujillo's mind, Andrews was a suspect too. He didn't know what Andrew's motive might be, but he sure had the know-how.

The detective spotted a familiar face as he proceeded down the sidewalk. He didn't expect to see anyone he knew.

"I would have gotten a cake if I knew we were going to have a reunion," JC Snow said to Trujillo when they met on the street.

"How is it that when a case gets weird, you end up in the middle of it?" Trujillo asked the reporter.

The Denver detective had come to know JC Snow roughly five years ago, during the investigation of some murders that wrapped up in ski country. Trujillo knew that JC would be a presence in this investigation. The reporter was not one to fade into the woodwork until things were resolved.

JC introduced the detective to Robin. Bip had met Trujillo on a few occasions.

"Can we shoot a quick interview?" JC asked.

"I suppose so," Trujillo told them. "But let me get something in my stomach first, then maybe I won't come off so angry."

"I'll call your secretary," Robin said, launching into her familiar role as JC's producer. "Can we do it after lunch?"

"I don't see why not. But it has to be quick. I have a lot of ground to make up," Trujillo said with neither joy nor angst. "Can you tell me where the Lady Moon Café is?"

"You've only got a half block to go," JC told him. "Cross the street and it's right there. We'll see you soon."

"No doubt," the special investigator answered.

29

"**W**hat if Hank Monk is lying?"

JC posed the question after he and Bip and Robin interviewed Special Investigator Steve Trujillo in his office. The detective made it clear that everyone in Cameron County was essentially a suspect.

"It does reset reality, doesn't it?" JC asked his friends. "It gives us a chance to look at John Washburn's murder anew and peer at the probable murder of Marv."

They stood at the base of the ski runs at The Craters. People passed them on either side, carrying skis or a snowboard. A growing throng was trying to get to the lift.

"So," JC asked again. "What if Hank Monk really did slip that paper with the HM initials under my door? The only ones who would know if Henry Marvin *didn't* do it are Hank Monk and Henry Marvin. And Henry Marvin isn't likely to be taking questions anymore."

"So, we're rethinking everything?" Bip asked.

"Yes," JC told him.

"Then I think *you* did it," Bip said with a growing smile.

"Very helpful," JC said, shaking his head.

Detective Trujillo said during the interview with JC that he felt he had a lot to do to catch up with the natural timeline of the investigation.

"I'm going to conduct my priority interviews with people," the special investigator said. "But I've also got the matter of Henry Marvin's body. If it's out there, we've got to find it. I'll be sending equipment to the top of the hill today, lights and that sort of thing. We're going to conduct a detailed search of the mine and its shafts and tunnels and see if he's in there."

"And who will be doing that on your behalf?" JC asked.

"Well, I'm allowed to use the sheriff's people," Trujillo said. "I'm told they have a pretty handy guy for this sort of thing. A deputy named Hank Monk has been loaned to me as my special assistant. He'll help me get the lay of the land."

The three journalists left the courthouse and headed south, turning onto Long Draw Road, the access road to The Craters. They passed a sign reminding visitors that they were guests in Roosevelt National Forest.

Bip hoped to get footage at the base gondola of the lights, cables, ropes and other equipment being taken to the top of the mountain to search the mine.

After parking their SUV, they were surrounded by skiers snapping into their bindings, and snowboarders strapping in one foot and shuffling for the lift line. JC, Bip and Robin wore their winter hiking boots and tried to stay out of the way.

"Are you making a Warren Miller movie?" Trigger Fischer shouted as he skidded to a stop on his skis near them. "I was in one of those," he said. He had a big smile on his face, indicating he just had a good run.

"It's amazing how quickly this mountain can spring back from two days of rain," he told them.

Trigger stood with them while Bip shot video of lights being loaded into the gondola for the ride up.

"Uh-oh, here they come," Trigger said, looking uphill at some resort guests he was skiing with. "The guy asked me to take him to some gnarly jumps and chutes. His friends are taking the safe way down from the top. But *he* bugged me to take him to something more extreme. He survived the first run and now he thinks he's Dan Egan."

"Can I ask you something?" Robin interjected.

"Sure, I can give you all the time you need until 'Not-Dan Egan' and his friends ski back down here," Trigger asked her. "Then I've got to go back up with them to make sure he doesn't kill himself."

"Okay, I'll get to the point," Robin said. "A friend of Loretta Sopris' says that Loretta was your girlfriend for a couple of years, that you and Loretta were 'a thing.'"

"Not really," Trigger smiled, boyishly. "We dated a couple of times, and it was kind of hot and heavy. I thought we might become 'a thing.' But then, she never went out with me again. She always came up with excuses."

The skiers chasing Trigger down the hill had now arrived at the gondola with him. They were eager to take another run with the ski racing champion.

"I've gotta go," he told Robin. "But to answer your question, I wasn't the focus of Loretta's attention anymore. Believe me, I know the difference."

"Thanks," Robin said as Trigger and the paying customers climbed into the gondola car and proceeded up the mountain.

"Oh man, did I just miss Trigger?"

Robin turned to see Horace Emerson, geared to go skiing.

"I thought you didn't ski inbounds," JC said to him.

"I hardly ever do," Horace told them. "But Trigger and I wanted to take some runs together today. That's always fun, because skiing with him is hell's bells. He rips!"

"Are you missing a tooth?" JC asked, noticing a change.

Horace laughed. His grin displayed the new gap in his dental display.

"How do you like my battle scar?" Horace asked, still laughing. "I lost it up on Colby's Couloir. I guess I should have zigged when I zagged."

Horace did not seem at all disturbed by the new disfigurement. It included some temporary scratches across his face. But JC thought Horace wore the missing tooth like a medal. He was a free spirit.

"Do you know Trigger well?" JC asked.

"We've been in PT together," the skier responded. "Physical therapy. He was getting his knee done and I had a busted shoulder, I think. You get to know people when you go through PT together."

"Did you know Trigger when he was dating Loretta Sopris?" Robin asked, leaping at an opportunity.

"I've known Trigger when he was dating about fifty women," Horace told them, laughing and showing off the new gap in his teeth. "Sometimes at the same time."

"What about Loretta Sopris, specifically?" Robin asked.

"She's the lady who jumped from the chairlift, right?" Horace said. He shook his head. "I've never known Trigger to date any woman for more than a week. Now, maybe he *has* dated someone seriously and I just didn't know it. But that's my answer."

"Hey, Whore House." That was Bob "Badass" Andrews' nickname for Horace. Emerson just laughed when he heard it.

Bob Andrews was holding his skis, saying he was going to take a few runs.

"Come on, Whore House," Andrews said to the extreme skier. "Let's take a run together."

"Docious, dude!" Horace said, the smile exposing his missing tooth again. "I'm as likely to bump into Trigger while I'm skiing, as while I am standing here at the bottom of the hill doing nothing."

"That is the strangest pairing I have ever seen in my life," Bip said as he watched the petty thief, and the ex-cop move away.

"We're not going bus-stop skiing, are we?" Horace asked Andrews as they walked out of earshot toward the gondola line. Andrews looked down on Horace like he had just spoken to him in a foreign language.

"What is bus-stop skiing?" Badass grumbled.

"Some people like to stop and chat all the way down the mountain," Horace explained. "In one run, they make more stops than the crosstown bus. I like to bomb. No stops."

As Horace and Bob Andrews headed for their first run of the day, other skiers were finishing their last run of the morning and stepping out of their bindings. Their day was done.

They were the "regulars." Most of the regulars were retired and lived near the mountain. They showed up every day before the lifts began to run. Many of them put their ski boots on in their cars, whatever it took to be at the front of the lift line when it opened.

They were rewarded with "first tracks." There were a lot of runs at a ski area like The Craters. Many of the first wave could get the thrill of being the initial skier to lay down tracks that day.

That first wave, those regulars would ski the best snow of the day and, after two or three hours, they'd call it quits. They had season passes that more than paid for themselves. And they'd be back the next day, to do it all over again.

Every ski mountain had their regulars. Most of them were older and purchased their discounted "senior" season passes before the prior season even ended. They served an important role at the mountain. Those early pass purchases helped pay the mountain's bills over the coming summer.

Still standing at the base of the gondola, JC's phone buzzed. He recognized the phone number and accepted the call.

"Charlie Washburn was just released from jail," JC was told by Deputy Hank Monk.

"On bail or did they drop charges?" JC asked his tipster.

"My understanding is that all charges are being dropped, for now," Monk said. "We can't prove her guilt, but they can't prove her innocence. Maybe I shouldn't tell you this, but I will. We looked at her bank statements and there is no indication that she was stealing the money with her husband."

JC thanked the deputy. Monk said he was calling from a chairlift, on the way to the top of the mountain, where he would lead the search for Henry Marvin's body inside the mine.

"It's going to be a long day," Deputy Monk said and ended the call.

JC told Robin and Bip about Charlie Washburn's release.

"What would you give to get her picture, right now?" JC asked Bip.

"That would be a nice picture to have," Bip conceded.

"Then turn around," JC said.

Bip and Robin did so, and they all watched Charlie Washburn, freshly released from jail, approach a chairlift carrying her snowboard.

Bip threw the camera back on his shoulder and began to shoot footage.

"Don't even think it," a voice said behind JC as he reached into his pocket for his notebook and began to approach the widow for an interview.

Maddie LaJeunesse stood behind JC and Robin with her arms folded and a look of satisfaction on her face. She also wore sensible insulated hiking boots, instead of the high heels she left in her office to be used in the courtroom.

"I'm still her attorney," Maddie said. "And I told her not to even breathe in the direction of you and the rest of the news media. The cops are still going to try to put together a case against her. They just haven't had any luck yet. Anyway, I've instructed her to be on radio-silence. That's something she is particularly good at."

"How did you get her out of jail?" JC asked.

"I motioned the court," Maddie said. "That's the beauty of law. Facts are facts."

"Can we interview you, then?" JC asked.

"I guess," Maddie allowed.

During the interview, she said that her client was innocent of murder and had no knowledge of her husband's possible embezzlement from the county treasury. The attorney said that her client was still grieving her loss and asked for privacy.

During the interview, JC remembered that Deputy Hank Monk, his tipster, was the public defender's boyfriend. He wondered if Maddie might be tied to Monk's role as informer, and how far-reaching that cooperation might be.

"And the first thing Charlie did when she got out of jail is grab her snowboard?" Robin asked when the interview was over.

"There is a light in the darkness of everybody's life," the defense attorney told her.

"Did you just quote *The Rocky Horror Picture Show*?" JC asked. "Seriously?"

Maddie LaJeunesse had a broad smile on her face and shrugged her shoulders.

"Carpe ski 'em," she added.

It began to snow.

30

T he snow came down in big flakes. It was a storm sweeping down from Wyoming.

But after the rain, real snow elevated the mood of the crowd. Man-made snow covered the ice. And nature's snow covered the wounds.

"How was your run with Badass?" Bip asked Horace when he arrived back at the gondola.

"Docious!" the extreme skier told him. "He skis like an old man, but I can have a good time skiing with anyone. He even asked me if he could help me with my occasional collisions with the law."

"What could he do for you?" Bip asked.

"I'd like to ask the court for a redo," Horace responded.

"How far back would this redo go?" the photographer inquired, wondering if the conversation was just pure nonsense.

"Luckily, I'm a retrovisional," Horace told him.

"What is a retrovisional?" Bip asked.

"I can see the past, man," Horace said in all seriousness.

"Remarkable," Bip responded, leaning toward the nonsense theory. "That's a gift."

"There is some good in the worst of us and some evil in the best of us," quoted Horace. "Martin Luther King Jr. said that."

"Wait a minute," Bip said. "I thought you were a high school dropout."

"Well, I showed up that day," Horace laughed, showing off his missing tooth. "I think I need a redo going back to sixth grade. All this bad karma I've picked up along the way, it's like I carry suitcases around now, full of ill deeds and dumb stuff I've done. The suitcases arrive with me when I get somewhere and leave with me when I go. I'm not a bad dude, dude. I just gotta check these suitcases at the train station and move on without them."

"Good luck with that," Bip said. He decided there was some sense in Horace's nonsense. Those suitcases had to be getting heavy.

The sheriff's staging area atop the ski mountain, organized by Hank Monk, attracted curious looks from skiers and snowboarders as they glided by. But the purpose of the sheriff deputies' presence was deep underground.

The gear was positioned under tarps and inside a fence of yellow police tape. The tarps were to keep the falling snow off of it.

Below ground, powerful lamps illuminated the old mine's tunnels. They exposed a few shafts that plunged hundreds of feet, and other exploratory holes that only went twenty or thirty feet down.

Deputy Monk enjoyed the work. He was happy that the special investigator, Detective Steve Trujillo, recognized his skill set and put him in charge of this detail.

Monk instructed his team not to trust any of the old wooden trusses or floors.

"Beetles and wood rot have had over a century to hollow them out," Monk told them. "Assume they will not carry your weight."

Monk was the first to rappel down the shafts that needed exploring. Some of them, he would declare, ended without reaching a tunnel and he'd ask to be pulled up.

"We expected some dead ends," Monk said. "This mine showed early promise when it opened in the 1880s or so, but the gold vein ran out and the mine shut down abruptly. I looked for some drawings or plans, but I didn't find anything."

In comparison, the Matchless Mine in Leadville was opened in 1878 and remained open for roughly ten years. Productive shafts were bored deeper and wider. Nearly a half-billion dollars' worth of silver was unearthed before being exhausted.

Monk concluded that they could finish exploring the mine they were in by the end of the night, if they kept working. Inside a mine, day and night didn't look much different.

The horizontal tunnels on the main floor were all inspected by noon. But all deputies had discovered were broken axe handles and a rusty canteen. Henry Marvin was still missing.

The first vertical shaft Monk rappelled down was the closest one to the overhead entry they were using to enter the mine. It wasn't the first shaft that Monk would have chosen, but the apparatus was already set up when he arrived at the top of the mountain that morning. He'd been delayed by a meeting with Detective Trujillo.

The shaft dropped about fifty feet into darkness before reaching a floor. Men with pickaxes had long ago chipped away a horizontal corridor going about eighty feet in each direction. After exploring the short tunnels, Monk told the deputies, waiting above, to raise him back up to the main floor.

Monk blamed himself for not telling his team where he preferred to set up the morning's first probe of a vertical shaft. He told himself that he would remember that the next time he had a chance to command a team.

Monk was most interested in the vertical shaft that was closest to where the glove was found, the one with the hand inside it.

"The killer wasn't going to drag that body any farther than he had to," Monk said.

Monk wondered why Marvin's gloved hand ended up at the old entry to the mine, the one that used to have scaffolding up the cliff and stairs allowing entry. He stared at the square hole from inside the mine. He watched fat snowflakes fall outside.

Perhaps, Monk thought, Marvin made a run for it. But he was caught at that opening where, from where he stood, it looked like a sheer drop.

A pair of steel augers were drilled into the floor of the mine tunnel, next to the shaft Monk was most interested in. He would secure his rappelling rope to the augers, rather than trust one of the old wooden posts or struts that had been holding the mine up for nearly a hundred and fifty years.

Running a rope through a carabiner on his harness, Monk lowered himself into the shaft. A light on his helmet provided the only illumination. He helped slow his descent by reaching out with his feet to jagged edges in the rock. He looked down, from time to time, searching for the floor of the shaft. But all he saw was darkness.

He spied something resting on one of the jagged edges. He pulled out his phone and took a picture of it. Then he reached out with his gloved hand and snatched it from its precarious perch.

It was a lift ticket, dated from the previous Saturday. In his mind, Monk determined that was the day Henry Marvin went missing.

Monk slipped the lift ticket into a pocket of his jacket. He looked down, but all he saw was blackness. He looked up and estimated he'd rappelled down about seventy-five feet.

He knew that he had plenty of rope left and continued to slide it through the harness wrapped around his waist and groin. He remained upright by sliding the rope through his leather gloves.

This was when he enjoyed his job the most. He was getting *paid* to exercise his rappelling skills. This was what he did on some of his days off, often right down the road on Highway 14. He smiled at the thought.

He wasn't wearing his gun. Why would he? It could interfere with his harness and if he met anyone at the bottom of this shaft, he'd likely not be breathing.

Hank could hear the voices of his team above him. They were joking about taking a ski run while he was down there. One deputy figured that Monk would never know the difference, as long as they were back before Monk wanted to come up.

Another deputy suggested they start raining pebbles down the shaft, just to make sure Monk was still awake.

"I see something," came a muffled voice up from the shaft. The deputies moved closer to the shaft, leaning over it to hear better.

"Send down a litter," the muffled voice ordered.

Monk had found Henry Marvin's body.

Deputy Monk studied the surface of the shaft's floor without letting his feet disturb it. He dangled about a foot off the ground. Monk shot more photos for the evidence techs. It was unlikely that they'd be lowered into the hole themselves.

The face of the corpse was swollen and unrecognizable. The cold would have prevented some swelling over the past five days, but the exposed flesh was probably battered during the fall down the shaft.

Monk saw that one hand was missing. And the remaining glove matched the glove Aguayo had recovered on Sunday. The hand inside that glove had already been identified as belonging to Henry Marvin.

Monk had to stretch to reach one of Marvin's ski boots and place it on his lap. The violence of the fall had pulled the boot, still fully fastened, off of Marvin's foot.

Satisfied that he could stand on the surface of the shaft without trampling any evidence, Monk stood and received the litter that hung from a separate rope. There wasn't room at the bottom of the shaft for Monk and more deputies. So, with difficulty, Monk leaned the litter against the shaft wall and lifted the body.

Monk wrapped his arms under the armpits of the body. The side of their faces met. Marvin's was cold and stiff. Monk finally leaned him into the litter, almost in a standing position.

With the corpse firmly strapped into the litter, and the loose ski boot wedged under one of Marvin's legs, Monk allowed the deputies above to pull the dead man up. Monk followed, always in contact with the litter, in case it became snagged on the wall of the shaft.

The deputies at the top grabbed the skeleton of the litter and pulled it up. Then they pulled Monk out. It had been grueling work and Monk sat alongside the shaft for a moment. Despite the cold and the breeze coming from the opening in the side of the mountain, he was sweating. He caught his breath, sitting on the floor, leaning against a wall, and watching the snow fall outside and the chairlift ride by.

"You'd better get the ski patrol to post that run," one deputy said, nodding toward the shaft. "I think it's a triple-diamond."

"Yeah," agreed another deputy. "I don't think Horace would have *any* teeth left after skiing this."

"Uh oh, here comes the night," Trigger said to himself as he walked away from the bar.

He'd had a couple of drinks with "Not-Dan Egan" and his friends at the end of the ski day. They were buying. That made it part of Trigger's compensation package.

Trigger was limping when he left the bar. It was the time of the evening when that sort of thing happened. But Badass had been true to his word. There was a new package of medicine waiting for Trigger back at his condo.

The snow had stopped. Trigger looked up and saw the stars drifting down the black sky until they landed on the mountains.

He thought about things as he walked through the ski village. He wondered what day it was that he clinically became a heroin addict. He felt no guilt. The pain overwhelmed him. He'd rather feel nothing.

He was still wearing his ski gear when he reached his condo and shot up. Relief came over him like a wave. For a minute or two, he was close to passing out. But he heard the knock at the door.

With the resilience his body had developed during this repeated practice of pain and restoration, he emerged from the bathroom and quickly acclimatized to the world, the way it is supposed to be.

A dazzling blonde was resting against the door jamb when he pulled on the knob.

"I followed you from the bar," she said in a Southern accent. "Do you remember me?"

"How could I forget?" Trigger said. And that's just what he was thinking. She was so gorgeous, why didn't he have any recollection of her?

He pulled the door open and she walked in.

He thought her name was Georgia. Or was that where she was from? She undressed him tenderly. He was in the mood for that. He felt like a baby yearning for an embrace from his mother. The medication had taken hold. The pain was gone, but he knew it would come back.

"Sometimes, I don't even know where I go when I take my meds," he told her as they lay next to each other in bed. "Sometimes, I don't even remember the next morning."

"That's scaring me a little," she said.

"No, don't be afraid," he said as he rolled closer to her. "I would never hurt a woman. Especially a pretty one."

31

"**D**o you think your sheriff killed Henry Marvin?" Detective Trujillo asked Monk.

"Do you?" the deputy asked, shocked by the question.

"Well, someone did," the detective said, getting comfortable in his role as special investigator. "If we drew up a list, he'd be on it. Don't you think?"

They sat in Trujillo's temporary office on the second floor of the courthouse. Monk sat in the only chair in the room besides the one behind Trujillo's desk, where he sat.

The dingy room was usually used for storage. It was quickly cleared out when Cameron County heard they had a special investigator on the way. There was no window and there wasn't time to repaint the dingy walls or clean and wax the old hardwood floors.

"You work in Denver," Monk said. "You must see a lot more murders than we do."

"But there are over seven hundred thousand people where I live," the special investigator said. "*This* county has a population of nine hundred and forty-three, and you have two murder investigations going on at the same time. I think your current per-capita murder rate is a little scary."

"So, you're asking me if my own sheriff murdered Marv?" Monk asked.

"I tell you what," Trujillo offered. "Let's make a list, in no particular order. The sheriff had a motive. He had a good reason to be mad. The victim was sleeping with his wife."

Detective Trujillo wrote the sheriff's name down on a piece of paper in a notebook. It looked like he had drawn two columns. Then he looked at Monk, indicating it was his turn.

"Is Mercy a suspect?" Monk asked.

"Is she?" the special investigator responded.

"Okay, she was sleeping with Marv. Maybe he wanted to break up with her," Monk suggested. "Or maybe she wanted to break up with him."

"Love triangles, of one nature or another, are responsible for about half of the murders we solve," the detective told him. He wrote something in the other column on his paper.

"How about Charlene Washburn, the suspect in the other murder you people are investigating? Could she work into this somehow? If she killed her husband, the odds go up that she killed someone else. What's the saying? The first murder is the hardest?"

"Charlie? That's what everybody calls her," Monk said. "The case against her in her husband's murder was based on one flimsy witness. That's how her attorney got her out of jail."

"There's also a chance this was a random killing," Detective Trujillo said. "Those killers can be hard as hell to catch, because there's no connection with their victim."

"But it's always a possibility," Monk agreed. Trujillo nodded in agreement and wrote something else in his notebook.

"Here's something to consider," the detective said while scratching his neck. "Henry Marvin has lived here about two years?"

"About that," Monk affirmed.

"So, Henry Marvin's problem may have nothing to do with Cameron County. This could go back to before he was around here."

"How do you go about finding that out?" the deputy asked.

"I remember a fellow in Denver who had a spotless record," the detective said. "He and his wife and their little baby went to church every Sunday and did all the right things. He didn't seem to have an enemy in the world. Then he was murdered."

"Did you find an enemy?" Monk asked.

"I did," Trujillo said. "It turned out that the guy had a past. He made some enemies out in Oakland. He belonged to a motorcycle gang there. They ran drugs. Our victim decided he wanted to begin life over again, a clean life. So, he bathed and shaved and stole some of the drug money from his motorcycle gang and disappeared. The problem was, they found him, in Denver."

239

"And they killed him?" Monk asked.

"They did," the detective told him. "Let's look into who Henry Marvin was before he got here," Trujillo said. "I'll make that my assignment."

The detective wrote something down in his notebook.

"What about Horace Emerson?" Monk asked.

"Horace. I don't know much about him," Detective Trujillo said. "I thought he was more likely to steal someone's underwear from the public laundromat."

"Well, yes. And he's probably done that," the deputy laughed. "But I'm just thinking out loud. Horace and his buddies are backcountry skiers. And they are upset that The Craters is here at all. Maybe they're trying to give the ski resort a black eye."

"By killing two people?" the detective asked, scratching his neck. "Okay, we'll put him on the list."

Monk liked Detective Trujillo. He felt like he was treated as an equal. Trujillo was the boss, but Monk felt like his voice was heard.

"Let me ask you something," the special investigator said. "It's not in my purview here, but the other murder you're investigating, Washburn. His car was found in Hailey, Idaho?"

"That's right," Monk said.

"Mr. Andrews, Bob 'Badass' Andrews," the detective said. "Did he not live in Ketchum, Idaho, until a few weeks ago? And isn't Ketchum right down the road from Hailey?"

"So which list do we add Bob Andrews to?" Monk asked.

"All of them," the special investigator said without smiling.

"That's all I can think of," Monk said, as he looked at their list of suspects. He was reading Trujillo's notebook upside down.

"And it probably isn't any of them," the detective stated. "But it's someplace to start."

"You said you're going to look into Marvin's background," Deputy Monk said. "Do you want me to start looking at these others?"

"Yeah, we both will. See what you can do," the special investigator said. He liked Monk. He hoped he didn't kill Marvin. But mentally, not in the notebook, the detective added him to the list.

"Come out to my house tonight," Scooter said when he phoned JC. "Bring Robin and anyone else. I want to get back in your good graces."

"That was my fault," JC told him. "I was in a bad mood. We'll be there. I hope you have a room with all your second-place ski racing medals from the high school races I won."

"What was I thinking?" Scooter said, laughing. "You're still a jerk. See you tonight."

Following JC's live shot on the Friday evening news, he and Robin followed the headlights of her car up a winding road. Bip and Sunny were behind them in the news car.

Robin's car was an older Japanese model. She liked to brag about how many miles she had on it. A dignified Ute chief bobblehead doll was adhered to the middle of the dashboard.

"You know that you can afford a new car, right?" JC asked. "You make more money now that you're a reporter."

"I know," Robin replied. "But this is more than my car, she's my friend. And she's not done."

She patted the dashboard. That made the Ute chief nod in agreement.

"And I don't believe in assisted suicide," she added. "My car will die a natural death."

They pulled into the driveway of Tommy "Scooter" Halvorson's substantial mountain home, parked in front and got out. They approached a wooden door big enough to drive their car through and Tommy Halvorson, JC's old high school friend, opened it up.

"Do I call you Tommy or Scooter when we're in the privacy of your own home?" JC asked.

"Call him Donuts," Bip said with a smile.

"Donuts," Scooter laughed. "That's what Badass calls me. He's got a nickname for everyone."

They walked into a luxurious home with stone floors and soft carpets thrown on top of them. Dark paneling covered the lower wall. It was met in the middle by bright wallpaper that stretched to the ceiling with scenes of pine trees and wildlife.

The windows were tall and arched, as were the ceilings of the hallways. There was an abundance of built-in bookshelves.

"Anyway, call me Scooter," he replied. "I've been called Scooter for so long, I probably wouldn't even answer to Tommy. Now, get in here before all that cold air coming from Cameron Pass gets into my house."

He welcomed them and took their coats. A warm blaze was burning in a large fireplace. The interior of the house was open and immense.

"I didn't realize how well you had done for yourself," JC said, taking in the beautiful home. "I apologize for thinking you were a moron."

Scooter laughed. He poured them a whiskey he wanted them to try. It was called 10th Mountain Whiskey and was distilled in Vail.

"It's really good," Bip said after taking his first taste.

"Your home is in touch with nature," Sunny said, admiring the stone and wood beams. She stopped in front of a small creek in the floor. It followed a shiny copper streambed and disappeared into a stone wall.

"I love that creek," Scooter said. "I designed it. It's really just a fountain lying on its side. The water recycles itself. In the winter, I actually tap into the snowmelt, so I don't even tax the municipal water supply."

"You designed it?" Robin asked.

"Yeah," Scooter confirmed proudly.

He gave them a tour of the home. It was tasteful and inventive. On the bookshelves, there were three volumes he authored. Two were written to demystify the nuances of computers and the internet. The other was a guide to help unravel the confusion over cryptocurrency.

"Didn't you say Marv was into cryptocurrency?" JC asked.

"Yeah, I told you the story," Scooter confirmed. "He was a swindler. There are people out there who believe he should have gone to prison instead of just paying a fine, even if the fine was in the millions of dollars. They won't shed a tear when they hear of his death."

"Care to share any names?" JC asked.

"Let me think about that," Scooter said after giving it some thought.

"Did you lose any crypto money to Marv?" JC asked. It was the second time, and Scooter remembered.

"I told you before," Scooter replied. "I can honestly say that I didn't lose a dime to Mad Marv. Besides, look around," Scooter said as a big smile appeared on his face and he raised his arms to show off his home. "Does it look like I'm losing money?"

Everyone laughed and Scooter refilled their glasses with 10th Mountain Whiskey.

32

"Have you felt these bed linens?" Robin asked JC in a slurred voice that came with just waking up. She was cradled in his arms as she ran her hand across the soft, slightly blue sheet beneath her.

Early morning sun was shining through three arched windows in the bedroom. The sun was warm against her bare skin. The sheer linen curtains in the window revealed a dreamy view of the Medicine Bow Range.

"Do you know where we are?" she asked JC.

"Kind of," he replied in a soft voice. His eyes were still closed. "Do you?"

"Heaven," she giggled.

"You might be right," JC said. "I smell coffee and bacon."

Friday night at Tommy "Scooter" Halvorson's house had extended into Saturday morning. The bottle of whiskey from Vail was emptied and replaced with another. Slippery roads and blurry eyes led Scooter to assign guest rooms to JC and Robin, and Bip and Sunny.

As the guests climbed out of bed, they followed the scent of the food to a bright, tiled kitchen with stainless steel appliances. There were more arched windows and more views of the mountains.

"Your home is so beautiful," Sunny told Tommy. "You have given us a night to remember, followed by a morning to remember."

"Can we have our honeymoon here?" Robin asked in a dreamy voice.

Scooter seemed happy to have the company and was the perfect host.

"I love it here," he said. "You should have seen my house in Puerto Rico. But Hurricane Maria flattened it. There are no hurricanes here. I think this house is safe."

"Why aren't you married?" Robin asked. "You're a catch."

JC admired the way Robin had of asking questions like that with uncontested innocence, questions that could be insulting if asked the wrong way.

"Divorced," Tommy said, smiling at her compliment.

They lingered at the breakfast bar for a long time. It was Saturday, after all. They sipped coffee and ate toast and bacon and scrambled eggs with lox.

"I've seen moose walk across my yard out these windows," Tommy told them.

CARPE Ski'em: a Murder on Skis Mystery

The five of them talked about architecture and old ski races that pitted JC against Tommy. They discussed Tommy's life in Cameron County and the gossip around The Craters Ski Resort.

"You said last night that you had stories to tell about Mad Marv and his cryptocurrency swindle," JC said.

"Did I?" Tommy laughed. "You remember more about last night than I do. I had a lot to drink."

"We all had a lot to drink," Bip laughed.

"You said there were some people who would not shed a tear at the death of Marv," JC reminded his host.

Halvorson looked at JC but didn't say anything. He was thinking. He chewed a piece of toast and took a drink of coffee.

"Alright," Tommy finally said. "What do you want to know?"

"Who wouldn't shed a tear, learning that Marv was dead?" JC repeated.

"Bob 'Badass' Andrews, for one," Tommy told him.

"He didn't like Marv?" JC asked.

"That's not a guy that I would want mad at me," Bip added.

"No," Tommy said. "Badass did not like Marv. Badass lost a lot of money in Marv's crypto scheme. I wasn't surprised when Badass showed up in Placer. I'm just surprised that Marv lived that long."

"You think Badass killed Marv?" JC asked.

"I don't know," Tommy said. "I'm probably wagging my tongue too much. I just know that Bob 'Badass' Andrews lost a considerable amount of money in the scheme that Marv was prosecuted for. I don't know if Badass got his money back or not. But I found it quite a coincidence when

Badass showed up in town. And I didn't get the feeling that Marv was too happy to see him."

"You and Marv didn't seem to get along," JC told Tommy.

"No, I didn't approve of what Marv pulled on his customers," Tommy said. "I know a little something about cryptocurrency. Marv was a crook. And he knew that I knew he was a crook."

"Badass, huh?" JC said, making a mental note of it.

JC and Robin said that it was time to go. Since they had the weekend off, they thought they would do a little skiing. Bip and Sunny said they would join them. Tommy said that he had things to do around the house.

"So, when am I required to call you Scooter again?" JC asked Tommy. "As soon as I walk out of your house?"

"As soon as you cross the threshold of my castle," Tommy said, slapping a friendly hand on his shoulder.

Giving their thanks, Scooter's four guests climbed into their cars and headed down the mountain. The sun was bright, almost blinding as they navigated the road. And there was fresh snow.

But they would get a late start. They could already see skiers and snowboarders on runs that passed Scooter's home and the other luxurious houses lining the slopes of The Craters.

"Do you think Badass killed Marv?" Robin asked JC.

"Gee, murdering someone for money. Has that ever been a motive?" JC asked sarcastically. "If you could get rid of love and money, there wouldn't be any murder."

"So, what now?" Robin inquired.

"Right now, it's Saturday," JC said. "We go skiing and think about how we can put Badass to the test, without him getting mad and killing us too."

Back at the Clark Hotel, the four of them collected their gear and headed for the ski mountain.

Walking to the lift line, they saw Sheriff Brush. He was puffing some, walking from the parking lot, which was down a hill from the lodge. Skiers and snowboarders rationalized the heavy breathing that hill brought on. They felt the climb got their heart rate going for the exercise awaiting them. Locals called the incline "The Cardiac Kickstart."

But the sheriff had a smile on his face, despite his panting. His wife, Mercy, was at his side, clutching his arm and wearing an even bigger smile.

"He's got his woman back," Bip said.

"His and his alone," JC added.

"It makes you wonder," Bip stated.

"Would he do it?" Robin asked. "Would he kill Marv?"

"Would you?" Bip asked.

"I wouldn't let it get that far," Robin told him.

"Sometimes, you find things before you know they are missing," Sunny reasoned.

"I'm sure you just said something really smart with that Ute head of yours," Bip said to her with a bit of a laugh. "But what does that mean to us white savages?"

"She probably wandered away without him noticing," Sunny said. "And by the time the sheriff realized it, he had a choice to make. He had to live with the situation or forfeit the woman he loved."

"Maybe he tried his best to live with it," Bip supposed. "But one day, he just snapped."

"We've seen people snap before," JC agreed. "It only takes an instant."

"The sheriff sure looks happy," Bip said.

"Happy," JC agreed.

It was the usual circus atmosphere of a Saturday at a ski resort. There was a long line at the base lifts. But once skiers got up the mountain, the smart ones didn't return to the base until the end of their day. Lines at the other lifts, further up the mountain, would be shorter.

The sun reflected off the frost on the trees as they rode the chairlift. It was a bright day with few clouds in the sky. A skier riding with them on their chair was ecstatic over the snow and the sun. He said he was from New Hampshire. He came on a trip with the Blizzard Ski Club.

"We got a great deal," the Blizzard Ski Club member said. "Discount room, discount lift tickets, and they threw in a couple of cocktail parties for us."

"It's the only way to go, man," Bip said. "You'll go broke if you ski for full price."

"Next year, we're coming back to Colorado," the man said. "We're going to Minnie's Gap."

"That's where we met!" Sunny told the visitor as she and Bip exchanged an affectionate gaze.

At the top of the lift, they decided to ski a couple of cruisers to another lift. The sign pointed toward "Laura's Love" and "Handsome Peter." From there, the four of them could catch a lift headed up onto the ridge. There was a steep run called "The Ditch" that they wanted to try.

The chairlift to the top was a six-pack, built to carry six skiers. One more skier joined them, from the "singles" line.

"Ready to rip? Where are we going?"

They turned to the enthusiastic skier who had joined them. It was Trigger Fischer. They welcomed him aboard and he decided to join them on The Ditch run.

Robin was sitting next to Trigger on the chair. When JC and Bip turned their attention to a gifted snowboarder they saw carving turns below them, Robin turned her attention to Trigger.

"So, what guy did Loretta Sopris think was hotter than you?" she asked. "You said she dumped you for someone else."

"Well, I'm pretty competitive in the 'hot guy' contest," Trigger laughed. "But this wasn't a fair fight."

"Was he rich too?" Robin laughed.

"That wouldn't be a fair fight either," Trigger laughed. "No, I lost to someone on the other team."

Robin gave him a quizzical look.

"Another woman," he finally said. "She fell in love with a woman. I liked Loretta. When she explained things to me, we remained friends."

"Did she tell you who the woman was?" Robin asked.

"She did," he admitted. "But I'm not sure I should say. She isn't 'out,' you know? People don't know she likes other women."

"So, she's local?" Robin deduced. "She's here in Cameron County?"

"She is," Trigger told her. "That's why I don't want to be the one who 'outs' her."

"I understand," Robin said, though disappointed. "You won't just tell me?"

"A television reporter?" Trigger laughed. "Yeah, who could you possibly tell? No, I'm sorry."

The run down The Ditch was steep and harrowing. Trigger took a line that appeared to follow gravity. JC tried to emulate him, but his survival instinct caused him to throw some more turns.

At the chairlift, Trigger bade them farewell.

"I've got to go make a living," he said.

He gave a nod to Robin and then introduced himself to a family of four. He asked them if they wanted to take a run together. First, the dad wanted a group photo. Bip took the picture with their camera so Trigger and all four family members could be in it.

Heading back up the six-pack, JC and his friends were joined on the lift by a coach for the mountain's junior race team.

"I've got the small ones," she said. She pointed at the bright pink helmet she wore with a red light on top.

"Like a police officer," she said. "I need to make it easy for them to find me."

"Are they any good at racing, at that age?" Robin asked.

"Some of them are," the coach responded. "But they have a limited attention span. I know they're bored with running gates when they start dropping skis off of the chairlift."

"They drop their skis off the chairlift?" JC asked.

"Only when they're about twenty feet above the ground. It's never anywhere treacherous," the coach laughs. "It's a scam. At the top of the lift, they tell me they dropped a ski. Usually, the friend with them on the chair has also dropped a ski."

"Both dropped a ski?" Robin asked.

"Right," the coach confirmed. "So, I have to lead the other little racers to the race course and tell the two con artists to climb down, get their skis and then catch up with us. But that gives the little schemers a chance to do some free skiing before they return to join the group practicing in the gates. I'll see them skiing through the trees and doing jumps. I guess they think they're fooling me, but they're not."

"Don't the other little racers figure this out and do the same thing?" Robin asked.

"Oh my, yes!" the coach laughed. "Sometimes, after I see one ski drop, about ten more fall. It starts raining skis. That's when I tell them that we're going to take the rest of the afternoon off and go ski through the trees and do jumps and let them behave like children."

33

Horace pumped his legs and arms as he ran across the ice. His heart was beating so hard, he felt his ears throb. The cold air burned as he inhaled.

He kept an eye on the surface under his feet. Sometimes he found traction and sometimes he found himself sliding.

He looked over his shoulder as he ran. Monk was still there.

The chase had started on terra firma covered by a crusty surface of snow. Monk had spotted Horace by the dam at Joe Wright Reservoir.

But Horace took off, racing along the shoreline and forcing Monk to abandon his patrol car.

Then Horace made a dash onto the thick ice. The pursuit took a comical turn, the two men slipping and barely keeping their balance until they found their footing.

As he ran, it actually occurred to Horace that there were thousands of lake trout, cutthroat trout, graylings and other fish beneath the ice. He wondered if they could hear his footfalls. He wondered if he was disturbing them, or if fish ignored what people were doing on top of the ice like people ignore the rumble of a train after living next to the tracks for a while.

"Fuck!" Horace finally shouted and stopped running. He slid to a stop. He was panting. He bent at the waist and leaned on his knees with his hands. His heart was beating so hard, he thought it might tear through his shirt. He gasped for air as Monk approached.

"What do you eat for lunch?" Horace said, still breathing hard. "Nitroglycerin?"

Deputy Monk walked the last few steps as he reached Horace and gently slapped him on the back, like he was tagging him. He knew Horace wasn't going anywhere.

"I'm fucked, man," Horace said, still sucking in cold air. "What did I do now?"

"You nearly gave a law officer a heart attack, for one thing," Monk told him. His hands were on his hips. The deputy was concentrating on replenishing his oxygen supply.

"I don't want to go to prison, man," Horace said. Panic was surfacing in the pattern of his panting. "I've been counting. That 'three strikes and you're out' thing can send you to jail for a long time. I don't think I can be arrested again, Monk."

Horace considered running away again. Monk sensed it and grabbed the back of Horace's jacket.

"I can't go to jail for like three years, Monk!" Horace shouted, as he got his breath back. "I don't care about summer, but I'd miss ski season!"

Horace's eyes began to shift rapidly. Monk worried that Horace was under the influence of drugs. He was afraid Horace was about to do something stupid, even for Horace.

"Just chill out, Horace," Monk said in a firm voice. "Just relax."

"I can't man," Horace pleaded. "You've got to let me go! I don't even know what I did. I can't even tell anymore. I'm sorry. I won't do it again, Monk."

Horace began to walk in a circle. His pace began to pick up. Monk was afraid his prisoner was going to take off.

Monk looked around. They were in the middle of a frozen lake. All spring, summer and fall, it would be dotted with rowboats and canoes carrying fishermen. Elk and moose would come up from lower elevations to graze on the unpopulated south side of the reservoir. Right now, the closest humans were ice fishers. And they were far away.

But there was an unattended ice fishing shack with a bench outside. Monk directed his panting captive in that direction, and they sat on the bench.

Monk pulled a small tin box out of a pocket in his jacket. The tin said "Altoids." He carried it for just this kind of occasion. Some offenders, facing arrest, found it to be just the thing to mellow them out.

"Take one," Monk said as he opened the can. It was intended to hold breath mints. The deputy extended it to within Horace's viewpoint. Horace looked up at the deputy, disbelieving.

"Take one," Monk repeated.

Horace pulled one marijuana cigarette out of the tin. Monk extended a hand that held a lighter.

"Are you going to arrest me for this now?" Horace asked as he took his first puff.

"No," Monk said. "But when you calm down, I have some questions."

Horace offered the deputy a toke on the joint.

"I'm on duty," Monk said, refusing the offer.

"This stays between us, right?" Monk asked, nodding toward the joint.

"Yeah, man. We're cool," Horace told him. The pot was having the desired effect on Horace. Monk could see his suspect relax. The panic was gone.

"I have some questions, Horace," Deputy Monk said.

"Okay," Horace said, paying more attention to his grass than his captor.

"Where did you get that watch?" Monk asked.

"Sweet, right?" Horace said, looking at the rose-gold watch with the vintage leather strap on his wrist.

"Pretty impressive," Monk agreed. "Where did you get it?"

"I found it," Horace responded and took another hit.

"Did you find it on Mad Marv's wrist?" the deputy inquired.

"Who?" Horace asked, looking at Monk for a moment. "Marv? No, I found it while I was skiing."

"Where did you find it?" Monk asked, already exhausted by hundreds of unlikely stories he had been told by criminal suspects.

"I was skiing, like I said," Horace stated. "It was by the side of the trail at The Craters."

"You don't like to ski at The Craters, Horace," Monk reminded him. "You only ski in the backcountry. It's some sort of political statement on your part."

"That's true," Horace agreed, taking a hit. "But Trigger and I agreed to take some runs together that day. I like skiing with Trigger because it's like following a Ferrari at Daytona. You do everything you can to hang on, just to keep him on this side of the horizon."

"And you skied past a watch store?" Deputy Monk asked. "Was it next to the waffle hut?"

"No, man. Listen to me," Horace said. "I was skiing on Heart Attack. I saw this glint, this reflection, in the rocks. But it was right by the snow. So, I skied over to it. I could see it was the face of a watch. It was a little scratched up, but I could always use a watch. So, I took off my skis, walked about ten feet into the rocks and picked it up. I didn't see anyone around who was looking for it, so I put it on. Nice, huh?"

Horace rolled up his sleeve to show the deputy the watch with the leather strap.

Monk took a close look. He saw spots on the crystal and more spots on the leather band. It could be blood.

"Was Marv wearing the watch at the time you found it?" Monk asked.

"No, man. It was just the watch," Horace replied.

"Do you know how much that watch costs, Horace?" the law officer said. "You found it? Like someone dropped it and didn't bother to come look for it, because it only costs eighteen thousand dollars?"

"Seriously?" Horace said and then whistled. He looked the watch over. "Eighteen-K? I could live two years on

CARPE Ski 'em: a Murder on Skis Mystery

eighteen-K. And he just wants to know what time it is?" Then Horace took another hit.

"He doesn't want to know what time it is, Horace," Monk said with a bit more weight behind his voice. "Because he's dead. He was murdered. And you're wearing his watch."

Horace looked at the watch and then looked at Monk. Then he took another hit, still looking at Deputy Monk.

"Oh shit," Horace said. "You think I killed him, don't you?"

"People have killed for less than eighteen thousand dollars, Horace," Monk said. He advanced on Horace with a pair of handcuffs.

"What do I do with this?" Horace asked, holding up the joint.

"Put it in your mouth," Monk said. Horace believed that to be a proper solution. He put the joint between his lips and placed both hands behind his back. Monk closed the handcuffs around Horace's wrists and read him his rights.

When they walked back to Monk's patrol car, they both stopped and admired the scenery. The mountains towered over them. Snow covered some, and old dark volcanic rock was exposed on others.

"Take one more hit," Monk said.

Horace obliged and Monk pinched the joint between his fingers and tossed it on the road, stamping it out with the sole of his boot.

"We ain't starting no forest fires," Horace said as he looked at the extinguished reefer.

Driving up Highway 14 toward Placer, Monk called Special Investigator Steve Trujillo.

"I've got Horace Emerson in the backseat of my patrol car, Detective," Monk said. "You're going to want to hear this."

"Why did you start chasing me?" Horace asked Monk from the backseat of the patrol car when the deputy ended his call.

"Because I saw the watch," the deputy told him.

"Why didn't you just ask me where I got it?" Horace asked.

"I did, Horace. That's exactly what I did," Monk informed him. "And you looked at me like a bull that just got castrated and took off."

"How did I get here?" Horace asked, looking out the car window as they pulled away from the boat launch for the reservoir.

"You tell me," Monk said. "You got a good jump on me. So, I got in my patrol car, and I spent the next hour looking for you. I saw you on the shore and you decided to enroll me in an aerobics class."

"You're in good shape," Horace told the deputy.

"So are you," Monk responded.

Horace Emerson was booked and fingerprinted and placed in one of the cells in the small county jail. He was charged with felony theft and obstructing a peace officer.

"He smells like weed," Special Investigator Trujillo told Monk. The two of them sat in the dingy special investigator's office.

"Yeah," Deputy Monk said as he framed his lie. "It took me an hour to find him after he ran. He must have stopped for a joint."

"You smell a little like weed too," Trujillo told Monk.

"You know weed," the deputy responded. "The stink sticks to everything."

"So, you think Horace killed Henry Marvin?" Trujillo asked.

"I think he was wearing Marvin's eighteen-thousand-dollar watch," Monk told the detective.

"Wouldn't he try to fence it?" Trujillo asked. "If he went through all that trouble to get it, what hippie living in a rental apartment would want to wear a watch like that instead of selling it?"

Monk thought the detective's logic made a lot of sense.

"So, you think he's telling the truth?" Deputy Monk asked the special investigator.

"I'm more asking than telling," the special investigator said. "Could he be telling the truth?"

"Most people who say they found something valuable belonging to a murder victim are lying," Deputy Monk responded.

"True," Trujillo said, and then scrubbed his chin as he thought. "Those rocks where Horace says he found the watch are below the opening in that old mine, aren't they?"

"They are," Monk agreed.

"And our murder victim, Mr. Marvin, had his hand cut off?" Detective Trujillo continued.

"So, the watch fell off Marv's wrist when his hand was cut off?" Monk asked. "And it bounced down the rocks until it landed by the ski slope?"

"Either that, or Horace murdered him," Trujillo said.

34

Indian fights, gunfights and gold miners had all come before them. JC, Robin, Bip and Sunny drove down the path along the Cache La Poudre River toward Fort Collins. They had been preceded by an exciting slice of the old Wild West.

"Are we going to stop at Mishawaka Inn?" Robin asked. "Isn't Kat performing there tonight?"

"Let's have dinner there and say hi to her," JC agreed.

"And why are we going back to Fort Collins?" Bip asked as he drove.

"Loretta Sopris," Robin told him. "Trigger is certain that Loretta had an affair with a woman. No one else around

Placer is a likely suspect. And that brings me back to Johanna Forbes."

JC's phone rang. He recognized the number and picked it up; confident he knew the topic of the discussion.

"We are reaching that point in our lives again, JC," said Rocky Bauman, the assignment editor. "This is getting to be a very expensive story you're telling our audience. It's a very good one, but hotel rooms and restaurants are expensive."

"I know, Rocky. I feel terrible about it," JC said, thinking that he'd try a different tactic, feigned guilt. And it worked momentarily. Rocky was silent for a moment.

"We've got to at least bring Robin home," Rocky said. "Is she getting anywhere with the Loretta Sopris story?"

"Rocky," JC said. "She is about to break it wide open. If we don't tell it, someone else will. The dogs are nipping at our heels. Do you want this story showing up on someone else's television channel?"

JC relied on Rocky's competitive nature. There was, in fact, no other television newsroom even showing interest in the suicide of Loretta Sopris. But JC had a feeling, and so did Robin.

"Success is for those who don't quit," JC told Rocky. It sounded a bit like a pep talk. It was met with more silence.

"JC," Rocky finally said. "I know there aren't any other TV stations up in Cameron County wondering how Loretta Sopris died. What makes you think there's anything more to learn?"

"You don't pay me to be stupid, Rocky," JC replied.

"No, we don't," Rocky acknowledged with resignation. "Remember that."

"You took me home to your place," the singer crooned into the microphone. "I punched you in the face."

A well-behaved crowd politely listened to the lyrics, accompanied by an acoustic guitar.

"You asked me my name; I thought that was lame."

Kat Martinez, the singer-songwriter who captured audiences across the Rocky Mountains with her raunchy, loud lyrics and combative attitude, was purring like a country music singer. She even sang with a bit of a twang.

"Don't I recognize this song?" Bip whispered to JC.

"Yeah, but the last time you heard it was at a hundred and sixty decibels, like a jet engine," JC told him. "And I think she was throwing beer bottles at her fans."

At the end of the song, the crowd erupted in applause. They stood and whistled.

The Mishawaka Inn was a landmark in Poudre Canyon for those who made the trek up from Fort Collins. Jim Morrison and The Doors had once played there.

It was a rustic tavern and restaurant that had been there for a century. It squeezed into a narrow portion of the canyon, with a porch that hung over the Poudre River.

The indoor concert venue, with a stage, was built of old dark wood and it was cavernous. It was large enough to fit tables for two-hundred people. When bands picked up the pace, like Commander Cody or a bluegrass band with a banjo player in a leopard-skin mini-skirt, tables got pushed aside and the crowd displayed a raucous brand of dancing.

But Kat, who could be fierce, was unusually tame tonight.

"Grab a tip and bite your server," Kat said sweetly into the microphone. "I'll be back soon and play a second set for you."

Kat stood up from the chair where she had been playing her guitar and walked down a set of stairs, stage right. She headed straight toward JC. This time, he got a kiss on the cheek.

"That sounded great," JC told her. "But what happened to Kat, the woman who wants to take a bite out of a beer bottle and spit the glass at her audience?"

"They love it when I do that," she told him. "This is my acoustic set. Cute, isn't it? Same songs, only with some 'come to Jesus' country influence. I think it fits the venue."

Kat still wore the clothing her audience expected. She had on her familiar bare-midriff pink tee-shirt that said "Boi Toy" on it and very short blue jean cut offs. But her hair was platinum blonde instead of brunette. JC wondered if it was a wig or if Kat dyed it.

Kat's audience used to be largely female. But Kat, even though her music lyrics still leaned toward the lesbian way of seeing things, had found a growing audience from all walks of life.

A server came and took the dinner order from JC and his crew. They started with an appetizer of Rocky Mountain oysters. JC and Robin decided to split a Mish Burrito for dinner. Bip and Sunny shared a burger called the Mish Monster.

"What, are you sleeping with twins?" Kat asked JC as she looked over Robin. "Does Shara know about this?"

JC's former girlfriend, Shara, was also a radiant redhead. Kat knew Shara and they got along very well.

"Robin and I are engaged," JC told Kat. "I think I told you that."

"That doesn't really address if you're sleeping with both of them," Kat said in her way. "It just tells me you're marrying one of them. Where's Shara?"

"She's in prison," JC told her.

"I knew I liked that girl," Kat said with a corrupt smile.

The server brought a round of beer, a couple of New Belgium's Fat Tire and a pair of Odell's Peach Rambler. Both beers were brewed in Fort Collins.

"So, what are you doing after the show?" Kat asked. "Maybe I want to sleep with her," she said, looking at Robin.

They all laughed. JC was fairly confident that Kat was only joking.

"We have to get down to Fort Collins," he told the musician. "We have work to do."

"Speaking of which," Kat said, lighting a cigarette. "Do you know anything about that suicide up at The Craters? She was a friend of mine."

"I don't think you can smoke here," JC said. He was quite certain that Kat was aware of that. She inhaled the smoke.

"I'm pretty sure I just proved that I can," Kat told him with a smile.

"Wait," Robin said. "You knew Loretta Sopris?"

Kat looked at Robin and took one last drag on her cigarette and put it out as a member of the serving staff approached to enforce the "No Smoking" edict.

"She really is hot, JC," Kat said, not taking her eyes off of Robin. "You must be rich. Why else would these hot women waste their time with you?"

"Wait," Robin repeated. "And thank you, by the way. You knew Loretta Sopris?"

"I did, Carrot Top," Kat said. "She was older than I was, but she was really pretty. She was my first."

"First what?" Robin asked. Kat looked at the other faces at the table.

"First woman, honey," Kat told her. "She took my hand and showed me around the neighborhood, if you know what I mean."

"Oh," Robin said. Sunny sat quietly at the table. She hadn't moved, other than to take Bip's hand under the table.

"Any idea why she'd kill herself?" JC asked.

"I hadn't seen her in a while," Kat said. "But it seemed like she had a bleeding heart."

"How do you mean?" Robin asked.

"She took breakups pretty hard," Kat told her. "Loretta told me about a woman she had a long affair with when she was in college. They were both in college."

"At Colorado State, in Fort Collins?" Robin asked.

"Yeah, I guess that's right," Kat responded. "She still considered this woman the love of her life. But she dumped Loretta when they finished school. I don't think they'd even seen each other since then."

"Do you remember her name?" Robin asked with urgency.

"No," Kat replied. "She told me this years ago."

"Does 'Johanna' ring a bell?" Robin asked.

"I don't know," Kat said. "I don't remember. I just remember how crushed she said she was when the other woman broke up with her."

"I think it's time, hon," a woman said over Kat's shoulder. JC recognized her as the drummer of the band, Kat's girlfriend with a stage name of Sojourner The Truth.

"Latoya, right?" JC used her real name. The Black woman smiled back, appreciating the recognition.

"Gotta go," Latoya said.

Kat got up and looked at the stage. Then, she looked back at Robin.

"Make him pamper you. Make him buy you things," Kat told her. "One look at you and I knew he was terrified of letting you get away."

"Pampered sounds nice," Robin said, brushing against JC.

"When did you know he loved you?" Kat asked, still not taking her eyes off Robin.

"When he nearly got me killed, a couple of years ago," Robin told her.

"Yeah," Kat said, nodding her head and looking at JC. "That is a sure sign, with him."

Kat walked toward the stage and waved her fingers over her shoulder, saying goodbye.

"I want her to play at our wedding," Robin said. "I really like her."

"She is one of a kind," JC agreed.

Their dinner came. They ate as they enjoyed Kat's second acoustic set. Then they climbed into the news car and continued down Poudre Canyon toward Fort Collins.

It was dark. There wasn't much of a moon and their headlights often crawled across the hard rock canyon wall, only feet away.

"How coincidental is it that Kat knew Loretta?" Bip asked as he drove.

"Well, look at Kat," Robin said. "She's gorgeous. I would guess she has a long waiting list."

"I learned a lot," Sunny said. It was the first time she had spoken in an hour. "I come from a small town. There's no one there like Kat."

"Now you live in a big town," JC said with a smile. "There's no one like Kat there either."

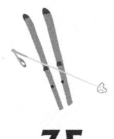

35

"I have to figure this thing out," Robin told JC. "Otherwise, management is going to bring me home."

They were just waking up at the Armstrong Hotel in Fort Collins. After their arrival last night, they'd returned to Ace Gillett's. But the bartender, Bobby, had the night off. They were told he'd be in the next day.

"We're close, though," Robin said. "It's here."

"I think you're right," JC responded.

They listened to the city awaken. Cars drove over the railroad tracks on South Mason. They sounded like horse hooves.

Street sweepers, garbage pickup, snow shoveling, car horns, a dog barking. They were all sounds of a city preparing for another day.

They got dressed and walked down to The Rainbow on West Laurel Street. It was a breakfast place across from the CSU campus. There was a sign hanging in the corner saying, "Serving Hippies Since Ford was President."

They left the car for Bip and Sunny, who said that they'd meet them later in time to knock on Johanna Forbes' door. It was almost that time. JC paid the check, and they walked through a residential neighborhood on Remington Street to Forbes' house.

"No, it wasn't Friday night," Johanna Forbes told them after inviting them all inside and offering coffee. "I went up to Cheyenne for the weekend. Loretta and I went out to Ace Gillett's on the Wednesday night before that. We nibbled on some hors d'oeuvres and had a couple of drinks and then went home. She said that a friend was coming to see her that weekend."

"Did she say who the friend was?" Robin asked.

"She didn't say, and I didn't ask," Johanna replied. "I thought she had made it clear in the past that if she didn't offer the information, I wasn't expected to pry."

"Can I ask you something?" Robin asked in an apologetic tone. "Were you and Loretta a couple?"

"No," Johanna said with a giggle. "That's not what I'm looking for."

"Do you think that's what Loretta was looking for?" Robin pursued.

"I don't think so," Johanna said with uncertainty. "But I'm not really sure, now that you asked."

"And you were not out with her on that Friday night, the night before she died?" JC repeated, just to be sure.

"Not me," Johanna told them. "I was up in Cheyenne at the Outlaw Saloon. They had a good band, good beer and some good-looking cowboys."

"May I impose," JC asked. "We're not having much luck with that picture of Loretta you gave us. How about I return it to you and let me pick out another?"

Johanna was agreeable and brought out a photo album. JC looked over the pictures and picked out one of Loretta and Johanna, standing next to each other.

"That was a fun day," Johanna told them. "We went cliff jumping up at Horsetooth Reservoir.

"I remember doing the very same thing when I was in college here," JC smiled.

He slipped the photograph into his pocket and returned the picture Johanna had loaned them before.

Upon their departure, JC walked next door and again peered through the window into the house that Loretta Sopris had rented.

"I hear they have a new renter," Johanna said, standing on the stoop to her own rented house. "I guess they're moving in next week."

Nothing had changed inside Loretta's home. It was the same as when JC peeked through the window last time. The walls and the floor were bare. It looked thoroughly scrubbed and ready for its next occupant.

"Were you home Thursday?" JC asked Johanna Forbes.

"Not really," she replied. "I left for Cheyenne that morning. Thursday morning."

Bip had brought the car to Johanna's. But driving down East Mountain Avenue, away from Johanna's house, JC realized they were only a few blocks from the public library.

"Let's make a stop there before heading downtown," JC said. "I've got a thought."

They turned down Mathews Street and drove through a neighborhood that was mostly residential. They passed a collection of old log cabins that were historic to the area. The structures had been re-located to the lawn of the old library, now a museum. Behind it was the new library.

Walking inside the new building, JC asked for directions to the periodicals section. There, he found the newspaper he was looking for and paid to have the front page copied. He folded the piece of copy paper and slipped it into a pocket.

"It feels like it's thirty degrees warmer here than it is up on Cameron Pass," Bip remarked as he slipped off his coat before climbing back into the car. They had dropped six thousand feet in elevation since leaving the ski resort.

The lunch rush had ended for the bars and restaurants in downtown Fort Collins. They drove to the Armstrong Hotel and parked in back. They walked around to the front of the block and down an outside set of stairs into Ace Gillett's.

They wanted to speak to Bobby, the bartender who remembered seeing Loretta Sopris on Friday night.

They stopped, waiting for their eyes to adjust to the low light.

"Hey, how's it going?" Bobby said in a jovial manner.

"You remember us?" JC asked. "I was in a couple of weeks ago, asking about Loretta Sopris."

"Yeah, I remember you," the bartender smiled. JC couldn't tell if the bartender really remembered him or if he told that to every paying customer who walked through the door.

"Loretta Sopris," the bartender said, leaning both hands on the bar in front of them. He moved his eyes toward Robin and held his gaze until it would be impolite. He turned his attention to JC. "That was a shame. You're the first one who told me she was dead."

JC pulled a picture out of his pocket and placed it on the bar.

"Is this the woman you saw with Loretta that night?" Robin asked.

"That's her," the bartender said, looking down at the picture. "Wednesday night. They've been in here together before. That's why I recognize her."

It was the photograph of Loretta with Johanna at Horsetooth Reservoir.

"What about Friday night?" Robin asked.

The bartender took a closer look at the photograph.

"Friday night? Nope," he said. "Loretta was in here with a different woman on Friday night. I remember because I didn't recognize her."

JC reached into the pocket of his jacket and pulled out a folded piece of paper. Unfolding it, he placed that on the bar.

"Could this be the woman who was with Loretta Friday night?" JC asked.

The man gave it a long look. The image was grainy. He picked it up to hold it closer.

"I'm pretty sure that's her," he said, looking up at them. "She wasn't wearing handcuffs, but that sure looks like her."

It was a picture of Charlie Washburn. It was the photograph that JC had copied from the newspaper at the public library. It was taken the day Charlie was walked into the Cameron County courthouse for her arraignment.

"Thanks," said JC and Robin.

They gathered up the picture and the newspaper copy and walked up the stairs into the sunshine.

It only took minutes to drive back up Mountain Avenue to Johanna Forbes' house.

She was surprised when she opened the door and saw them again. JC pulled out the newspaper photo.

"Have you ever seen her before?" JC asked.

Johanna took the photo in her hands and stared at it.

"I've seen her," Johanna said. "I saw her with Loretta. I was looking out my window and I saw her at the door once. I don't know who she is. Like I said, Loretta would tell you something if she wanted you to know."

"Do you rent your house from the same landlord that Loretta rented hers from?" JC asked.

"Yes. She's an older woman. She's nice. She tries to keep things repaired. Do you want her phone number?" Johanna asked. JC was eager to get it.

"Tell her that I want a nice neighbor, like Loretta," Johanna said after she wrote down the number for him.

Bip was outside, shooting video of the former house of Loretta Sopris. JC walked along the side of the house, glancing into the windows. He saw two bedrooms.

In the back, there was a carport and a window looking into the kitchen. He eyed some cleaning supplies, neatly lined up along the back wall of the home. He asked Bip to take pictures of the cleaning supplies too.

After recording his images of the home, Bip opened the doors to the news car to let it air out. The winter sun had heated up the interior. JC made a phone call as he stood by the curb.

A woman answered the number that Johanna Forbes had given to JC.

"Did you see anything out of the ordinary when you were straightening up, after Loretta passed away?" JC asked, following the exchange of pleasantries.

"No," the woman answered. "You see a little bit of everything when you're a landlord. But I can't remember anything unusual."

"Did you meet any of her friends?" he asked.

"No, I don't pry into their lives," she said. "As long as they respect my property, I leave them be. She was a very good tenant."

"She always paid her rent on time?" JC asked, not certain what he was fishing for.

"Oh yes," the woman said. "In fact, when I came to inspect the property after poor Loretta passed away, there was nothing really for me to do. It looked like she had been on her hands and knees scrubbing the floors and walls. I've never seen them so clean!"

"Was she planning to move out?" JC asked.

"No," the woman said. "At least, she didn't tell me she was moving."

JC had called Robin over by that time and put the woman on speakerphone.

"Are those your cleaning supplies on the back porch of Loretta's rental?" JC asked.

"No, they're not mine," the landlord answered. "I saw them too. Loretta must have put them there. I don't clean until a tenant moves out. As I said, Loretta never told me anything about moving out."

"So, you didn't scrub the rooms inside the house?" Robin asked. "That was Loretta?"

"It must have been," she answered. "You don't find many renters like that."

Ending the phone call, JC stared into the window of the rental again. Robin did the same, standing next to him.

"Is there any evidence that John Washburn was killed inside his home in Placer?" Robin asked.

"No," JC said. "There isn't."

36

"You need to convince your client to speak with us," JC told the public defender. Robin was at his side in the small public defender's office in the county courthouse.

"The hell I do," said Maddie LaJeunesse. "I think we've already covered this ground. The answer is no."

"I think you'll regret it, if you don't," JC said.

"Is that a threat?" Maddie said in a very serious tone.

"Not at all," JC said. "But if you don't get Charlie to talk to us, we'll just go straight to the police. And then you'll learn what their case against your client is when *they* want to tell it. And it will only be *what* they want to tell the public, until it's too late."

JC, Robin and the others had rushed back to Cameron County from Fort Collins before their newsroom could order Robin to return to Denver. The order would probably still come, but it bought the journalists time to nail down their suspicions.

"And if I let you speak with my client, you won't go to the police?" Maddie inquired.

"I didn't say that" JC responded. "I'm going to the police, whether or not you let us talk to Charlie. But this way, you'll know what you're dealing with. She's going to be criminally charged. It's going to be *your* job to see that she isn't punished for *more* than what she did."

"So now you're telling me how to do my job?" the attorney asked. A small fuse was burning in LaJeunesse. And it was burning in the direction of a bigger fuse.

"When they know where to look, the sheriff is going to find John Washburn's DNA," JC told Maddie. "It may be embedded in a mop or maybe splashed on the side of a pail. But they're going to find it. Your client is going to be arrested again. And this time, it's going to stick."

"They've already scoured the Washburn house," Maddie reminded him. "They didn't find anything."

"That's because he wasn't killed there," he responded.

"And the ghost town?" she suggested.

"Manhattan? Not there either," he told her.

Maddie LaJeunesse's face soured.

"You're sure about this?" she asked, rubbing her temple.

"We're sure," Robin said. "If we're wrong, the story will fall apart, and you'll have nothing to worry about."

Maddie took a few minutes to consider their proposal. Then, she acquiesced.

The interview would take place at the Washburn home on Never Summer Street. But the attorney said there would be no camera allowed in the discussion. And Maddie would make no comment when it was over.

The public defender telephoned her client and made arrangements. Then they climbed into their cars and proceeded to Charlie's house in Placer, less than five minutes away.

The sun bounced off the snow, intensifying the glare as they walked up a shoveled walk to the house. JC spotted what might be a bald eagle spiraling above Joe Wright Reservoir.

Charlie Washburn answered the door to her home and stepped aside to let them in.

"Hello," was all she said.

She led them into the living room. It was where JC and Bip had interviewed her before her husband's body was found.

Charlie sat on one end of a sofa. Her attorney sat on the other end. Robin took a seat in a chair next to the sofa and JC leaned on the side of a sturdy desk.

"Just hear them out," Maddie told her client. "Then decide if you have anything to say."

The attorney explained to her client that she was free to speak, but she didn't have to say anything.

"These TV reporters seem to think they know something," Maddie said. Her version of the arrangement didn't show much admiration for the fourth estate.

"Thank you for seeing us, Charlie," Robin said. "We know what happened, and we're going to tell the sheriff what happened. But we don't think it's all your fault, and we don't want to talk to the sheriff until we have a chance to speak with you."

Robin proceeded to tell Charlie what they knew and how they had come to know it. Charlie, during the telling, sometimes looked at Robin and sometimes allowed her eyes to wander across the room to a window. The sun was shining through the lace curtains.

Sometimes, as Robin described their discovery, Charlie's eyes seemed to linger on pictures and pieces of furniture in the room. Sometimes, she would tear up.

JC recognized the signs as surrender. He wondered if Charlie was lamenting that she would soon have to leave this home and her furnishings behind.

Robin finished her version of their findings. In silence, she looked to Charlie for her response.

There was none.

Maddie also looked at her client, waiting to see if Charlie wanted to respond. When it became apparent that the widow would maintain her silence, the public defender leaned forward on the sofa, preparing to get up and end the gathering.

"On Friday," Charlie suddenly said in a soft voice, "Loretta was scheduled to be in Sun Valley for a business conference. It was for accountants."

Maddie leaned back in the sofa, paying careful attention to every word that came from her client's mouth.

JC and Robin didn't move. They wanted to do nothing to disrupt Charlie's train of thought.

"I came down to Fort Collins on Thursday," Charlie continued. "We had two seats on a flight to Sun Valley early Friday morning. We were going to use the trip as a long weekend away together. We were both very excited."

She spoke as though she were describing a dream. She rarely made eye contact with the others.

"We were in bed together, sleeping at Loretta's house, when John showed up," she said. "It was Thursday evening. It was dark outside. He pounded on the door and woke us up. He screamed my name. We got up and opened the door to let him in.

"He told us that he had looked in the window. He had seen us in each other's arms. He was so angry. Maybe he had suspected for a while. Looking back on the past two years that Loretta and I had been together, John and I had drifted apart. We were friends, but we were not lovers.

"John began to cry, and I went to him," Charlie said. "But he became furious. He pushed me away. But then he came at me and grabbed my arms. I told him that he was hurting me. And he pushed me away. I fell against a table in the kitchen and then fell to the floor. I was hurt.

"But he stood over me. There was such anger in his eyes. He raised his hand and balled it into a fist. I knew he was going to hit me. I covered my face and closed my eyes. But he didn't hit me. I waited, but he didn't hit me.

"I opened my eyes, and I saw John. His face looked like he was in agony. He just hovered over me for a second. He looked at me. And then he fell on the floor next to me. A knife was in his back.

"It was clear what had happened," Charlie told them. "I looked at Loretta, who had a horrified look and covered her face with her hands. She had stabbed John to prevent him from hitting me. She did it for me."

JC and Robin continued to watch Charlie. A long silence followed. They feared that she had said all that she was going to say. Instead, she abandoned any further resistance.

"We wrapped John's body up in a rug that I had covering the floor, and we came up with a plan," Charlie told them.

"Charlie," Maddie said abruptly. "You don't have to say anything more. In fact, I'd advise against it."

"It's okay, Maddie," Charlie replied. "It's going to come out anyway."

The defense attorney stared at her client but then resigned herself to what was probably inevitable.

"I wanted to call the police," Charlie said. "But Loretta didn't want to. And she stopped John to save me. I couldn't betray her. So, we devised a plan.

"I drove John's car back up Poudre Canyon, with John wrapped in a rug in the back of the car. We reasoned that there would be nothing unusual if police found my DNA in John's car. Loretta stayed behind to clean up her house. She wanted to remove the blood and any sign that John had ever been there.

"I turned off Highway 14 in Rustic and drove up Red Feather Lakes Road," Charlie stated. "I just wanted to get off the beaten path. I thought of the ghost town. He was still inside the rug when I stopped the car and dragged him to the spot where they found him. But I took the rug with me because I didn't want them to track it to Loretta's house. I drove John's Citroën to Idaho. It took all night. I dumped Loretta's rug in a dumpster, and I parked the car at the airport in Hailey. I figured that John's car would eventually be tagged as an abandoned car and towed away.

"It was a long drive," she said. "But Loretta was driving from Fort Collins in her car, after cleaning her house up. That was just as long a drive. She got to Sun Valley just in time for her breakfast meeting. She said that she was right on time.

"At the meeting, Loretta pretended that she was feeling ill," Charlie told them. "It wasn't far from the truth. She had driven eleven hours to be there. She felt and looked awful. She told the conference that she was going home. Then she picked me up at a coffee house in Hailey and we drove back to Fort Collins.

"It took us all day to get there. We had been up for more than twenty-four hours. But when we got to Fort Collins, we wanted it to seem like we'd never left. So, we got dressed up and went out for dinner. We ate at a restaurant called Ace Gillett's and made sure that we were seen. That would be our alibi.

"Finally, we returned to Loretta's house. We were too tired to reflect on the horrible thing that had happened there. She had cleaned it all up. The house smelled like ammonia. But we opened some windows and went to the bedroom and fell asleep.

"On Saturday, we drove to Placer in her car. She dropped me off a few blocks from my house and Loretta checked into Home, that nice hotel at the ski resort. We didn't want to be seen together, and we didn't want her to be seen at my house. We had kept our relationship a secret for two years. We knew that would work in our favor."

Charlie stopped talking. Maddie told her that she had said enough.

But Robin didn't think the whole story had yet been told.

"What happened to Loretta?" Robin asked in a gentle voice.

Charlie slowly turned her head to look into Robin's eyes.

"I was scared, and I was tired and I was disgusted by what we had done. I loved John. Not like I loved Loretta, but I loved him," Charlie told her.

"That night, I put on a hat and a scarf over my face and came to Loretta's room at the hotel. I told her that we shouldn't be seen together," Charlie creaked, nearly breaking into tears. It was plain to see that she was emotionally spent. "Then I said that I didn't think we should be with each other anymore. I said that seeing each other would just remind us of the terrible thing we had done."

"Nothing fixes in the memory so intensely as the wish to forget it," JC said.

"That's Montaigne," Charlie acknowledged. "John's favorite philosopher."

Charlie smiled at the reference. But then she seemed to brace herself for what she was about to say.

"Loretta was distraught," Charlie continued. "She begged me not to break up with her. She said that we could go somewhere together, that we could finally be together. She told me how hard it was when I broke up with her before. She said that she couldn't go through that again. But I said that we couldn't be together anymore. I was terribly upset and very tired. I probably would have changed my mind. But the next day..."

Charlie stopped talking. Everyone in the room knew that on the next day, Loretta Sopris threw herself off a chairlift and plunged one hundred feet to her death.

37

"Did you find bruises on her back or on her arms?" JC asked the public defender. "It would assist your claim of self-defense."

JC and Robin had just walked up to the second-floor office of Maddie LaJeunesse after telling their story to Sheriff Brush and Captain Bush.

"I didn't know to look for bruises," Maddie admitted. "Charlie wouldn't talk to me. But today, when you left her house, I asked her to let me look. If John did leave bruises when he grabbed her, they're gone. Enough time has passed."

JC looked out the lone window of the public defender's small office. Dark clouds were moving in. It looked like snow was on the way.

"What did the sheriff say?" Maddie asked.

"As you can imagine, he showed a lot of interest," JC told her. "I would guess they'll check out what you've discovered. They'll check to see if Loretta and Charlie had booked a flight to Sun Valley. They'll check to see if the bartender in Fort Collins saw them. And they'll look for John Washburn's DNA at Loretta's house in Fort Collins. Loretta was never on their radar."

"So, in other words, you gave them their case," Maddie said with some bitterness.

"They were going to figure it out anyway," Robin responded. "You are better off knowing."

"So now *you're* telling me my job?" the attorney asked her.

"No," Robin responded. "I think you believe it too."

"And we know what comes next," JC interrupted. "You're going to admit Charlie was there when John was stabbed. But you'll say that she didn't' know Loretta was going to kill him. In addition, you'll say Charlie was a victim of abuse. It's almost self-defense. If she hadn't hidden the body, she'd walk."

"I don't expect the sheriff or the district attorney to demonstrate your forgiving nature," the defense attorney stated.

"This isn't my first rodeo," JC told her. He was an experienced legal-issues reporter. "You'll be able to get manslaughter or negligent homicide. She could be out of prison in five or six years."

"Or sooner," Maddie said softly, smiling a knowing smile and organizing some things on her desk.

JC heard the brakes huff on the large television satellite truck as Jem Norvell pulled it to a stop outside the county courthouse. It was time for the journalists to prepare their story regarding the shocking facts of John Washburn's murder. They would share it with their viewers in Denver in a matter of hours.

As JC opened the door to the public defender's office, preparing to leave, Maddie LaJeunesse spoke up.

"I asked her, you know."

JC stopped and looked at her.

"I asked Charlie if she was involved with another man," Maddie informed him. "She said no. My fault, I guess, for not asking her if it was a woman. She was protecting Loretta, I think. Even after her death."

Robin's phone rang as she stood outside the courthouse after their live shot.

"You could have been more forthcoming," Robin answered into the phone.

Robin mouthed to JC that it was Agnes Mason, Loretta's sister.

"You didn't have to tell all those secrets," Agnes said angrily.

"How could we not?" Robin asked. "If you didn't want that story told, you shouldn't have asked for our help. It is why John Washburn was killed and led to the reason why your sister killed herself."

"Well, you didn't' have to say it," Agnes repeated.

"I'm sorry that you have a problem with the way your sister lived," Robin told her.

"Oh, I don't, really," Agnes said, after exhaling. "It's Daddy. He couldn't accept it. It made him so angry. It caused a major rift in our family."

"Well, I'm sorry for that," Robin said. "But we did what you asked us to do. And we don't tell half-truths."

The next day, Charlie Washburn was arrested a second time. She was accused of manslaughter in the death of her husband and remanded to jail. She was now on suicide watch.

"You live by slim margins," the assignment editor told JC over the phone. "I was about to drive up there and bring Robin home myself. But we're all pleased with how the story turned out. It was another home run by you two."

"Thanks, Rocky," JC said.

"Are you ready to come back too?" Rocky Bauman asked.

"Not while the killer of Mad Marv is loose," the reporter said. "There is still a bankable story to be told here."

"Mrs. Washburn didn't do it?" the assignment editor asked.

"Nope," JC replied.

"Who did?" Rocky inquired.

"Beats me," JC answered. "That's why I can't leave. We're not done."

"Alright," Rocky replied. "We'll keep you and Bip there. But we expect to see Robin in the newsroom tomorrow morning. Her assignment up there is over."

The snow was falling in small flakes. But it was accumulating. Perhaps an inch had collected on the sidewalks and pavement. JC, Robin, Bip and Sunny decided to dine at the Home, the expensive hotel where Loretta Sopris spent her last night on earth.

On the walk from their hotel, they heard the scraping sound of snow shovels. To business owners, it was the sound of money. There were a few thousand people in nearby hotels, restaurants and stores who gave no thought to murder or suicide or sadness.

JC and the others toasted their success as they ate dinner. Their meal reflected the ecology of Colorado. There was buffalo meat, elk and lamb and small bowls of green chili. There was trout and sweet corn.

There were peaches from Palisade, and they sipped a blue corn bourbon distilled by Feisty Spirits in Fort Collins.

Robin would be leaving in the morning. So would Sunny, who said she needed to get back to work.

"What is your game plan in the murder of Mad Marv?" Robin asked at the dinner table.

"I was hoping the special investigator would announce an arrest and we'd all drive home together," JC said with a smile. "Failing that, I'd like to talk with Horace. I've got to find out who his attorney is."

"What do you hope to get from him?" Bip asked. "You think he'll confess, like Charlie did? Do you think you've acquired new powers and people will confess their sins to you?"

"I just don't see Horace as the killing type," JC said, dismissing Bip's sarcasm.

"Did you see Loretta as the killing type?" Bip retorted.

"Good point," JC said. "My new powers do not seem to include psychic abilities to spot killers."

The snow was piling up outside. The forecast now said snow would fall all night. There was a buzz in the dining room. Most of the people eating there had gone to a great deal of trouble to be at The Craters. They were excited by the prospect of having fresh Colorado powder to ski in the morning.

JC exchanged a wave with Tommy "Scooter" Halvorson. He was sitting near the restaurant's best window. He was on a date.

"Do you think he greased a few palms to get that table?" Bip asked.

The window at Scooter's table looked out on the ski mountain. The PistenBully grooming machines were parked at the bottom, almost a standing salute to nature. The powder would be allowed to pile up unmolested.

Across the dining room, they saw Sheriff Brush with his wife, Mercy. They were both smiling, sitting close together.

"It looks like a special occasion," Robin said.

"The sheriff looks like he's getting used to having his wife back," JC said.

And at a table in a dark corner, Bob "Badass" Andrews sat alone. He worked on his dinner and occasionally raised a glass of red wine to his lips. He looked content.

"Do you want to stay for a couple of hours and ski fresh powder?" JC asked Robin with a mischievous smile.

"Rocky will take away my allowance," Robin said with dread. "He wants me there at nine a.m."

"That's not an allowance," JC pointed out. "It's a salary. And, in his words, you just hit a home run."

JC looked at the clock on his phone. He thought that he still had time to place a phone call to the jail.

"I want to schedule a talk with Horace Emerson for mid-day tomorrow," JC told the jailer over the phone. "How do I arrange that?"

"I'm advised that you have to go through his attorney," the deputy at the county jail said.

"And who is that?"

"He is being represented by the public defender's office," the jailer replied.

"And who will that attorney be?"

"Maddie LaJeunesse," the jailer informed him.

"Is she the only public defender in the county?" JC asked.

"If you hear of any others, you let me know," he was told.

JC ended the call and dialed the number for the public defender, while the others at the table worked on their dessert.

"No," was the greeting at the other end of the line.

"You don't even know what my question is," JC protested.

"You want to speak with my client, Horace Emerson," Maddie said.

"Yes," JC replied. "Lucky guess." He knew that it wasn't.

"You remember my last client?" Maddie asked JC. "The one who wouldn't talk to me?"

"Your client of only this morning?" JC asked. "Yes, I remember her."

"Well, *this* client, Mr. Emerson," Maddie said. "He won't shut up. I don't even have to ask, and he will tell me the names of all the pets he's ever had, his favorite foods and, of course, his favorite backcountry ski runs."

"That's not what I want to ask him," JC told her.

"I'm not even sure that's my concern," Maddie said. "I'm afraid that if you start him talking, he'll never stop."

"Well, does he say that he killed Mad Marv?" JC asked.

"He does not," Maddie answered. "He insists that he did not kill Mad Marv. It's nice to have a client who just comes out and says it."

38

There is a grace and rhythm that comes with skiing through a foot of Colorado snow. JC thought there was nothing else quite like the feeling. A man visiting from Mississippi watched from the base lodge. He likened the motion of powder skiing to that of a dolphin.

The Craters Ski Resort was situated in the same weather pattern as the Steamboat Ski Resort to its northwest. And The Craters enjoyed the same kind of legendary champagne powder that Steamboat was known for.

There was an enthusiastic turnout at The Craters. Long lines of skiers and snowboarders proceeded toward their chairlift.

"This is what turns people into ski bums," said the voice of a man who squeezed next to JC and Bip in the lift line. It was Trigger Fischer.

"Look at Scooter Halvorson," Trigger said. "He's a zillionaire. But he came skiing here one day and never left. Now, he's a ski bum."

"Why do you guys call him Scooter, anyway?" JC asked.

"He told us that's his name," Trigger responded, chuckling at the obvious answer.

"I thought he told me that you guys gave him that nickname," JC replied.

"Maybe we did," Trigger said agreeably. "I probably skipped class that day."

After skiing uncompromised first tracks for an hour, JC and Bip reluctantly returned to their hotel rooms and prepared for a day of work.

They reconvened in JC's hotel room. The fireplace between the living room and the bedroom burned.

"Are you going to get romantic?" Bip quipped sarcastically.

Snow continued to fall outside, piling up on the porch that overlooked the heated outdoor swimming pool.

The giggles of children could be heard. They had never gone swimming when it was also snowing. Steam rising from the pool was as thick as opaque glass.

"What does Monk say?" Bip asked JC.

"He's gone silent," JC told him. "He didn't seem to mind talking about someone else's case. But he's in the thick of the investigation into what happened to Mad Marv. He probably doesn't want to risk compromising it."

"Have they charged Horace with murder yet?" Bip asked.

"Nope," JC told him. "That tells you something, doesn't it?"

"So, if it isn't Horace, who is it?" Bip inquired.

"I don't know," JC admitted. "The killer could have murdered him in his sleep. He could have been shot or stabbed. But it was someone who knew where the opening of that old mine was. That tells me it was someone who lived here, which narrows our list of suspects down to slightly under one thousand."

"Great," Bip cracked. "You've almost solved the crime."

"No, I haven't," JC agreed. "And I don't even know where to start."

"Our bosses in Denver aren't going to let us wait here in front of the fireplace until something happens," Bip pointed out.

"No," JC agreed. He thought things over as he watched the snow fall.

"Your girlfriend, Sunny, can be very insightful," JC aloud.

"She says the Ute people have a greater understanding of the world," Bip told him.

"Her reason for dying may tell why she lived," JC recited. "That's what she said about Loretta Sopris. And it turned out to be true."

"So, we look into why Mad Marv lived?" Bip offered.

"Yep," JC responded. "I think we need to do a deep dive into why Marv was here and what he was doing before he got here."

"Didn't Scooter say that Marv was hiding here?" Bip recounted.

"He did," JC said. "So, for a start, let's find out who he was hiding from."

"You're a lot better at that than I am," Bip said. "In fact, I'm a lousy research assistant."

"Luckily, I know where to find one," JC replied.

Robin answered the phone on the second ring, at her desk in the newsroom.

"I'm sitting in a room that could use a bathtub," Robin told JC. "This newsroom will never be mistaken for a luxury hotel with a fireplace at the foot of the bed."

Their office space at the television station was typical of the industry. The metal desks were scratched, and the rugs were faded by constant foot traffic. That included boots that had just come in from the snow, the rain and the mud.

The walls of the newsroom were a brownish color that was chosen as a compromise during a management meeting. The closest thing to art hanging on the walls were a few logos of their television station and various mug shots or courtroom sketches taped up by news photographers who had a keen eye for visual mischief.

There were no fireplaces and there was no outdoor swimming pool.

Robin listened over the phone to JC's wants and needs.

"I have a story I'm working on for tonight," she told him. "But, after work, I can see what I can find on my laptop when I get home."

Following the phone call, JC settled in on the couch with his own laptop. Bip brought his camera to the room and stepped onto the porch. He knew that the meteorologists at their TV station would be elated by new pictures of weather happening in the mountains.

"Are you game for a little scavenger hunt?" JC asked Bip when he returned inside.

"Sure," the photographer replied, brushing off the snow piled up on his shoulders and head.

"Could I send you to the county building?" JC requested. "If Tommy owns that house, he had a lot of paperwork to file. Maybe he even took out a loan. I wonder which name all of that is under, Thomas or Scooter?"

Bip seemed to like the change of duties. He grabbed his coat and left, saying he was only a phone call away.

JC spent the next few hours in his hotel room, exploring Mad Marv's online biographies. Henry Marvin's GPS software made him an overnight sensation in the world of tech inventions. And that notoriety drew investors to launch more projects.

A magazine devoted to asset growth said that Marv, after making a fortune with his GPS gizmo, dedicated himself to the cryptocurrency market and blockchain investments. Henry Marvin bragged that no one understood the digital algorithms of crypto like he did.

Mad Marv became a crypto cover boy. The investment firm he started posted impressive profits. And he told anyone who would listen that the sky was the limit for cryptocurrency.

"Get on early," he urged investors. "Or get left out entirely."

For a number of years, Marv sat on a pile of money that grew beneath him. He was a multi-millionaire. And the business industry said he had reason to eye a billion dollars in profits before the next new year.

Then, the bottom fell out. All the unknowns about the new digital currency began to arise, like ghosts from their graves. Fortunes were lost, including those belonging to some of Mad Marv's investors who had thrown their caution to the wind.

JC read about lawsuits that tried and failed to get money repaid from Marv's investment firm. Marv's lawyers successfully argued that investments are not guaranteed. It was as true when it came to crypto as it was true a century ago when it came to stocks sold by IBM or General Motors.

One audit, however, caught some bad math in the books at Mad Marv's crypto business. Accountants who worked for the government insisted that things didn't add up.

A newspaper account reported that a federal lawsuit was filed in U.S. District Court in San Juan, Puerto Rico, where Henry Marvin had moved his business office. Criminal charges followed. Henry Marvin pleaded guilty and agreed to pay tens of millions of dollars in restitution.

Mad Marv, as part of his guilty plea, was prohibited from participating in the investment game again. But he avoided jail time, and his investors were repaid a portion of their losses.

A portion. It was always unclear to the court how much of the losses were legitimate and how much Marv had stolen. The justice department agreed on a sum and Marv paid them.

JC glanced at a picture, taken outside the courthouse. Some people in the newspaper photograph held protest signs.

They were hard to read. The photos were grainy. One sign, held by an older woman, said, "Give me my money!" Another said, "Where is the rest?" The caption beneath the photo implied that investors didn't get all of their money back and believed Mad Marv had more to give.

JC took a harder look at the photograph. He tried to read a third protest sign. But his eyes were drawn to a man behind the woman with the sign demanding her money.

The man's features were partially hidden behind the woman's shoulder, but his grainy face was visible. He wore sunglasses. But the face looked like the one belonging to Bob Andrews. Badass.

JC picked up his phone and dialed.

"Would an Idaho state trooper be placed on duty in Puerto Rico?" JC asked. "On loan, or something?"

"I don't see that happening," Special Investigator Steve Trujillo said on the other end of the line. "Idaho is Idaho and Puerto Rico is Puerto Rico. They have their own law officers, commonwealth officers and U.S. federal marshals. They don't need Idaho's help."

"Then what was he doing there?" JC asked.

"You've given me something to look into," Trujillo said evenly, sitting at the desk in his temporary office in the Cameron County office building.

"I am told that Badass lost a lot of money to Marv's crypto scheme," JC said.

"I was wondering when you were going to get around to that," the special investigator responded.

"So, you're aware of all that?" JC inquired.

"We have a handle on that, yes," Trujillo told him.

"And if Bob Andrews was in Puerto Rico outside the courthouse, that was on his own time?" JC asked.

"That is our belief," Trujillo declared.

"You're aware of Badass' falling-out with his former employer?" JC asked.

"The terms of Mr. Andrews' departure from the state police up there?" the detective asked. "I am."

"Have you already arrested him?" JC asked.

"Mr. Andrews?" Trujillo asked back. "We have not."

"Do you know where Bob 'Badass' Andrews is, currently?" JC asked.

"I do not," the special investigator divulged. "And if I did, I would not be at liberty to share that with you."

"Are you about to arrest him?" JC inquired.

"Same answer as before," Trujillo said before ending the call. "I'm not going to share things like that with you."

Trujillo ended the call on his end. JC still held his phone and said to himself, "I think something is about to happen."

39

"There are dark clouds over your head," Robin told JC on her cell phone as she looked west from the window of her apartment in Denver. "I can see them from here."

"Yeah, we're getting a lot of snow and wind," JC told her over the phone. "Or are you applying a metaphor? You kind of sound like you've picked up some Ute wisdom."

"Maybe," Robin said in a quiet voice. "I do see that snowstorm that's stalled over the Divide. But, yes, I also feel a storm gathering above the two of us. Maybe it's Dad, moving so far away from home."

"But he likes his new life in North Carolina," JC said, trying to bring her some peace.

"Well, maybe I don't," she said. She sounded worried. "I have two men who are beyond my reach right now."

"Call your dad," JC suggested. "You'll feel better knowing he's okay."

"I will," she replied.

Robin continued looking at the mountains from the window of her apartment in RiNo. It was the fashionable River-North district of Denver, revived in an old light-industrial area.

Beneath the dark cloud line, Robin looked at a building with a large mural painted on it. A woman clutched a cat to her chest for comfort. It was painted on a wall across the street from Robin's apartment.

Snow wasn't falling in Denver, but it was windy. Restaurants had just opened their doors for the evening. People were finding spots where they could park their cars and walk to popular RiNo attractions like The Beacon, Barcelona Wine Bar and Epic Brewing. Those on the sidewalks below Robin were pulling their jackets snug against the sudden cold breeze.

JC told her about what he found in the newspapers regarding Henry Marvin's conviction on charges related to his crypto-investment firm. He told her of the picture that looked like Bob "Badass" Andrews.

"Did you happen to look at the newspaper from Miami?" she asked.

"That's a good idea. Miami is the closest American mainland city to Puerto Rico," JC said. "But I stuck to Puerto Rico papers."

Bip walked through the door and sat himself down on a chair, watching JC converse on the phone.

"There's another picture I found interesting," Robin told JC. "There are a few paragraphs about a woman. It's in the Miami paper that reported Marv's conviction.

"She says that her husband had died, but she thought he had invested with Marvin. At least, that was her assumption, because she found all sorts of information about Marvin's firm in her husband's files. She wondered if she was owed money."

"Any connection to what we're doing?" JC asked.

"Maybe," Robin said. "She's identified in the newspaper as Matia Halvorson. She said her husband's name was Thomas."

"Do you think Tommy still has a wife?" JC asked, surprised.

"He said he was divorced," Robin said.

"And she thinks she's a widow?" JC wondered. "Remember that story about Tommy being killed in Hurricane Maria?"

"I found a phone number for her," Robin told him. "Would you like it?"

JC jotted down the number.

"I'll be back in Placer Friday night," Robin said, still sounding apprehensive. "Take care of yourself, Jean Claude."

"Call your dad," he repeated in a soft voice. And they ended their call.

JC turned his attention to Bip and accepted a cup of coffee that the photographer had picked up for him from the hotel's dining room. There was complimentary coffee all day long.

"Thanks," JC said. "How is the weather out there?"

"That snow is piling up," Bip told him. "And sometimes it's blowing sideways. Our meteorologists at the TV station say you can only call it a 'blizzard' if certain accumulations and wind speeds are attained. But that's a blizzard out there."

"How did it go at the county building?" JC asked.

"Interesting," Bip said. "They've never heard of a guy named Thomas Halvorson. But there's lots of paperwork filled out by *Scooter* Halvorson. He paid cash to build the house, so he didn't have to prove his true identity to the bank.

"Everything has Scooter as his name," Bip said. "The taxes, everything. No sign of 'Thomas.' It's like Scooter is his real name. Here's the weird thing, though. Scooter has a social security number. He has all the documentation to prove he's Scooter, not Thomas."

"How did he accomplish that?" JC wondered.

"I don't know. But I got to thinking," Bip told him. "If he's trying to make Tommy disappear, he can't be too happy about you showing up out of nowhere. You know he's Tommy."

"Meaning what?" JC asked.

"Sleep with one eye open, my friend," Bip said with a grin.

JC laughed a little laugh.

"I saw that deputy too," Bip continued. "The one who speaks Ute to Sunny. He's a pretty nice guy."

"Does he know anything?" JC asked.

"He didn't seem interested in telling me what he was doing," Bip replied. "But he seemed to be doing something in the same office as I was. Aaron Aguayo. That's his name."

JC said he had another call to make. He collected his thoughts, looking at the driving snow, and picked up his phone.

The conversation took only a few minutes for JC to be convinced that he was talking with the wife of Tommy Halvorson. And she thought he was dead.

It took longer to convince Matia Halvorson that Tommy was alive.

"I'm not mistaken," JC told her. He thought that he heard a slight Latino accent in her voice. "I don't blame you for thinking that I'm nuts. But I've known Tommy since we were in high school. I heard that he was dead too, but then I saw him here."

"We were living in Puerto Rico at the time," Matia said. "Hurricane Maria struck when Tommy was away from home. He'd gone to a remote area that was hit very badly. Many people died. Survivors had seen him there as the storm struck. But he was never seen again."

"What about credit cards and bank accounts?" JC asked. "Did he ever try to get money after the hurricane?"

"No," she said. "Not his bank accounts, credit cards, phone. Are you sure that you're not mistaken?"

"It's impossible," JC told her. "It's Tommy. I've had dinner with him. We've exchanged memories from high school days. I'm sorry."

"I don't understand why he would do this," she said.

"Did he know Henry Marvin?" JC asked the woman.

"I don't think so," she said. "I never heard Marvin's name. But then I was going through his things after he'd died. I found a whole notebook with things about Henry Marvin's investment company. There are pages that just have numbers and mathematic equations. I don't understand crypto things. But I couldn't imagine why he would have all that unless he made an investment with that criminal. That's why I went to court that day, to get answers."

"And did you?" JC asked.

"No, I didn't," she said in a disappointed voice.

"You might think this to be an inappropriate question," JC said. "But how was your marriage at the time Tommy disappeared in the storm?"

There was silence on the other end of the line. JC thought he might have crossed a line.

"Not the best," Matia finally said. "His business was failing, and he wasn't very pleasant to be around. He seemed to hate his life with me."

"Do you think he might have *faked* his death?" JC asked her.

"If what you say is true, anything is possible," she replied. "I've been trying to have him declared legally dead. There's an insurance policy that would help me. I have a serious boyfriend. I'm ready to move on."

"One more thing," JC said. "Has he ever called himself Scooter?"

She was quiet for a moment. He wondered what chord he had struck.

"That was his brother's name," she finally said. "He told me about it when they were children. His brother died very young."

JC agreed to keep her up to date and ended their call.

"It's his brother's social security number," JC concluded, sharing Matia's insights with Bip. "He's taken on his brother's persona, on the paperwork."

JC drank from his coffee and picked up his laptop. He found an article about the aftermath of Hurricane Maria in 2021. It said that hundreds of bodies were never found. Many were believed buried beneath mudslides.

"Who was going to quibble about one body?" JC asked aloud. "Including Tommy Halvorson's."

He thought about the manifestation of Scooter Halvorson in Cameron County. Tommy had said himself; it was a good place to hide.

In addition to using the alias of "Scooter," JC had noticed that Tommy didn't use a credit card. He paid cash. That was almost unheard of in the post-Covid days of hands-free currency.

"It has all the markings of someone who is trying to drop off the grid," JC said.

But where did Tommy's money come from? *Scooter* Halvorson was a wealthy man in Cameron County. Matia Halvorson said that *Tommy* Halvorson's business, when he disappeared, was failing. Was his change in fortune tied to Mad Marv?

Halvorson and Marv did not seem to like each other. JC had seen their dismissive manner when bumping into one another. Tommy told JC that Marv was a swindler. But Tommy also swore that he hadn't lost a dime to Marv's schemes.

JC thought back to the note passed under his door. It said, "Houston, we have a problem. Find me."

When Hank Monk vigorously asserted that the note signed "HM" was not from him, JC came to reason that it was from Henry Marvin. But before JC could find Marv, he was dead.

"So, you think the killer is Scooter Halvorson?" Bip asked, taking a sip from his own coffee.

"He's lied about a lot of things," JC said. "And he's working awfully hard to hide who he really is."

"Toss your wallet on some rubble as the floodwaters recede and walk off to your new life," Bip said.

"I wonder if Matia could take pictures of the mathematics that Tommy was scribbling on those pages," JC said. "You like to study unusual things. Have you ever studied crypto?"

"Enough to be ashamed to admit it," Bip told him.

Back on the phone, Matia was agreeable to their plan. Fifteen minutes later, JC received ten emails. On his laptop, they could be enlarged.

The two men studied the scribbling.

"Some of this is code," Bip said. "And some of it is phrases and some of it is just math."

JC felt a headache coming on. Visions of high school algebra and logarithms began to haunt him.

"Before this requires us to pull out our slide rules, I'm going to get us some dinner," JC said. "I admit defeat. I'm leaving this to you. Math is not my strong point. To this day, I can't understand how crypto becomes a valuable commodity. It strikes me as a pyramid scheme."

JC walked down the hall, looking at old pictures of the miners and lumberjacks who made their wages on land just outside of the hotel.

"Were any of you banking crypto?" he asked the images of men, dead for one hundred years.

JC looked out the windows as he proceeded down the hall. It looked like the snowstorm had shut down the ski area. Buildings were dark and nothing seemed to be moving, not a single person and not a single vehicle.

He could hear a commotion coming from the lobby as he headed downstairs.

"The highway just closed," the concierge told him. "We're being swamped by people who want a place to stay for the night. Residents in town are being asked to take stranded motorists into their homes, if they have a spare bedroom."

JC resumed his search for sustenance. He ordered two to-go dinners at the desk of the restaurant.

"Have you heard?" a hostess at the desk asked him as he waited for his food. "We've been asked to inform all of our guests that an 'interlodge event' has been declared. That means no one may leave any of the lodges because of the storm."

When JC arrived back at his hotel room, Bip's spiked hair looked as though he'd dragged his hands through it.

"I thought you were good at math," JC quipped.

He passed Bip a plate with a large burrito wrapped in foil. It came with a fork and knife. JC had the same.

They took a few bites, remembering how long it had been since they'd eaten.

"The kitchen was almost closed," JC told him. "But the staff is stranded here by the storm, so they've just kept on working."

"No beer?" Bip asked with a longing look.

"I can't drink and add at the same time," JC told him, then nodding toward the laptop, asked, "What have you figured out?"

"There is code and there are phrases," Bip explained. "They could be passwords. But some of these pages aren't about crypto, they're about simple revenues. And these figures don't seem to be losses, they seem to be gains."

"Is it telling us anything that we can understand?" JC asked.

"It some cases, no. There's an equation or encryption that I can't even begin to explain. But I've seen something like it before, on a site on the dark web that I will deny ever having seen."

"You say it looks like something," JC stated. "What does it remind you of?"

"It reminds me of this hacker I know about. I watched his video. He was hiding his identity and explaining how he ripped off a crypto account," Bip said, looking at him. "I couldn't duplicate it. I was just sitting in on a dark web seminar about doing things like this. It was pretty interesting."

"Do you think Tommy was hacking Mad Marv?" JC asked.

"If I had to guess, I'd say it is possible that Tommy set up something like a fake trading app," Bip said. "If that were the case, Marv would have thought he was buying assets on a crypto exchange. But he was really sending his money to a dummy hacker account that Tommy had set up."

"Would Marv have fallen for something like that?" JC asked. "Didn't Marv write books about cryptocurrencies?"

"Some of the biggest crypto exchanges in the world have been tricked by hackers," Bip told him. "Billions of dollars have been stolen."

"And I suspect it's going on even more than we're told," JC said. "News like that could kill cryptocurrency."

"It would explain where Scooter's money came from," Bip agreed. "And his wife told you that the last time she saw him, he was broke."

"And it's not like Marv could call the cops," JC said. "Tommy was taking money from Marv that Marv wasn't even supposed to have. He hid millions before he was arrested and deceived the United States Justice Department."

"The perfect crime," Bip said.

"Tommy was stealing stolen money," JC agreed.

40

"Then why is *Marv* dead instead of Tommy?" Bip wondered aloud.

"Maybe Marv caught him," JC suggested. "Maybe he threatened to do something about it."

"If it came to a fistfight, I don't think Marv would stand much of a chance against Scooter, er, Tommy," Bip said.

"Tommy was a pretty ferocious football player," JC said. "I think you're right."

JC's phone rang.

"I'm going to do you a solid," Deputy Hank Monk said. "Trujillo is on his way to the ski resort to bring Bob Andrews in for questioning."

"Badass?" JC confirmed. While getting wrapped up in Halvorson's mysterious behavior, he'd forgotten about the arrows that pointed at Andrews.

JC also wondered if Monk's first tip in days had to do with the fact it would help his girlfriend's client, Horace Emerson.

"Yeah," Monk said. "Badass rents a condo near the base lodge. The special investigator figures the weather will keep everyone inside, including Andrews. It's less likely that anyone gets hurt, if Andrews tries to resist. He has sort of a reputation for violence."

"Alright," JC said. "Thanks."

"And you didn't hear it from me," Monk reminded him.

"Hear what?" JC answered. "How are the roads?"

"They suck," the deputy said, then ended the call.

JC stood and picked up both of their empty paper plates, placing them in a trash can.

"I fed you, so you belong to me," JC said to Bip. They grabbed their coats. Bip picked up his camera and put two more batteries in his backpack. He also grabbed a plastic laundry bag out of the closet. He slipped it over his camera.

"When I need to shoot something, I'll tear a hole and stick the lens through it," Bip told JC. "The rest of the camera will be under plastic and protected from the storm."

"Desperate times call for desperate measures," JC said.

As they stepped out into the hallway, the lights flickered and then were extinguished altogether.

They heard an anguished cry from the crowd in the bar where a Denver Nuggets game was being watched. The hotel's generator kicked on and the lights came back to life, as well as the televised basketball game. The crowd in the bar cheered.

Instead of using the main door in the lobby of the Clark Hotel, they found a side door. It was a shortcut that would spare them from being in the storm for an extra hundred yards.

The ski village was dark. The only sign of human life was some children building a fort out of snow. A parent, armed with a thermos of something warm and taking shelter under an overhang, was ignoring the "interlodge event" but keeping an eye on them. Two snowmen had already been constructed to help stand guard.

JC and Bip squinted to keep the blowing snow out of their eyes. There wasn't much to see, the visibility was only a dozen feet.

"We should have worn our ski goggles," JC hollered.

"Is this a squall or a blizzard?" Bip asked, raising his voice.

"I think this has graduated beyond being a squall," JC shouted.

It was better as they walked through the village. The buildings protected them from the gusts, somewhat. There were even a few lights on, powered by generators. The generator engines roared, though barely perceptible as the wind wailed.

It grew dark again as JC and Bip pushed themselves toward the main base lift and away from the village. They were looking for any sign of a police presence. They wanted to record the arrest of Bob "Badass" Andrews.

The wind picked up loose snow and blew it in waves across the open space until it hit something. They heard a garbage can blow onto its side. The sound of metal posts, leaned against some out-of-view building, resembled chimes as the wind threw them to the ground.

315

JC's fingers were growing cold, despite wearing gloves. His face was growing numb.

"This isn't a happy place for my camera," Bip hollered into the wind. "It's freezing up. And my batteries aren't going to last long in these cold temperatures."

"You're right," JC said, snow stinging his face. "Why don't you get inside somewhere. If you see anything, give me a call. I'll do the same."

They walked away from each other in different directions. Bip retreated to the village. JC walked toward a multi-story building containing condominiums, perhaps one belonging to Bob Andrews.

He thought he saw movement ahead. He knew the likelihood that it would just be more children, impervious to freezing temperatures.

Then he heard the crack of a gunshot.

He thought the sound came from straight ahead. Maybe those figures in the blowing snow were not children.

But the howl of the storm, and the velocity of its snow, was disorienting. Nothing quite looked like it had before the storm began.

JC wondered if it was a bird chirping that he heard. He thought of Mercy, mimicking the call a robin makes when there is danger.

JC pushed through the snow, now up to mid-calf. He headed toward where he had heard the gunfire. He fought to keep his footing. He could make out the figure of one person, large enough to be an adult. As JC approached, he could see one arm extended toward the ground. He seemed to be pointing at something.

"Are you alright?" JC yelled into the wind. The figure wore a hat pulled down and a scarf pulled up over his face to protect himself from the blizzard.

He glanced JC's way and then ran away into the darkness.

JC took a few steps and recognized what the figure had been pointing at, a man lying in the snow. He was wearing a deputy's uniform. Taking a closer look, JC saw blood was seeping from his chest.

Dropping to his knees alongside the man, JC recognized the deputy as Aaron Aguayo. JC could see the deputy's eyes moving, but he couldn't speak.

JC unzipped the deputy's jacket and saw the wound. He pressed with one hand on the spot to create some pressure and pulled out his phone and dialed 9-1-1.

"You have a deputy down," JC hollered over the storm. "He has a chest wound. His name is Aaron Aguayo. We're about one hundred yards north of the ski lodge. Hurry."

JC ended the call and applied pressure with both hands on the source of the blood.

"You're going to be okay, Deputy," JC tried to say in a calm voice.

He was thinking about what he had observed at a dozen crime scenes he had been to, the bleeding victim still lying in the street. He'd picked up a little knowledge about applying pressure to a gunshot wound.

The deputy's eyes locked on JC. He tried to say something but was unable.

"Dammit!" Deputy Monk hollered as he ran and slid to his knees next to JC and Aguayo. "Keep applying pressure. We've got to get him to the hospital!"

Monk got on his phone and demanded an ambulance in a commanding voice. He provided the location and the situation. And he ordered for more deputies.

"JC!"

The voice came from the darkness. JC turned his head away from Deputy Aguayo and looked into the storm.

Deputy Monk pushed JC aside and took over applying pressure to the wounded man's chest.

"JC!"

It was a man's voice, coming from the darkness. It sounded like Bip.

From the other direction, Captain Bush appeared in the blowing snow and kneeled down next to Monk.

"You got this?" JC asked Deputy Monk.

"Yeah," Monk said, not paying much attention to anything other than his injured comrade.

JC rose and assumed a trot through the snow toward the voice. He reached the corner of the building. The condominium units were dark, because of the power outage.

"JC!"

The voice was closer. He could barely see Bip's outline, until he could see that it wasn't Bip. It was Tommy Halvorson, who was pointing a handgun in JC's direction.

"That's close enough," Tommy shouted through the storm.

JC recognized Tommy as the man he had seen moments ago. "Did you shoot that deputy?"

"I had to," Tommy said, raising his voice to be heard. "He'd been snooping. He probably wanted a promotion. But now, that makes you the only one who knows who Scooter really is."

"You mean because Marv is dead?" JC asked. "You killed him too?"

"No one is going to miss Mad Marv," Tommy yelled. "He stole millions of dollars from good people. All I did was steal from a thief. I'm Robin Hood."

"And what's that got to do with me?" JC asked. "You lured me over here. Are you going to kill me now? Your perfect crime is getting a little complicated."

All JC could think of was to keep Tommy talking. Sheriff's deputies weren't far away. Maybe they'd come looking for the gunman who shot Aguayo.

"What was the deal with cutting off Marv's hand?" JC asked.

"That wasn't part of the plan. It just happened," Tommy laughed over the wind. "I was certain the fall into the mine would kill him. But when I climbed down, he'd gotten up. I think he was going to die anyway. He had to have internal bleeding."

A gust of cold air hit JC and Tommy like a punch. A vinyl banner advertising Stockli skis rolled over the snow past them.

The wind tossed aside two metal posts. Red ribbon attached to them was intended to herd skiers to the chairlift. It sounded like a bell when the posts landed on each other.

JC and Tommy stood, leaning into the gale, only feet away from one another.

"I picked up a rusty ax and swung it at Mad Marv," Tommy shouted to be heard. "I almost missed him, but I cut off his hand and the ax handle broke. Whatever. He collapsed and died right there. I dragged him and tossed him down that shaft. I just forgot about the hand."

"This has nothing to do with you and me, Tommy," JC hollered. Hard pellets of snow hit his face. "Let's get out of this storm or it's going to kill us both."

"You know who I am, JC. Sorry," he shouted. "You and that photographer of yours. You haven't had time to tell anyone else. You're the only ones who know Tommy Halvorson is still alive. Get on your phone and give your photographer a call. Tell him to get over here."

"You're dreaming," JC yelled. "I'm not going to do your dirty work."

"It doesn't really matter," Tommy replied. "I'll take care of you and then I'll use your phone to call him. He'll come."

A gust of wind and snow hit them so hard, it nearly knocked them to the ground.

"It's over, Tommy," JC hollered. "Let's get out of this storm."

"No, I'm just going to kill you," Tommy yelled. "Don't you remember what you used to say before those high school races? It would be raining or icy. You'd say, 'There's no such thing as bad snow.'"

"Yeah, I remember. I spoke to your wife, Tommy," JC told him. "She knows you're alive too."

"You what?" Tommy yelled. "You had no right! She was about to collect on a big insurance policy. She would be taken care of! You had no right!"

"It's not the perfect crime, Tommy," JC told him, hard snowflakes battering his face. "You're going to be caught."

"Well, you'll never know," Tommy said as he raised his gun to eye level.

The impact of metal on bone made a sickening crunch, and a slight metallic ring.

Tommy lurched and fell, face first, into the snow. Flakes instantly began to settle on the back of his coat.

"Donuts," Bob Andrews grumbled. "What an idiot." The former Idaho state trooper held a heavy metal post in his strong hands, a piece of red ribbon hanging from it. Badass turned Tommy onto his back so he wouldn't suffocate.

The ex-lawman had approached JC and Tommy unnoticed, hiding in the blur of snowflakes blowing sideways.

"My condo is right over there," Badass gestured over his shoulder. "I was home. Who would go out in this weather? Anyway, I could see you two from my window. Lucky for you that Donuts wanted to make a speech instead of just doing what he intended to do. Criminals are stupid."

"Mr. Andrews?" a voice shouted from near the building.

JC recognized the man pushing through the snow toward them. It was Detective Steve Trujillo. He was flanked by four deputies.

Arriving, Trujillo looked at the pronate figure of Tommy Halvorson and then at JC.

"Why am I not surprised that you're in the middle of this?" the special investigator said.

"Badass isn't your man," JC told him. "Scooter Halvorson is. His real name is Thomas Halvorson."

"Got any proof?" Trujillo asked.

"You'd be surprised," JC responded.

"Did you kill him?" Trujillo asked former Trooper Bob Andrews.

"Nah," Badass responded. "He's just taking a nap."

"We've got a deputy who needs our attention. Then, regardless of what happened here, we're going to want to interview you," the special investigator told Andrews.

"I'm always happy to share a cup of coffee with a colleague," Andrews replied.

41

"He's going to make it," Special Investigator Steve Trujillo told JC at Poudre Valley Hospital in Fort Collins.

Deputy Aaron Aguayo had been rushed there during the storm. They had to use an ambulance. Helicopters couldn't fly. He was given vital blood inside the ambulance and was now improving.

"Ah gah rah u̅?" Sunny asked the deputy at his bedside. There was concern in her voice. Bip noticed it.

"Toŏ ī e̅ in," the deputy told her in a weak voice.

"He says he feels good," Sunny translated. "He's a tough guy."

"Mwe√gah pwē cah va nē," she told him with a gentle smile. "I told him to go to sleep," she said as they left the room.

Through the windows, they could see that dawn had arrived. The sun bounced off a fresh layer of snow, though there was nothing near the accumulation as up in the mountains on Cameron Pass.

JC and Detective Trujillo stood outside Aguayo's room. JC filled in the special investigator on all they had learned about Tommy "Scooter" Halvorson.

"I'll want you to give us a formal statement when we get back to Placer," the special investigator said. "We have Halvorson in jail on charges of shooting Deputy Aguayo. I'm sure there will be some more charges."

Robin stood at JC's side; her arm threaded through his. She was happy to have him home, safe. She and Sunny had made the midnight drive from Denver to Fort Collins when they heard what happened.

"Are you okay?" she asked JC.

"Yes, ma'am," he responded. He caught her eye as her expression of annoyance turned to one of affection.

Sheriff Brush walked down the hospital hallway and joined Trujillo and JC. Trujillo updated the sheriff on Aguayo's condition. Jerry Brush took off his cowboy hat and ran a hand over his red hair.

A nurse raised a finger as she entered the deputy's room, asking the sheriff to wait in the hallway and give her a moment before he went in.

"Everything that you told us about Loretta Sopris and Charlie Washburn checks out," the sheriff told JC. "We confirmed they had a room booked for Sun Valley. Loretta was seen there at a breakfast meeting. And a camera at the airport in Hailey captured an image of Charlie with John Washburn's car."

"Are you going to take a look at Loretta's house, here in Fort Collins?" JC asked.

"Later today," the sheriff said. "We also have a waitress at the hotel at the ski resort. She says that on the morning of Loretta Sopris' death, the decedent had a *few* mimosas and was seen popping some pills. She probably did a pretty good job of dulling her senses for the task ahead."

A memorial could finally be arranged for John Washburn. The court allowed Charlie Washburn to attend, in the company of her jailers.

"Have you released Horace?" the sheriff asked Trujillo.

"All charges against him have been dropped. He was informed about an hour ago that he was free to leave the jail. He told your overnight deputy, though, that he wanted to go back to sleep and leave in the morning," the special investigator said with a chuckle.

Robin and Sunny had moved down the hall to sit on a bench.

"Are you alright with this?" Sunny asked Robin in a quiet voice. "All the killing?"

Robin looked at the intuitive woman and searched for an answer.

"I don't know," Robin replied. "I don't know if I can do it."

"He's a good man," Sunny said, turning her head to JC. He was standing down the hallway with the law officers. "But he seeks a lot of adventure."

JC and Bip were ready to leave. They came down the hall and, together, they headed for the hospital's exit.

But Sunny gently touched Bip's arm.

"I'm going to stay," she told him in her voice that was almost a song.

Bip looked at her. He comprehended what this quiet, caring woman was telling him.

"Okay," Bip said. He kissed her cheek and turned to go.

Sunny returned to Deputy Aguayo's hospital room.

When JC and Bip arrived back at The Craters Ski Resort, it was mid-day. Before returning to Denver, they had been told to deliver live reports from the resort for all of the evening shows. They had a lot of work ahead in the next few hours.

"What's up with Sunny?" JC asked Bip.

"I think she wants to go back home," Bip told him. "All the way home."

"On the arm of a handsome Ute deputy?"

"Something like that," Bip said. "He'll have more in common with her than she'll ever have with me."

"You okay?" JC asked.

"Yeah."

The two men looked with envy at the day of powder skiing everyone else was enjoying. JC and Bip had work waiting for them. All they could do was watch as skiers and snowboarders arrived at the chairlift with a crust of snow on their goggles and tangled in their facial hair. A new day was becoming legend.

"Why did Tommy risk it all?" Bip asked. "He could have worked something out with Mad Marv. Tommy had money, a great house at a great ski resort. He had it all. He blew it."

"On the highest throne in the world, we still sit only on our own bottom" JC said. "That's Montaigne."

"Live today. Because you never know what you'll screw up tomorrow," Bip added. "Carpe Ski 'em."

A Note from the Author

The suicide note that begins this novel is real. It was printed in the *New York Herald Tribune* in April 1942.

A thirty-two-year-old woman was found dead on the floor of her Brooklyn apartment. The gas jets on her stove had been opened.

The same newspaper, on the same day, reported the death of a woman of similar age who jumped from a sixth-floor window of her Brooklyn apartment.

The two souls lived only a short distance from one another, on either side of a small park. They could have met there.

The newspaper was at a loss to explain what had driven the two women to their ends. If there was a connection between the two, it went with them to their graves.

The Names

Many of the names of the characters in this book once belonged to real people. They were amongst the early settlers on Cameron Pass and in the Poudre Valley.

Jared Brush was elected sheriff of Weld County in 1870.

Horace Emerson came to Cameron Pass in 1868 to work as a tie hack.

John Washburn was a pioneer in Big Thompson Valley in the 1860s.

Thomas Halvorson was a former Danish soldier who came to the Poudre Valley in 1881 to farm.

Robert Andrews settled in Fort Collins in 1879, coming from Pennsylvania via Wyoming.

The LaJeunesse name belonged to the Rev. G. Joseph LaJeunesse, pastor of St. Joseph's Catholic Church in Fort Collins. He came to Fort Collins from Montreal via Denver in 1899.

Frank Steen is not a real name. But he represents families of freed slaves who really settled to farm the Pawnee Grasslands in the 1880s.

Rock Bush, a hunter and beaver trapper, filed a squatter's claim on land along the Poudre River in 1859. He lived in peace with the local First Natives and sometimes secured four hundred beaver pelts in a month.

Johanna Forbes married Mr. Bush in the 1870s.

Arthur Patterson donated the largest piece of land to help found Colorado Agricultural College, now Colorado State University.

Hank Monk, a veteran mountain man of Browns Park, was a stagecoach driver in 1859. He drove the famous newspaperman, Horace Greeley ("Go West, young man") on a trip from Denver, across the Poudre Valley, and on to California.

Acknowledgements

I first read *The History of Larimer County Colorado,* in 1975. Ansel Watrous wrote it in 1911. It is still a great resource.

Thank you to the estate of Edward Lynch for the loan of Horace Greeley's rare edition of *An Overland Journey to California in 1859.*

The Poudre River booklet was published in 1976 by The Gro-Pub group. The great thing about history is that it doesn't change much when it gets older.

A publication by Colorado State University told the story of New Belgium's 1554 beer.

Uncompahgre Ute Words and Phrases, by Hazel Wardle, published by the American West Center at the University of Utah helped me try to pay tribute to the great history and language of the Ute people.

The lyric, "There is light...in the darkness of everybody's life," is from the legendary stage musical, *Rocky Horror Show,* written by the brilliant Richard O'Brien.

And thank you to the University of Wisconsin Arboretum for their interesting research on what birds say to each other. For more information, go to Journeynorth.org.

Dean Micheli is our Digital Sorcerer. Sometimes, he laughs at us. Deirdre Stoelzle is our editor. She is fluent in my sometimes gibberish and translates it into English for everyone else. Debbi Wraga is our talented formatter who continues to educate us.

And thanks to residents, and ghosts of residents, on Cameron Pass for allowing me to incorporate their small plot of earth into my fictitious Cameron County. I can now bequeath the land back to Larimer County.

I invented the imaginary county so that I could tell my story without twisting the true and fascinating history of the upper end of Poudre Canyon. Aside from the characters who lived in my novel, this book is full of people who really lived and died in a land of immeasurable beauty.

About the Author

Phil Bayly was a television and radio journalist for over four decades. He lived and worked in Denver, Fort Collins, the Eastern Plains and the Western Slope of Colorado, as well as Wyoming, Pennsylvania and New York.

He was a reporter and anchor for WNYT-TV in New York's state capital, Albany.

He attended the University of Denver and is a graduate of Colorado State University.

For a brief time, he carved tombstones for a paycheck. He's been a ski racer and a ski bum. It's too late to stop.

He was born and raised in Evanston, Illinois, and now resides in Saratoga County, New York.

You can learn more about Phil and his books at murderonskis.com.

Made in United States
Cleveland, OH
24 December 2025

29952978R00204